PRAI

THE

STA   S HEAD

"*The View from Stalin's Head* is a view of life and loss, desire and despair, coming of age and running away. In short, this stirring debut is a view of everything that matters, accomplished by a brilliant young writer with tremendous gifts."

–BEN MARCUS, author of
Notable American Women and
The Age of Wire and String

"With a sharp eye for outlandish details, absurd turns of phrase, and quiet but monumental moments of realization, Aaron Hamburger lures you into the most intimate worlds of young Czech schoolboys and jaded expats alike. This is a marvelous and honest collection of stories about people searching for identity in a country searching for the same."

–JESSICA SHATTUCK, author of
The Hazards of Good Breeding

"We're definitely not in Paris anymore. *The View from Stalin's Head* is a triumphant collection of stories chronicling the loves, the losses, and the dreams of denizens of Prague. With charm and wit and force of life, Aaron Hamburger takes us deep inside the city walls. Poignant and laugh-out-loud funny, these stories are as good as they come."

–BINNIE KIRSHENBAUM, author of
Hester Among the Ruins

"A provocative and often striking first collection."
–*Library Journal*

THE VIEW FROM STALIN'S HEAD

RANDOM HOUSE TRADE PAPERBACKS   NEW YORK

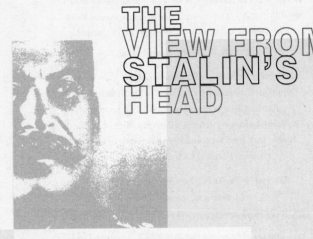

THE VIEW FROM STALIN'S HEAD

STORIES

AARON HAMBURGER

A Random House Trade
Paperback Original

"A Man of the Country" was originally published in *Salt Mill*, Vol. 14.

Library of Congress Cataloging-in-Publication Data
Hamburger, Aaron.
The view from Stalin's Head : stories / Aaron Hamburger.
p.   cm.
Contents: A man of the country—Jerusalem—The view from Stalin's Head—This
ground you are standing on—Sympathetic conversationalist—You say you want a
revolution—Garage sale—Control—Law of return—Exile.
ISBN 0-8129-7093-4
1. Prague (Czech Republic)—Fiction. 2. Americans—Czech Republic—Fiction.
3. Europeans—Czech Republic—Fiction. I. Title
PS3608.A5496V54 2004
813'.6—dc21   2003047063

Random House website address: www.atrandom.com

Printed in the United States of America

24689753

Book design by Barbara M. Bachman

Dedicated to my mother and father,
and to Meggin Silverman

CONTENTS

A MAN OF THE COUNTRY   3

JERUSALEM   23

THE VIEW FROM STALIN'S HEAD   51

THIS GROUND YOU ARE STANDING ON   71

SYMPATHETIC CONVERSATIONALIST   100

YOU SAY YOU WANT A REVOLUTION   122

GARAGE SALE   149

CONTROL   175

LAW OF RETURN   188

EXILE   221

THE VIEW FROM STALIN'S HEAD

ALL FAIRY TALES HAVE IN common not "once upon a time" but an unlikely pairing of characters who under normal circumstances would never have met. Like a former waiter from Madison, Wisconsin, and a giant.

Jirka is tall and *tlusty,* which translates roughly into "thick." It is an equally useful word for describing people who weigh over two hundred pounds as well as books that clock in at over a thousand pages. His nose, chin, and fingers are fleshy and full of life. The only subtle thing about his looks is his smile, which curls up in the corners of his lips as if he's winking at you.

We met on a subway platform. I was standing under an ad for the new Pizza Hut, my nose buried in a book with the cover wrapped in brown paper. A guy from Minnesota advised me to cover all my English books to avoid being hassled by undercover ticket inspectors on the subway.

Jirka picked me out of the crowd to ask if he could take a picture of my nose.

"It is regret I do not understand what you have said," I told him in Czech.

"Where are you from?" he asked. He wore a bright yellow knit cap over his mangy curls and a dull blue winter jacket that looked like he'd slept in it. I wore a full-length Czech gray raincoat to hide my American clothes.

"I am a man of America but I speak a little of Czech."

His eyes, already big and round like moons, widened. "You are American and you can speak Czech?"

I said, "Is it contrary to a law for an American to speak Czech?" Sometimes I was reckless in languages that were not my own.

"*Wir können* to speak the English," he replied.

We rode the subway to Dejvice together and then transferred to the tram. Jirka, who worked in construction, wanted me to be his English teacher. After fumbling around in his coat pocket, he fished out a pencil stub and a wrinkled Dunkin' Donuts napkin so he could write down his phone number. How much did I charge for lessons? Could I give him a list of books? He would buy them the very next day. He knew a good bookstore.

"Wait, wait," I said.

"I no can wait," he told me and pulled my arm. The other passengers in the tram stared. "I must *besser* speak English. It is important to make my fortune."

"But this is my stop. I have to get off. *Moja zastavka.*"

Jirka looked deep into my eyes. "Please call to me tomorrow," he begged.

■

A YEAR PASSES, and I'm going home. Jirka the giant and I stand in front of a pink and green castle on a hill that inspired a novel by Kafka. We are not lovers and Jirka has no idea I ever wanted to be, but he has taken the day off work to spend it by my side like a lover would. The smog has melted, as if in honor of my leaving, and we have a clear view of the trams, the tourists on Charles Bridge, trees dragging their leaves over the water, paddleboats on the Vltava River, shadows, islands.

After a last look over the city, we walk down the craggy steps of Nerudova ulice into Mala Strana, a neighborhood of narrow streets where the buildings are painted in pastels and trimmed with scallops and curls like wedding cakes. Jirka scratches his chest with a proud, satisfied smile. His size and rocklike good looks turn heads everywhere. Even the American tourists wearing the red-and-black-checkered velvet hats for sale on Charles Bridge stop to look at him. I can't decide if he's unaware of the attention he's getting or if he enjoys it.

We turn right onto Malostranske namesti and Jirka puts his hand on my neck. His touch feels cold and heavy, like a metal clamp. "Please, my friend." He slips his whole arm around my shoulders and pulls me against his hip. I try not to get hard because we've never talked about it openly, this propensity of mine to be attracted to him.

Three teenage boys dressed in oversize sweatshirts and backwards baseball caps like the hip-hop artists they watch on Euro MTV are heading straight for us, but Jirka doesn't drop his arm. He points at the show window of a store that imports Levi's. "It is funny *reklama* for slips. How you say *reklama*?"

"Advertisement." The ad in question, for men's underwear by Diesel, consists of three close-up shots of crotches in various states of arousal as seen through white briefs. The word for underwear in Czech is *slip*. I ask him, "What kind of *slip* do you wear?"

Jirka hikes down the waist of his pants low enough for me to see his paisley-print bikini briefs.

The boys walk by and take no notice of us.

■

HE USED TO live in an apartment in a complex of high-rise cement buildings called Cerveny vrch, or Red Hill. When you came over, you had to phone from the corner. Instead of letting down his golden hair, he'd open his window and throw you his keys.

"Why don't you fix your buzzer?" I asked when I visited him the first time.

"I like to give keys out window," Jirka said. He took my raincoat and pointed to a towel spread on the floor where I could leave my shoes.

Jirka rented his spare bedroom to Jason and Teal, a Canadian couple whom he never saw except passed out on their mattress, once next to a pool of vomit. Their backpacks, still stuffed with clothes, lay unzipped next to a stack of books covered in candle drippings, books like *On the Road* and *Zen and the Art of Motorcycle Maintenance.* Jirka had taped an index card to the phone for them: "*Jirka neni doma* = Jirka no home."

Pots of basil and thyme and baby tomatoes grew on the windowsill in Jirka's kitchen. I sipped a glass of carbonated water while he consulted a water-stained cookbook his mother had given him when he moved to the big city from his village. The black-and-white illustrations showed ecstatic families in peasant clothing sitting down to a traditional Czech meal after a hard day's work on a collective farm or the People's Steel Factory. Jirka nodded thoughtfully as he leafed through a few pages, then tossed the book aside and scrubbed five potatoes in the sink. After boiling them into a mash, he mixed in two sticks of butter and a small tub of sour cream.

We ate without speaking. I stared at the tiles on the floor, the color of piss, and tried not to touch the sticky table. When Jirka finished, he wiped his bowl clean with a hunk of wheat bread. "If my English is no so good, you must say me, okay?" he said, licking the corners of his mouth for crumbs.

"Okay."

"I want show you some things." He wouldn't let me wash the dishes so I piled them in the sink.

Jirka stored his treasures in a scratched china cabinet with its left door missing. I nodded my approval as he held up a few specimens from his collection of design magazines from Austria, a couple of crystals wrapped in rags, and incense.

"Smelling sticks are good for relaxation or when you must meditate. And here is my favorite auto." Jirka reached over my head to grab a Mercedes ad tacked to the wall, and I inhaled a whiff of his spiky body odor, warm and honest. As I admired the car he wanted and could never afford, he grinned as if he was ready to offer me anything. "I like your nose," he said and pointed a lamp at my face. "It is Judish nose, no?"

"Yes." I braced for an insult.

"I like it." He spread out his palms to frame my nose, and I smelled his armpits again. "Some-when I want take good photo of your nose. *Ja?*"

After I promised he could take a picture of my nose, Jirka lay back on his double bed and stretched his legs. He had a massive chest and thighs like horse flanks. There was so much of him, it was really impressive. "You want use toilet maybe?" he asked.

"No thanks." I sat on the edge of the bed and stared up the folds of his shorts hanging loose. "We don't say toilet in English. We say bathroom."

"Why? When you no want bath, why say bathroom?"

"It's softer, more suggestive. Maybe more polite." Jirka shook his head to tell me he hadn't understood. *"Zdvorily."*

He snorted. "I think is strange, Americans must say they want take bathroom when they want take toilet. Is no normal."

Amazingly, in all the time we've known each other, Jirka hasn't yet managed to take a picture of my nose. But then he still has one day left to try.

■

WE STOP BY my flat, which after today I no longer rent. My bags are sitting by the door, ready to transfer to his place where I'll spend the night before waking up early to catch my plane. Pan Cerny, the landlord, has given up renting the flat because he can make four times as much money letting it out week by week to tourists or Western businessmen. He's eager for me to go so he can accommodate a pair of insurance agents from Rome.

"Can we make sit?" Jirka asks and wipes his forehead with his arm. We stretch out right on my gray felt carpet. When I moved in, pan Cerny brought a roll of it and cut off a square with a pair of scissors he'd borrowed from a neighbor.

Jirka unbuckles his belt, then opens the top few buttons of his pants, a brand of Levi's knockoffs called Lee Cooper, which he is surprised to learn are not available in America. He opens his pants everywhere, even in pubs or restaurants. I used to try to convince him to button himself back up, but he'd say, "Why? I like it. It is easy."

I stare at his briefs out of habit and feel nauseous. "Is cool color, no?" he says and stretches out his waistband. "But I want find yellow. Yellow for me is the favorite color." Jirka explains he has been searching for a pair of yellow briefs but has never found any and if only some-who would buy him yellow underwear, then he would be really happy.

I nod and he nods too. "Why you all the time with head . . . ," he says.

"I guess it's a habit from teaching. To make sure people understand."

Jirka smiles blankly. He unbuttons an extra button on his pants, kicks off his shoes, and props his wide stockinged feet, sweat-stained along the toes, next to mine as if we're married. "Ahh," he says and folds his thick fingers over his stomach.

But we can't stay like this forever.

I ask if he's ready to go and then leave the keys on my

bed, next to my old Czech raincoat. I bought it for cheap in one of the Vietnamese street markets and it began falling apart a week later.

"You want call taxi or take *tramvaje*?" he asks outside.

"A taxi is too expensive."

Jirka laughs. "You are really Jew," he says.

I drop my bag. "Jirka, that's terrible. That's a terrible thing to say."

"Why?" he says. "I think is nice compliment for you."

"Would you say to a Czech person who is stupid, You are really Czech?"

He shrugs. "I think is nice compliment for you," he repeats stubbornly.

■

A YEAR AGO, back when I left the States, my mother took me to Kmart to load up on toiletries. (Prague had a Kmart too; they sold Oreos and peanut butter in the "imported foods" section.) As we wheeled past a rack of condoms, she asked out of the corner of her mouth like Humphrey Bogart in *Casablanca*, "You need any of those?" I shook my head. The day before at that same Kmart, I'd bought a packet of them, sandwiched between *Sports Illustrated* and *Car and Driver*, both of which I threw away in the parking lot.

She smiled. "I didn't think so."

When my mother was young, black-and-white movies faded out after kisses. Women wore gloves and men fedoras. "Graphic," "direct," and "explicit" were obscene words. "Everything was suggested," she'd marvel when *Now, Voyager* or *Random Harvest* came on TV. "There was no need to come out and say everything. That was the beauty of it." Still,

I dreamed of the day I'd wake up in a pink T-shirt glued to my chest that said FUCK ME, I'M GAY in capital letters. How wonderful to walk down the street with FUCK ME, I'M GAY printed on your chest in pink. Instead of guessing and hinting and winking, men would simply run out of buildings and give you their phone numbers, or throw down flowers from their windowsills. A prince in gold armor would swoop down on a vine from the roof of a gay bar with a sunflower in his hand.

After Kmart, my mother took me to lunch at a Greek diner. Our waiter caught my mother wearing her newly acquired reading glasses. They were light and thin, almost transparent. She'd whip them out and glance through them at menus, programs, newspapers. After gleaning whatever information she absolutely needed, she'd shove them back into her purse, where they clicked against her compact mirror and lipsticks.

In the middle of our meal, my mother leaned over her Greek salad and said in a low voice, "When you're over there, be careful what you tell people about yourself, that you're Jewish or, you know, who you go around with. People there are different. It's not the States."

She sat back against the vinyl booth and stared at her salad, dripping with oil. I faced a skewer of fat gray chicken kebab chunks on an overflowing bed of pale rice. "They have big portions here," I said. We dug our forks into our food as quickly as we could.

■

JIRKA AND I are riding the subway toward Haje, a neighborhood of crumbling housing projects on the edge of town that's so dirty and poor, Czechs insult each other by saying, "Go to Haje!" Jirka claims to know a good pub there.

A friend of mine, a Slovak named Petr, once said to me about Jirka, "Your friend is a real man of the country. He carries the dust of the small town wherever he goes."

I wonder, if he's a man of the country, what does that make me?

I've never been as far as the Haje station. We get off the escalator and emerge from a cavelike mouth of crumbling concrete. The air is damp with fog that smells like oil. Jirka leads me down a dark narrow space between thick gray walls fifteen stories high. Overhead, the lines of laundry block out the stars.

A sign flashes NON-STOP BILIARDY next to the pub entrance. All the pool tables are taken so we sit at the bar, next to a row of video games with flashing lights and names like "Hard Drivin' " and "Terminator X." The bartender, talking into his cell phone in a corner, waves a cigarette at a tired-looking waitress when Jirka snaps his fingers for service. Our beers come in Coca-Cola glasses. Jirka winks at the woman as she shuffles away in her tight Levi's and slippers. "What you think of this servant?" he asks.

"She's pretty." I utter a silent prayer of thanks that I don't wait tables anymore. Of course I might have to do it again when I get home.

"How is type girl you like? Yellow hairs or black hairs?"

"I don't know." I think of the men I've been with, different types and ages, some attractive, all liars. "Nice girls. They're all the same."

Jirka almost falls off his stool. "No are all same," he insists, almost angrily. "Some girl you like, some no. How can you say are all same? It's crazy!" Then he laughs deep and loud. *"Hloupy americany."* Silly Americans, indeed.

■

SOME MORNINGS I woke up and could actually feel my personality evaporate into the smog I breathed each day. As I shaved, I stood dumbfounded in front of my reflection until the glass fogged up with my bad breath. In class, I bit my words into chewable syllables and watered down my 99th-percentile-on-standardized-tests vocabulary. I became an expert on talking about the weather.

"*A* cloud, *a* storm, but you can't count rain unless you have *a* drop of rain."

"She is from Germany. She is *a* . . . does anyone know?"

"Few means not many. But *a* few means some."

A few of my students invited me over for dinner and I learned it was unofficially part of my job to accept. I smiled a lot, made polite comments about weather and Czech dumplings, stretched the bit of their language I knew to its fullest extent, which prompted much initial admiration and then quicker tongues. I smiled on, determined to concentrate and get back on track, but my brain invariably fogged up until the native speakers realized I wasn't paying attention and then it was time for me to go.

Few of them ever invited me to come back.

How had I become this robot (Did you know a Czech invented the word "robot"?), this impersonation of a man, who breathed, ate, paid crowns, all without passion?

I'd been this way long before coming to Prague. Even as a kid in school, I used to dress to blend in with the cinder blocks, slink through classes and bathrooms and the backs of libraries. My disguise proved so successful that when the principal called my name during high school graduation, I heard several classmates say, "Who is *that*?"

■

JIRKA AND I order a second round of beers, and then I take out my portable magnetic checkers/backgammon set. "I want sex two girls," he tells me. His nipples keep peeking out from the thin straps of his Chicago Bulls tank top. "I meet nice girl in *tramvaje* yesterday. She say she like girls. I say to her, okay, I will watch, but she say she will only have sex when she is *allein* with other girl, not for show to man. I say why not? Why you don't want at least to try it? She is crazy, I think." He jabs one of his stiff fingers into my chest. "You had sex with two girls some-when?"

I shake my head and finish setting out the pieces for a game of checkers.

"Hey, you like girls?"

"I *like* them," I say.

"Only girls? Or girls and boys?"

I swallow and search his eyes, afraid he might hit me. "I guess, girls and boys."

He nods.

"Do you like girls and boys?" I study the checkerboard.

"Only girls," he says. I should have figured.

When we finish our game, we turn over the board and play backgammon.

Every month I breathe in this pollution is probably costing me a year of my life.

.

THE YELLOW-AND-RED TRAMS thread their way slowly through this city, a slow network of lifelines connecting to subways that shoot like torpedoes under our feet. Early in the morning, men and women in suits and schoolkids with pink backpacks jam into the aisles. Sometimes I look over their shoulders as they memorize the names and dates of Czech kings and Austrian emperors. During the day, pensioners hobble up and down the steep tram steps with canes and shopping carts, unmoved by the drivers' dirty looks. Late at night, drunk teenagers sit on each other's laps at the back of the cars.

Because of my irregular hours as a teacher, I have experienced each of these crowds and claim none of them as my own. I show my season pass to the undercover ticket inspectors, and they wave me along. I am rarely in a hurry to get anywhere. My students often come late, and no one else would have checked on me.

The trams give you the feeling of constant movement until you realize you are simply going around in a circle. The moving itself has become stable.

.

JIRKA AND I ride the subway from Haje back to the neighborhood where we live, or rather where I once lived and he still lives.

I close my eyes and press myself against the seat. I want to become invisible.

"Haje is very stupid place for living," Jirka says. "But I like for drinking. Is no so expensive like the downtown. What are you thinking on?"

He leans over my face as if he is going to kiss me. I want to tell him either kiss me or go to Haje. "One day I buy flat. I want yellow kravat and yellow *slip* and yellow car."

"In America, yellow is the color for taxis and not private cars."

"Really!" His eyes widen. "Is cool color for myself, I think. I like it. When I am graphic designer I will design only yellow things."

My chest feels tight from trying so hard to breathe in this underground train.

"Why do you work in construction if you want to work in graphic design?"

"Just now I am not work in constructions. I have work as waiter in Planet Hollywood restaurant in town center."

"Fine. But why don't you find work in graphic design if that's your goal?"

He looks up at the ceiling of the train as if to look for the answer there. "Because I have no so much education for graphic design just now. I read all magazines, all books, but just now I think school for graphic design is a little expensive for myself."

"What is your degree in? I mean, what did you study in school?"

"Electrical technician." Jirka pulls out a dirty yellow handkerchief and sneezes.

I smile. "That's a little different from graphic design."

"Why?" he says angrily and wipes his nose. "When you are fourteen and your father say on you, you must choose career for life, how is possible to know what you like? Just now I know but I am twenty-four years old. I have no more money, no more time to do other things. Why you say you like girls and boys? You like only boys, I think."

"Because." I can't say I've been afraid to tell him because he is a man of the country. "I thought I liked girls and boys but now I know I just like boys."

Jirka makes me get out at Wenceslas Square and look at his favorite boutique, across from DKNY. It's a holdover from Communist times named *Dum Mody,* or "House of Style," with an unattractive display of old-fashioned ladies' hats in the window.

The lights from a disco on the second floor blink across his rapt face. They're playing the Macarena. Two teenage girls next to us stare up at the glittering windows and slap their hips in time to the music. Jirka asks me, "Which you like? I think this one is good design. Yeah." I'm not sure which one he's referring to. He's gawking at all of those ugly hats with regret.

■

MY MOTHER WROTE me a letter from home about love in response to my lament that I would be alone forever. "You'll find real love. Just make sure whoever it is listens to you and respects your opinions." My mother across the ocean. End of story.

■

"WHY YOU CAME here?" Jirka asks as we stare at the ugly hats.

"I don't know."

"Why? You must choose to come here, no? Is no accident."

"I don't know."

My parents asked the same thing when I told them the good news.

"Lots of people go," I said. "There's lots of jobs and it's cheap, you know."

"No, we don't know," my father said. "Are you sure?"

"He says he's sure," my mother tried to say. "Maybe he did some research . . ."

"I'm asking him, not you."

"Oh." She put her hand over her embarrassed smile.

"Of course I'm sure," I said.

My mother drove me to the airport, where we shared a sickeningly sweet "Cinnabon" in the O'Hare food court before I left, first for Newark, then Europe. "Have fun. Take care," she said. As we ate, I wanted to cry and she looked like she did too. We stuffed our mouths with sugar and dough, and I didn't know who loved the other more or when we'd see each other again.

Now I know: tomorrow.

■

JIRKA LIVES IN a new apartment now, on the top floor of a private house. He shares with a woman who often travels to Denmark on business. The oven is silver and made in France. The furniture is from Ikea and the faucets have gold handles. He turns them all on for me, then shows me to the toilet. For a few seconds, he stands in front of it and strokes his chin as if he's trying to remember something. Finally he asks, "You need to take a bathroom?"

I'm tired from our beers, the smoke, the smell of oil fry-
ing. There are two mattresses next to each other on the floor
of his bedroom, one for each of us. The pillow feels cool
when I lay my head down.

Once upon a time I imagined I could move somewhere
and dissolve like an old newspaper in a stiff rain. But I'm
horribly lonely now, not just for love, but for people to tell
everything that's bubbling inside me in full-blown, gor-
geously complicated language, with the generosity of a big
portion. I'm more than an asexual sidekick or polite, helpful
English teacher. If I don't know yet exactly what I can do or
who I am, at least I can settle for eliminating the things I am
not.

"Hey," Jirka whispers from his mattress. I don't answer,
but then I feel a rough pat on my shoulder. "Hey, you want
be make sex with me?"

I roll over and open my eyes. "What? Are you serious?"

"What does it mean, serious?"

"Is this a joke? *Je to vtip?*"

"Neni vtip." And to prove he isn't joking, he lifts his down
comforter. His "slip" has disappeared. He's not erect. "I want
try it."

As if I'm a new American breakfast cereal.

I should roll over and close my eyes, but I crawl across
the carpet to his mattress anyway. He pulls me into bed with
him and undresses me like a doll, peeling off my shirt, then
stretching out my boxers.

"Your penis is missing something!" he exclaims.

"It's because I am Jewish," I say. He nods as if he's just

remembered. For a second we lie there and inspect each other and I've almost forgotten how to have sex, but then I think to kiss his thick neck. His mouth gapes open as if I'm hurting him. He shuts his eyes and shivers as I rub my erection against his (which isn't as big as you'd expect from a giant). I suck his nipples, pull his hair, blow into his ears.

Then Jirka pushes me over so I'm on my back. He inches his way down to my waist and sucks on my hard-on like a professional, without scraping his teeth. I have to wonder if this is really his first time.

"I'm going to come," I gasp.

He takes my penis out of his mouth. "What does it mean, come?"

"Never mind. I won't now."

Jirka shrugs, then lies back so I can blow him, but I go back to grinding against his prostrate body until I come all over his chest. He pushes me aside and goes to the bathroom to wipe himself off. I wait, wet and naked, wondering if I've dreamed this up. When Jirka comes back, he puts on a pair of bikini briefs printed with Hawaiian masks.

"You didn't have an orgasm," I say.

"I don't want."

His body is warm. I nestle into his stinky armpit, and my skin sticks to his fur on his chest and arm. I know I should go to America and wait tables, but why? Just because it's my country? Maybe I haven't tried hard enough to make a life here. I could move in with Jirka, in the apartment with gold faucets. We could pretend to the world that we're just friends and make love at night with our eyes closed like we're sleep-walking.

Then Jirka says, "Can you sleep alone, in your bed?"

"Sure." I crawl across the floor again, skinning my elbows. Jirka falls asleep in seconds, but I'm wide awake. It was stupid of me to think I could have been happy here. In order to be happy you have to find someone to care about and a career and a family, all the stuff to help you steer your life. A dick is not a compass.

■

IN THE MORNING, I say I want to take a bath.

"I think is good idea for you," he says. What's that supposed to mean?

I come out of the bathroom, dry and dressed.

"What you think of our sex?" he asks, still wearing the bikini underwear with the Hawaiian masks. "I think is no so good idea."

I grin as if I agree; it's easier than trying to explain. I'm ready to go home now.

Jirka puts on a yellow T-shirt and red shorts, slings a camera around his neck, and walks me down the hill to the tram I'll take to the Ruzyne Airport. He even carries my bag—a real romantic. The tram stop is on a small rise and you can see all the way to the new twenty-four-hour Esso station with an inflated tiger on its roof. They have good ice cream.

"I want take photo," he says, "of your nose."

"No. I want to take your photo." So he submits, standing

in the road with his Mona Lisa–constipated half-smile as if he's the lord of all he surveys.

The tram pulls up. There's no time left for him to take my picture. I offer him my hand, but he takes me into his arms. "I think we will see each other again," he whispers.

RACHEL GOODSTEIN LEARNED about the Israeli folk-dancing class from an article clipped out of the *Cleveland Jewish News*. Her mother had scribbled in black marker above the headline: "Worth a try!!!"

At first Rachel called her mother and said she wasn't going, that she'd moved to Prague for adventures, not boyfriends. But somehow that Thursday evening, she found herself leaning against the empty stage in the ballroom of the Old Jewish Town Hall and muttering to herself, "This is so stupid." There were plenty of empty chairs but Rachel preferred to stand. "Standing burns more calories than sitting," her mother always said.

After several outfit changes, Rachel had settled on her reliable black cardigan with the matching knit skirt and a white collared blouse. I look like a librarian at a funeral, she thought. Still, at least she looked professional, a member of something. She certainly looked good enough for the handful of men who ignored her as they milled around the room. Bucktoothed, bald, pimply, and, worst of all, American, they cowered behind pillars and immediately looked away if she happened to catch their eye—as if she were still pathetic enough to hope one of those losers might ask her for a dance!

When Rachel first came to Prague, she'd had trouble fitting into her jeans and breathing at the same time. And then for a variety of reasons, she got smaller. First, she disliked Czech cuisine. Second, she didn't know where to get pot, which she gave up as well as the snacking it caused her to crave. Third, the ticket machines in the metro intimidated her, so she got into the habit of walking everywhere she could, up and down steps to castles, museums, and opera houses. Finally, her anxiety about sampling non-FDA-approved meat products inspired her to experiment with vegetables.

Tired of waiting for a boy to ask for her name, Rachel had begun studying the refreshments (orange soda and Danish coated in a gluey glaze) when she noticed a man staring at her. He was tall, with puffy cheeks and wavy brown hair dense and tangled like a nest. She quickly pulled out her sweater and stood up straight, but the man looked away. No big loss, she thought, grabbing a couple of Danish—they were small. She didn't really enjoy dances anyway. They were too completely seventh grade.

Recorded klezmer music blared over the speakers as a man in a gold tie called everyone up onto the stage in English: "Join our circle! You don't need a partner!"

The tall stranger with puffy cheeks seemed to be ambling in her direction. He hesitated at the refreshment table, tapping the corner twice as if to test its strength, and then sidled up beside her. He's probably hungry, she thought. You're in his way.

But then the man stuttered, "I-I-I am Lubos." He squeezed

her hand roughly and affected a slight bow. "Please pardon my boldness. You would like a dance?"

He wore a blue-and-white knit yarmulke and a thin gray sweater powdered with crumbs from the free pastries. His narrow body thickened ever so slightly at the middle.

Rachel, who couldn't seem to find her voice, had to nod her assent.

"May I inquire personal question?" Lubos asked as he led her by the trembling hand to the circle of dancers on-stage. "Are you actually Jewish?"

She cleared her throat. "Of course. Aren't you?"

"No, no," he said and almost tripped over the American who took his other hand. "I study in Charles University in"—he paused to place his tongue between his teeth—"theology department, in new specialty of Hebrew Studies. Unfortunately, many students laugh about the impracticality of such a study."

Rachel shook her hair out of her face. Her roommate Eve claimed she had pretty eyes; to accentuate them, Rachel had begun brushing her bangs into brown wings that constantly fell into her view. "Your English is amazing!" she gushed. Calm down, she told herself. She had a tendency to gush.

"Oh, no, not well. Very few of Jewish books are translated into Czech, in which case I must learn to speak English, or more correctly to *read* English."

This struck her as a new idea, that something as natural as being Jewish could be an object of study, even envy.

"And you?" he said. "May I ask what brings you to my homeland?"

"I teach English at a high school, to bored kids who don't pay attention."

"How brave you are!"

"Not at all," said Rachel. "Everything was arranged before I came by one of my professors at NYU. That's where I got my master's. All I had to do was show up."

Not entirely true. She'd also had to endure months of advice from her mother, who reconciled herself to the job by referring to it as a "fellowship."

"Still," Lubos said, "you were brave enough that you actually showed up."

They stopped talking to focus on the man in the gold tie, who was drilling them on a move he called *"Mayim mayim v'sason."* ("Remember, these are more than dance steps. These are the dance steps of your forefathers.")

"Isn't this fun?" Rachel exclaimed, trying not to make too many mistakes, but Lubos seemed confused enough for both of them. He clapped to his left and not his right. He stepped with the wrong foot or a few seconds too late and then landed on someone else's foot. "Oh," he'd say, shaking his head as he tried to correct himself. Rachel managed a fair imitation of proficiency until the last few bars of the song when she collided into Lubos. He fell on one knee.

"Please accept my apology for clumsiness," he said as he stood up again.

"It's my fault," she said sadly. "I'm too heavy to make a sudden move like that." Her cheeks flaming, Rachel hopped down from the stage and sank into a folding chair.

"No, it is my fault," he called after her. "I cannot really dance in highly skilled way." Just then a rail-thin girl came over to Lubos and jabbered in Czech.

"She is tired," he explained a few minutes later as he sat in a chair next to Rachel's. "We live in close proximity so I must escort her homeward."

"Don't worry about me," she sang. "I go everywhere alone. I went all the way to Karlstejn Castle and back by myself." He sounded like one of her students giving a long excuse for not turning in his homework. She wasn't stupid. She could take a hint.

"Perhaps we meet again. Do you attend regularly Jewish functions?"

"Only if my mom guilt-trips me into it."

He shook his head. "Guilt-trips? Er, I'm sorry, what it means?"

"My mom gives me guilt until I go," she said, enunciating slowly.

Lubos blushed. "I am sorry. My English is in very poor fitness tonight. But perhaps your mom would guilt-trip you soon and you would go to some other services. I know interesting old synagogue called Jerusalem which not many tourists visit."

Unsure of how to reply, Rachel shook his hand. "Well, I enjoyed meeting you."

He rubbed his forehead. "Er, yes," he said and then took off, which didn't surprise her because she was a realist. At least she could take comfort in that.

She was considering the Danish again when suddenly

Lubos ran back in and tapped her arm. "You gave me a heart attack!" she said, dropping a paper plate on the floor.

"Lubos is stupid tonight," he replied. "He forgets to ask for telephone number. And here I will write for you mine. My maminka speaks no English but if she says, *'Neni doma,'* it means I am not home but she will tell me some *americanka* has called."

■

ALONE IN HER apartment, Rachel treated herself to a plump little orange she'd managed to score at the fresh market in Hradcanska and had been saving for a special occasion. She let the juice dribble down her chin and fingers so they smelled tropical. Her roommate Eve, recently engaged to a tourist from Hamburg, had disappeared in a whirl of German classes and spontaneous visits to the Fatherland. Rachel's only other friends in Prague were the two middle-aged women from school who shared her office, which they called a "cabinet."

Her mother called, eager to know if Rachel had worn her red sweater set or her cardigan. "He may be more interested in your passport than you," Mrs. Goodstein said when she heard the good news.

"But he could be interested in me, right?" Rachel suggested.

There was a long pause. "Have your fun, then. Just be realistic about the future."

"If this is because he's not Jewish, I don't care about synagogue or lighting Hanukkah candles."

"What does going to synagogue have to do with being Jewish? Do you think Hitler cares if you go to synagogue?"

"No." She hadn't thought of Hitler. "But isn't Hitler, like, dead?"

Her mother breathed heavily on the other end, and she wasn't even on her NordicTrack. "Rachel, when are you coming home?" she said, even though she knew very well Rachel's contract expired in June.

"Who knows?" Rachel said. "I may decide to stay for a while now."

■

THE NEXT AFTERNOON Rachel went out for a ten-minute jog. When she came home, she received a call from Lubos, who invited her to Sabbath services that evening.

"Sounds fun!" she said, hoping the services wouldn't take too long.

At the appointed hour, Rachel waited on the front steps of the Jerusalem Synagogue with its red-and-tan-striped facade and slimmed-onion steeples. She blew on her mittens and stared up into the arched windows, all dark. Had he given her the wrong address? What a waste of a weekend! She could have gone somewhere instead of freezing on these steps. Berlin and Vienna were only four hours away by train. All of Europe was at her fingertips, though the farthest she'd traveled from Prague was for that day trip to Karlstejn Castle she'd bragged about to Lubos. Unfortunately, she'd taken the wrong train and had had to come back without seeing anything. Still, she'd enjoyed the train ride.

Rachel molded her bangs around her fingers and reached inside her coat to pull at her blouse, which had been rolling up on her all evening. Just as she'd decided he was playing a cruel joke on her, Lubos himself came trotting up the steps, his hair flying up in the cold wind. *"Shabbat shalom,"* he panted.

She was unsure of the proper reply. "The same to you," she said.

Her stomach dropped. He was real again.

"Please excuse lateness because I was finishing delicious dinner which Maminka baked for me," he said, then knocked on a side door. A bald, stocky man in a blue blazer let them in. "Services are in small room in back, not main sanctuary," Lubos huffed as he bobby-pinned his yarmulke to his wild hair. "Would you like to see main sanctuary?"

Rachel forgot how annoyed she was as they climbed a set of marble stairs and entered the women's balcony, which had the best view. Above them, stained-glass windows glowed dark blue, almost purple, from the dusk. Marble pillars trimmed with silver held up the central vault, painted in interlacing gold coils. A pair of silver candlesticks twice as high as a person stood next to the Holy Ark, capped by two stone tablets with gold Hebrew letters Rachel couldn't read: the Ten Commandments. She tried to remember what they were. Do not falsely obey thy father and mother. Do onto others and they would do onto you.

"It's beautiful," Rachel whispered and saw her breath in the cold air. Like a cathedral, she thought, or a mortuary. "Why don't they use it?" She gripped the polished wooden railing tightly as she looked out; she was afraid of heights. "If it's okay to ask."

"Congregation is small and old. Many were in Holocaust.

Sometimes they use sanctuary like in case of High Holidays. Even then it's not full."

Lubos leaned halfway over the railing with no fear, like the captain of a ship. She liked his profile at that moment: handsome, definite.

"Let's go," she said, afraid someone might lock them inside to freeze to death.

Lubos held the door for her as they entered the real chapel, which doubled as the library and was the size of her parents' TV room. The Holy Ark, on wheels and made out of plywood, was stationed slightly askew next to the windows, covered in felt blackout curtains. A few old men sat in the front row of folding chairs and licked their thumbs.

"Excuse me," Lubos buzzed as Rachel sat down. "Women sit in separate place."

"They still do that here? You're joking."

He shook his head. "I am sorry that I am not joking. It is the rule."

So these men didn't want to see her while they groaned to God. Old men like her grandfather's friends who ate herring and horseradish on pumpernickel bread.

The women's room was a narrow closet across from the ark. A shower curtain hung in the doorway, and the only light came from a squat purple lamp with no shade that sat on the floor. Two women with wrinkled faces and stiff peach-colored wigs chatted together as they slipped their bunioned feet out of low-heeled shoes. The room smelled like their perfume: a heady mix of lilac and lilies. As Rachel sat down, they protested in Czech.

"They say you are sitting in occupied chair," Lubos explained. "You are permitted to sit only in chair in corner. All other chairs are reserved for synagogue members."

"Why do women have to sit in the 'bad' room?" she asked, moving over and shooting a resentful look at the old ladies. "We're good enough to cook, clean, and get fat having your babies, but we're not fit to sit in the same room?"

"Men should not be tempted by beauty to forget God," he said and sniffled.

Rachel was about to think up a flirtatious reply when she noticed a clear thread of snot dripping from his nose to his upper lip. It could have happened to anyone on a bad day. She looked away as Lubos wiped his nose with a handkerchief.

"I like your shirt," he said. "Maminka has one similar, but it's prettier on you."

"Why, thank you!" she said, but the singing began, and he abandoned her for the men. Rachel opened her book the wrong way. One of the ladies reached over with a frown and turned it around.

The last time Rachel had spent this much time in synagogue was when she was sixteen and her parents had sent her to Hebrew School at the Greater Cleveland Humanist Temple. Her mother said it was a nice way to meet boys who weren't blinded by hormones to someone's inner beauty. Mrs. Rosenzweig, a newlywed with orange skin and blond-streaked hair, spent the first day of class sharing her honeymoon pictures from Aruba. Then she asked her students what they thought it meant to be Jewish.

Rachel considered the issue seriously. What was Jewish?

Tuna fish on challah was Jewish. Passover, High Holidays, Jewish. Chocolate coins, hamantaschen, particularly poppy seed, all Jewish. Anything old and stale-smelling, like matzo or prayer books. Grandparents. Especially grandparents! Bar (don't forget *bat*) mitzvahs. Good shoes you wore to the parties, shoes that you left under your chair once the dancing started. That's when you switched to gym socks over panty hose. Rachel was usually left to sit out the slow dances, except at one party when her mother whispered into the ear of a sullen-looking son of a friend of the family. Within minutes her mother was enjoying the sight of two adorable young couples holding each other at arm's length and shifting their feet back and forth as they moved in place, beat after merciless beat.

SHE MET LUBOS down at kiddush, like a little wine reception at the base of the marble stairs. There were pickle slices, herring, shot glasses of red wine, and tea cookies shaped like moons, the kind she loved. Rachel took one and then a couple more.

An old man came over and greeted Lubos, whose mouth was full of mashed tea cookies. "From America?" the old man asked Rachel. He had anxious gray eyes like chips of ice. Did his memories of Communism keep him up at night, she wondered, or the Holocaust? "You know maybe some Jewish men?" he asked.

Feeling vaguely guilty, she shook her head.

"If you meet any, please tell them about us," he said. "We need men."

Lubos tried to explain the old man's perceived insult on

the street, cold and silent except for a rusty Coca-Cola sign swinging over a dark grocery store. "Service requires minyan, community of ten brothers, in order to start. It is shame I am not really Jewish, so I am unable to be counted."

"Always brothers!" Rachel made a fist in her pink mitten and her bangs fell into her face. "Why not count sisters?" She almost marched into the oncoming Skoda and Lada cars, but Lubos grabbed her sleeve.

"Oh," he said, "I am afraid you are feminist."

"What, may I ask, is wrong with the notion that women are equal to men?"

"Of course they are equal. But not better. You are not lesbian, I hope."

Why were people always accusing her of being a lesbian? Once for an adventure, she'd visited a lesbian bar with a friend named Violetta from her master's program at NYU. When Rachel walked in, she thought she'd stumbled into a fantasy world. There were fat women everywhere, pounding the dance floor, shaking their hips, laughing and screaming as they downed beers and peanuts and potato chips. One woman pinched Rachel in the ass and offered to buy her a drink, but Violetta stepped in. "She's with me."

"Let her buy us beers," Rachel giggled. "Free beer!"

"How about free pussy?" asked Violetta, tall and bony with her hair in a buzz cut that Rachel thought very becoming and attractive, though not ever for herself.

"Well . . ." She wrinkled her nose.

∎

RACHEL TOOK LUBOS to Blatouch, an expat café in Old Town. She ordered in English: a hot chocolate and a brownie.

"Please, what is it, brownie?" Lubos asked.

"You've never had one? You poor thing. It's wonderful! Think chocolate."

Lubos blushed and knocked his menu onto the floor. "I will have exactly what she is having," he stuttered in English to their waitress.

"Your yarmulke is still on," Rachel said and grabbed it off his head. A curl of his hair stood up like a horn so she reached across the table again and tamped the curl back down. "You probably know more about being Jewish than I do," she said with a wink. "Basically all I know is that my mom would kill me if I married a goy."

"And what would be Mom's feelings if that goy converted?"

Suddenly Rachel felt so full she wanted to vomit. Of course even if they got married, she and Lubos would never *live* in Ohio. They'd sweep in and out of town for quick holiday visits, like bombing raids.

"Well," she said, "you might . . . I mean, he might have to slap her occasionally."

He scratched his ear. "Yes, I think I could slap her, if it is required."

When their food came, Lubos closed his eyes and said the blessing for bread.

"It's the strangest thing, but I'm too full to eat one bit," she said, so he ate hers too.

He rode back with her on the tram to her neighborhood, Borislavka, down the hill from where he lived, Vetrnik, or "windmill," with his mother. Even though Rachel couldn't pronounce "Vetrnik," she loved the way it sounded.

"You guys are always being invaded," she said. "Germans, Russians, now us."

"In that case," he replied, "how much more pleasant is your occupation."

As they picked their way down the icy sidewalk from her tram stop, the dark streetlights ahead flashed to life as if by magic and then extinguished automatically behind them. A legacy of Soviet engineering, Lubos explained, to save electricity.

They paused at the rusty gate in front of her bunkerlike gray building. Rachel could only think of her stomach swimming and her head splitting with the cold and him standing there. This man is kind, she thought. Even good-looking at times. So what if his socks don't match, or if he still lives with his mother? That's normal here.

She remembered a line Eve said she'd often used in this type of situation: "I'm thinking that I'd really like to kiss you." But before Rachel could decide whether to use the line herself, she realized she'd said it aloud.

"Yes," Lubos said. "That could be nice idea."

He bent down slightly and waited. I guess I have to do the work, Rachel thought. She hadn't kissed much either except for a guy-friend of Violetta's from NYU who came over sometimes to have sex and then didn't call for weeks unless he wanted to have sex again. It was better than letting the condoms in her bathroom go to waste.

Lubos was waiting, eyes closed, nostrils steaming in the cold air. Her mother was waiting too. She'd asked Rachel to call when she'd made it home safely from the date.

Rachel put her hand on his shoulder for balance and kissed his chapped lips. He pressed his head against hers too firmly, and she had to stop to whisper, "Open your lips."

"Oh." He stepped back and scratched his forehead. "I am sorry. I forgot."

The kiss after that felt pretty much extremely nice, though his breath tasted like weak tea. She forgot how long they'd been standing there before she pushed him away. "I want to ask you . . . Do you think I'm too fat?"

He put his finger on his cheek like he was thinking. She was afraid she'd ruined everything. "No," he said. "You are of course not skinny but you are not either *too* fat."

"Let's walk more," Rachel laughed and offered her hand. He squeezed it tight and took her down a road she pretended she'd never noticed before.

■

"THAT'S NICE," HER mother said, sounding peeved. "Now we'll just have to see when he calls again."

"I'm sure he will," said Rachel, not at all sure. "He's as good as hooked!"

Luckily he called that afternoon to make sure she'd arrived home safely.

"You walked me home, remember?" she said. "Do you know how silly you are?"

"Er, no."

Rachel phoned her mother back. "He just called," she said. "See?"

"I guess you're going to have your fun," her mother said. "I can't stop you."

They met again on Friday. Rachel paced up and down the synagogue steps and when Lubos came out of services, she plucked off his yarmulke and kissed his cheek. They walked through Old Town Square, lit orange in the glow of electric streetlamps and the occasional blaze of a camera flash. Horse-drawn carriages waited for tourists under the Gothic spires of Town Hall. The drivers wore black top hats and Nikes.

At Café Blatouch Rachel was too nervous to order anything besides herbal tea.

"Me too," Lubos told the waiter. "Exactly what she is having."

Rachel explained why she'd decided to teach: "I love kids, but I don't want any of my own to get in the way of my professional and personal growth," she said in the way she'd practiced. "So does it bother Maminka that you're . . . Jewish?"

"No real objection, excepting of at Christmas she expects attendance to family dinner in nice way and no commentary such as, 'Oh, foolish idol-worshippers.' Even though I have no Jewish relations, I always feel as if I am Jewish."

"I bet you're the black sheep in your family," Rachel said with a coy smile.

"What it means, 'black sheep'?"

"The rebellious son. The trouble causer." Lubos shook his head but she patted him on the hand. "Don't look so embarrassed. I like it. It shows you're independent."

They met again on Saturday. She wanted to see something new. He took her to an exhibition of Jewish artifacts in the City Museum near Florenc bus station, where all the grids of power lines for trams and streetlamps crisscrossed over their heads like nets. Lubos pointed out the detail-work on a soot-encrusted building covered in scaffolding: a sleeping owl, a dancing skeleton.

On the tram back, they had to squeeze to fit into two seats side by side. The seats were always so cramped, as if Communist butts had been smaller than capitalist ones.

Lubos described his schoolwork in detail, and she was bored, no, distracted by the hope that he might hold her hand, until he told her his dream. Apparently, it was possible to study for free in Jerusalem with the Orthodox. They'd give you housing and food. All you had to do was read Jewish books, which Lubos did anyway, and buy a plane ticket. "In spite of expensive ticket, Maminka would give me money. Still, I must think about it."

"What's to think? Go, go, go! Or you'll never realize your dream."

"But to leave home for such long time. To be away from Maminka."

"I'm away from my maminka," she reminded him.

"This is true," he said. "But if they find out I am not Jewish it could be trouble."

"Are you circumcised?"

"Yes. For reasoning of health Maminka asked for it."

"Then how could they find out?" She seized the earnest-advice-giving-moment to grab his hand. "Go, Lubos. Sometimes caution is a bad thing. Think of the Holocaust. If the Jews in Europe had just left, gone anywhere, they would have survived."

"You cannot compare," he said. "It was impossible to know what would happen."

"Okay, maybe that's a bad example. The point is, don't be so afraid all the time."

He seemed to be listening. In fact, she could already see him on the plane to Israel, which made her sad until she imagined herself next to him, the two of them riding matching camels across desert wastes and no phones for miles, no way to reach home.

On the ride home, Lubos sang Communist songs from his childhood that made her laugh. He told her about a neighbor, a Mormon from Utah who'd prayed to God to find his stolen car. Two days later, a miracle happened: his cherry-red Buick with the JESUS SAVES, CHRIST DIED 4 U, and I ♥ USA bumper stickers had been found.

"See you tomorrow?" he asked after he kissed her good night.

"Yes!" She kissed his cheek. "And tomorrow and the next day if you want to."

But when he came over the next afternoon, they couldn't think of anything to do or talk about. "Do you know about any unusual exhibits or lectures?" Rachel asked, but he didn't. Also, Eve wasn't back from Germany yet. Rachel wanted Eve to see she wasn't the only one with a foreign boyfriend.

"I feel hungry," Lubos said. "Can you make something for me to eat?"

Rachel decided then and there to teach him how to cook. What would he do without his mother in Israel? And yet as she stood in front of her kitchen counter surrounded by withered vegetables, Rachel felt helpless herself. She wanted to make something new and healthy and delicious though she wasn't sure what yet. Hopefully not a disaster like the tomatoes and mushrooms she'd tried to stir-fry in water instead of oil (her mother's advice), or the mashed-peas-and-rice mixture she'd burned the other week.

"Chop these carrots," she ordered Lubos. That sounded nice and authoritative. And whatever the dish turned out to be, it would probably need cut-up carrots. "How long does it take to convert to Judaism?"

"I am not sure. I think not such long time." Lubos held a carrot up to the light. "Why do I suddenly forget proper blessing for carrots?" He gave a little cry of "Oh," in surprise, as she rested her head on his warm back. She couldn't wait to hit the road with him. It didn't matter where, as long as they left everyone else behind.

"Lubos," she sang, "let's go to Jerusalem."

"Now?" he asked, alarmed.

"When the school year's over. You can study Judaism, and I will too. I have too much exploring to do to go home now." She loved the warmth of his body on her breasts.

"Yes," he said like he was considering it. "It could be nice idea."

■

RACHEL WROTE HER mother explaining that she and Lubos had fallen in love, and they were moving to Israel because they were explorers, with bigger horizons than growing old and fat bringing up babies in Ohio. She kept the letter in her pocket instead of mailing it. If she dared to bring up Lubos on the phone, all her mother would say was, "Whatever happens, you've had a nice little affair."

To prepare for the hikes in the Judean desert, she ran up and down the stairs in her building every night and skipped dinner afterwards. Eve went jogging with her once, but they both pooped out after fifteen minutes. "This is stupid," Rachel said as they panted on the curb. "Why do we do this to ourselves? Why can't we enjoy life like other people?"

That night, Rachel was so hungry she decided to grab a Hershey bar from a stash under her bed and not feel like a criminal for doing it. The sugar and caffeine kept her awake brooding about Jerusalem, which she had a hard time picturing. Mostly she thought of it as a place where instead of chocolate she would eat a variety of succulent fresh fruits her mother had never heard of.

EVE'S FIANCÉ FRITZ came in from Hamburg for the weekend. The two couples planned a double date at Joe's Pub, a dark expat bar with American waiters and free postcards. They sat in the basement, at a corner table carved with graffiti in English, and played German drinking games. Lubos came late, after synagogue. Even though Rachel had asked him to wear a special outfit, he looked as shlumpy as ever in an old argyle sweater and a pair of corduroys worn at the knees. Rachel yanked off his threadbare yarmulke and threw it into a nearby ashtray, possibly by accident. She didn't want Fritz of all people to think she was obsessed with being Jewish. She mentioned that she was only moving to Israel because she'd always dreamed of going on an archaeological dig.

A Gypsy woman came around with roses for sale. Rachel wondered how you became a Gypsy.

"*Kolik?*" Lubos called out, but the woman didn't understand Czech. He repeated himself in English. "How much?" Rachel smiled at Eve and Fritz.

"One hundred crowns." Three and a half dollars.

A ridiculous price, but Rachel was glad to get her rose (even though she'd had to lend Lubos thirty crowns to buy it for her) and glad Lubos hadn't thought of a blessing for it in Hebrew, especially in front of Fritz. She planned to press the flower between the leaves of a book so that years later she'd find the petals there, dried out like the Dead Sea Scrolls.

■

"WHAT NOW?" RACHEL asked after Fritz and Eve went home. The smoke in the bar bothered her eyes. She looked for something to do in *Do Mesta/Downtown,* the weekly entertainment guide, printed in Czech and English. Nothing appealed to her. If only they'd ended their evening a bit earlier, they could have run to the train station and whisked off for the weekend to a castle or something.

Lubos shrugged. "Shall we go home?"

"Home, home, home," she droned, dipping her nose into her flower.

"Excuse me? I don't understand."

"No, nothing," Rachel sighed. "Let's go home."

They were staying at his place to give Fritz and Eve some privacy. It was Lubos's idea. "Are you sure Maminka won't mind?" Rachel kept asking. She preferred to imagine him without a mother, even though Lubos made that impossible.

He and his mother lived in one half of a private house with a fenced garden. The first snowdrops were starting to appear. His father had planted the bulbs before he died. "It is beautiful in summer with nice bench where to sit and read," Lubos said as he unlocked the back door. "I like to stay at home." They left their shoes on a rack of spare slippers in the hall. Rachel stepped into a red pair with flowers embroidered over the toes, which belonged to Maminka. Rachel offered to put them back, but Lubos said, "No, no, I like them," and kissed her. His breath smelled, even though he was sucking a mint she'd given him, and once again his socks didn't match. *"Brucha Ha'ba'ah,"* he whispered.

"Lubos," she hissed back, "you know I don't speak Czech."

He blushed. "It is Hebrew," he said. "It is blessing to welcome guests."

The lights came on and Lubos's mother padded downstairs in slippers and a frayed pink robe. Rachel had hoped to sneak in and out of the house without anyone noticing, but Maminka turned out to be genuinely friendly, even in translation. Also, Rachel was glad to see she was a bit plump, with round, smooth cheeks and bright eyes without lines in the corners. "She says she is happy to meet you," Lubos said as his mother wagged her finger. "And I must clean my room instead of wasting time reading."

Upstairs, Maminka winked and wished them good night. Lubos opened his door for Rachel and cleared a path to his bed by kicking aside clothes, books, and a plate of bread crusts on his bedroom floor. They sat together as he described the Wailing Wall, which he called *Kotel,* and Me'a

She'arim, where the Ortho-crazies stoned women who didn't wear long sleeves, even tourists. Rachel wanted to visit the gold dome in one of the postcards he showed her, but he said it was a mosque and officially Jews were not allowed to enter other religions' houses of worship.

"The rules are always on your side," she complained. "You go to synagogue all you want and you're not Jewish. When are you going to start your conversion anyway?"

"I am content without conversion," he said. "In my heart I am Jewish."

"But what about Israel? How can you get a work permit if you don't convert?"

"Perhaps I will find another way." Before she could argue, Lubos kissed her and turned the lights out. He promised his mother couldn't hear them, even though her room was next to his, and even if she could hear she wouldn't have cared. "Maminka is realist," he said. He opened his nightstand and produced a condom, a Czech brand she'd never heard of. The grainy portrait of a ram on the package didn't inspire much confidence.

"No, never use those," she said. "I have some American ones in my purse."

They kissed for a few minutes and then took a break to strip. She was surprised how much hair grew over his toe-knuckles. Also, his penis was smaller than she'd expected. Rachel had to help him put on the condom and then guide it inside her. He hummed, pushing it deeply for a minute, and then slipped out. Afterward, the two of them in bed were a tight fit, though she liked being held. His sheets smelled like bad butter.

Lubos rolled over against the wall. Rachel, unable to fall asleep, shook his arm. "Do you like me just because I'm Jewish?"

"No, of course," Lubos said, yawning. "You are not only pretty Jewish girl I have known. But you are kind person and not extravagant. And you choose to live in foreign country and live in own apartment away from parents. I wish I am so brave."

"It's not brave," she scolded him. "This place is just like home, I'm telling you. It's easy to live here. And anyway, you'll be brave too. In Israel, right?"

He didn't respond, except to sigh a little.

Long after Lubos had lapsed back into snoring, Rachel lay awake and brooded over their conversations about Israel. He'd never made any explicit commitments and was perfectly free to chicken out on her. How could she move to Israel on her own, without friends or a job? But then if Lubos wasn't coming, why go to Israel at all? That was Lubos's fantasy. She'd have chosen a place that wasn't Jewish at all, like India or Turkey.

In her dream that night, Rachel visited a blue mosque and flirted with old men who hated Israel and sold purple dates and figs out of their carts. Full-figured women in black robes invited her to sit on their floors Indian-style and dip fresh-baked pita into hummus flavored with purple curry. They insisted she eat until she was full. Afterward, they all exchanged addresses so they could write each other postcards for years.

She woke up just before noon with her bangs in her face.

Lubos was sitting at his desk and reading a book about Maimonides. On their way downstairs, Rachel was about to say she had to go home to do her grading when Lubos paused in mid-step and sniffed.

"Oh, something smells cooking. You must surely stay for Maminka's lunch."

"All right then, if I have to," Rachel said. "Ask her if I can help."

"No, she would not want it."

"Ask her anyway."

He said something in Czech and then translated Maminka's response: "She says you must make yourself comfortable and I must help because I am lazy. It is true. I am quite lazy. But in spite of laziness I help sometimes." He translated back to his mother who laughed and said something in Rachel's direction. "She says truly I am lazy and I must learn to contribute in homely way if I expect to find good wife."

Rachel amused herself by staring at a wall of Lubos's baby pictures in the living room. She never understood why people got so worked up about babies. Kids were much more interesting when they were old enough to talk. Then she noticed a shelf of books with titles in English: *A Guide to the Church of Jesus Christ of Latter-Day Saints,* a biography of Martin Luther, and *Hare Krishna!: Facts and Myths.*

Lubos slid around in his slippers as he set the table while his mother called out directions. *"No, no, no,"* he said, which Rachel knew meant, "Yeah, yeah, yeah," in Czech. "She is afraid I will break glass plates," he said, pressing them tightly against his stomach. "She says don't forget spoons." "She says, 'Oh, Lubos, always dreaming.'"

"What are these books for?" Rachel asked, touching the spine of *Buddhism for Dummies.* "I thought you were only interested in Judaism."

"Before my current interest in Judaism, it is true I visited few times my Mormon neighbor," he admitted. "But after stupid belief of God returning to him stolen car I wanted no more with this man, although he kept coming to our house. I hid in bedroom while Maminka instructed him he must never call again."

When Lubos finished setting the table, he settled in the rocking chair. "Ah," he said. "It is comfortable in this room."

"You'll miss your mother's cooking when you're in Israel."

"It is true, if I really go to Israel, I will be sad for house and mother's kitchen."

"But you are really going, aren't you?" she asked, determined to trap him into coming out with a flat refusal.

"Certainly I am thinking about it." Lubos closed his eyes and stretched his legs. "Though I do not want Maminka to be alone."

"Does Maminka have a boyfriend?" Rachel asked. It was strange to talk in the third person about someone who was straining spinach in the next room.

"One, but he was alcoholic and she left him. She says now I am her boyfriend."

"Tell her she's pretty enough to have any boyfriend she wants."

"But she doesn't want boyfriend anymore," he said.

Exactly, Rachel thought. Boyfriends were worse than anchors.

Lunch was baked chicken, spinach, stuffing, and bland cake with sliced apricots inside. Lubos ate his food in heaping forkfuls. Rachel was too disgusted to watch. Across the table, Maminka smiled at her and said things which Lubos translated. She shoveled food onto Rachel's plate without permission.

" 'Eat! Eat!' she says," Lubos explained with his mouth full, his chin dotted with crumbs of stuffing. " 'It's healthy.' "

Her mother would have advised her to take a no-thank-you bite and then sip for dear life at her fucking water glass, so she'd be thin enough to marry a balding mama's boy, so she could show up to the Passover seders with him and a low-fat chocolate mousse cake which would never be as good as her mother's, so she'd munch on macaroons all night for solace and then go on a high-protein diet and join a gym and huff miserably on a treadmill, knowing full well no matter how far she walked, she'd never get anywhere.

Suddenly Rachel felt free, as if her bones were hollow enough to fly—a flying turkey maybe, but flying just the same. She didn't care if she never dated anyone else again, even if the entire Jewish religion died out because of it, even if Lubos cried.

She was a liar and a cheat, a thief of hugs and kisses she didn't need anymore. But he'd get over it. Rachel ate well, dug into her food until she was satisfied. The thick, heavy meal, plain as milk, stuck to the roof of her mouth and gurgled in her stomach.

Maminka winked as Lubos paused to say a blessing over

their meal. She understands me, Rachel thought. We understand each other. Outside it was snowing again, but in that living room with the buttery yellow walls, the air was warm from the kitchen, where Maminka had been baking all day. When Lubos finished his prayer, they went on chewing in silence. Their faces gleamed in the heat and the lights.

On May Day, 1955, two years after the death of Joseph Stalin, a fourteen-thousand-ton granite memorial statue (the largest monument ever built in honor of the great leader) was unveiled on the edge of Letna Park, a bluff above the Vltava River and the heart of Prague's Old Town.

Stalin stood thirty meters high in front of a line of workers, his right hand stuck inside the flap of his trench coat, Napoleon-style. The pose inspired such jokes as, "Why is Stalin reaching into his pocket? He's getting out his wallet to pay for the statue."

Otakar Svec, the monument's sculptor, chose an obscure electrician from the Barrandov film studios as his model for the late Party chief. The electrician, who earned the nickname of "Stalin" for the rest of his short life, became an alcoholic and died three years later. Svec himself committed suicide the day before the statue's unveiling.

A week after Nikita Khrushchev's 1962 speech denouncing Stalin as a mass murderer, the Czechoslovak Communist Party received orders from its Slavic big brethren to dismantle the monument. Too heavy to move, the statue had to be blasted apart with eight hundred kilograms of explosives and one thousand six hundred fifty detonators, set off over the period of a month.

Legend has it that during the first series of explosions, Stalin's head broke off cleanly at the neck and rolled down the bluff into the river, right to the bottom. Minnows darted into his ears and eyes and under his nostrils, looking for sustenance.

The remains of Stalin's body were paraded in an open truck through the narrow streets of Old Town. Seven months later, the truck driver died in an accident on the highway to Poland.

The space on the bluff has remained empty ever since, except for a twenty-five-foot statue of Michael Jackson, which stood there for a week in 1996.

NOW YOU CAN understand why young Franta Smolenek, upon hearing from his best friend Javor that he'd actually seen the legendary head of Stalin in a friend's apartment, reacted in a somewhat doubtful fashion. Then again, Javor was the kind of boy who could say he'd killed a man and make you believe it.

When Javor began at their secondary school three months before the incident in question, Franta had no close friends his own age. Instead he had his doting mother, who dressed her thirteen-year-old darling in short pants with pleats and peasant blouses with blue flowers embroidered on his breast. His nickname in school was "Daisy."

Franta spent his free time helping his mother with the housework. He'd often tie her apron around his own waist and fix their meals while she rested on the sofa after a hard day. They kept no secrets from each other. Franta knew all the names of the students in her chemistry class and which ones she favored. She knew he hoped to be either a painter or a ballet dancer when he grew up. If Franta's father walked in on them huddled together, he'd say with a smirk, "I do hope I'm not interrupting anything."

Franta's father was an ironic, distant man who affected the airs of a scholar. For example, if he wanted to look at one of the pornographic magazines he kept under the woodpile, he hid the porno behind his gold-stamped, leather-bound copy of *The Iliad.* Franta had browsed through these magazines once while his father was at work. He studied them like anthropological evidence of life and manners on another planet. Though he fully expected to have sex someday, he didn't see the point in making a big fuss about it like most of the other boys his age. He classified sex with alcohol, video arcade games, pop music, and other modern annoyances.

When Javor appeared out of the blue at school that fall, no one liked him. He was thin and sandy-haired, with an insolently twisted mouth. Every day he wore a pair of polished black boots with his pants tucked into them, like a Nazi.

"I'm no Nazi," Javor said coolly when Aleksandar, the class thug, pushed him against the bus stop outside their school. "I'm a Communist."

Which struck them all as a good joke, because the only Communists they knew were old people, always complaining about their increasingly worthless government pensions.

Javor never spoke in class except when the teachers' backs were turned. Then he'd disguise his voice and call out: "Mickey Mouse!" "Michael Jordan!" "Hamburger!" He wore old-fashioned wool suits in dingy shades of gray or blue, and square brown sunglasses until the teachers insisted he remove them. He pickpocketed girls. He lit cigarettes in the hallways, and blew smoke rings right in the face of the headmistress.

"Why are you a Communist?" Franta asked him after school one time. He'd followed Javor onto a tram going in the opposite direction of his own home and studied the back of Javor's head for several minutes without saying anything when Javor turned around unexpectedly. They bumped noses.

"I'm no Communist," Javor said and glanced at Franta's shoes. "It's just something to say. Hey, where did you find your shoes?"

Franta was wearing brown Oxford-style dress shoes with laces. "My mother bought them for me in Austria," he said.

"I've been looking for that same kind of shoes. All the old party bosses used to wear them. Do you want to come home with me?"

"I should call my mother first."

"Why should you call your mother? I forbid you to call your mother."

They spent the rest of the afternoon digging mud with loose branches in the woods behind Javor's apartment building. Javor claimed there was a box of vodka buried somewhere by Soviet soldiers before the Velvet Revolution.

"Do you like vodka?" Javor asked.

Franta admitted he'd never tasted it.

"It's delicious, though I prefer a good whiskey. How big is your penis?"

"I don't know."

"You mean you've never seen your penis before?"

"I've never measured it in centimeters."

Javor handed him his stick. "Go behind that tree and hold this stick next to your penis, then come back and show me the mark."

Franta did as he was told, adding a few centimeters.

"That small?" Javor asked.

"It's bigger when it gets, you know, stiff."

"Do you want to try some whiskey at my house?"

Though Franta was slightly afraid of his new companion, he didn't want to show it. "Why not?" he squeaked.

Javor lived on the fifth floor of a monstrous gray *panelak* in a public housing complex formerly known as Red Bridge. The elevator was always out of order, so they had to take the stairs. His mother's apartment was crowded with antique chairs and tables broken and piled on top of one another, a tray of tarnished silverware, a dirty breakfront with cracked windows, and rows of elaborately carved armoires, some with doors missing. From the bottom drawer of one of these armoires, Javor removed a bottle of whiskey, almost empty and wrapped in yellow newspaper. Franta downed half a capful. It tasted like perfume and scalded the roof of his mouth.

"The best stuff on earth!" Javor declared after downing a shot and beat his chest. He took off his boots and began to shine them with paint thinner, right on the living room floor, without even a newspaper underneath.

"Where's your room?" Franta asked.

"I don't have one. I share the place with my mother. I'm the man of the house."

"What about your father?"

"What about him?"

Franta liked that, the easy recklessness of "What about him?"

An hour later, Franta's father slapped his cheeks red for coming home late, then kissed him on the cheek and sent him to his room with no dinner. As soon as she heard her husband snoring in front of the TV, Franta's mother brought her son a plate covered with a pot lid to keep it warm. She also brought some leftovers for herself and they sat on the bed together, eating and laughing.

■

SO JAVOR REMAINED Franta's school friend only, despite attempts to lure the latter to Red Bridge with Nazi medals, sadomasochistic pornography, marijuana, a mythical American slut neighbor with big boobs who Javor claimed gave blow jobs as a hobby. It wasn't until he promised to produce Stalin's head that Franta paid attention.

"Stalin's head is at the bottom of the river," Franta argued. "Isn't it?"

"You mean you actually believe that old legend? Why don't you join me some time for a visit to pan Novak's flat?"

"Who is pan Novak?"

"Just a man I know." Javor raised his left eyebrow.

They arranged a date for the following Thursday evening. "And don't forget to wear your shoes!" Javor called out as he hopped onto the tram.

Franta picked Thursday because his father worked late on Thursdays, though really he was visiting his girlfriend, a woman from the office. Franta and his mother knew all about the girlfriend, but they never mentioned it to each other.

On the morning of the appointed day, Franta kissed his mother's cheek as she sat on the edge of her bed and pulled on stockings. "Maminka, I'm going to be late from school," he said. "You know you're my best friend, don't you?"

"Me? I'm an old woman. I don't know anything. I don't even know who your friends are. And why don't you wear that little hat I made to match your blouse?"

He smoothed her hair and let his fingers trail down the sides of her face.

"Where did you go that day when you came home late, the other time?" she asked him. "Was it a girl or something?"

"Yes," he said absentmindedly. "A girl."

"Is that where you're going today?"

"Exactly." He looked glum.

"You don't have to be so touchy about it. I won't tell your father."

"Thanks."

"He'd only make stupid jokes."

"Can I go now?"

"Why are you so touchy today? Yes, you can go."

∎

AT SCHOOL, JAVOR remained aloof all day until a few minutes before the final bell when he handed Franta a bulky paper

shopping bag with red plastic handles. "Good, you remembered to wear the shoes. Take this into the bathroom and get
dressed. I'll meet you at Karlovo namesti by the tram stop in
fifteen minutes."

The bag contained: one (1) sky-blue double-breasted
suit that smelled stale like an old newspaper, one (1) starchy
white dress shirt, and one (1) solid brown tie with an oil
stain. Locked in a bathroom stall, Franta took off his frilly
white shirt with the blue bow at the neck and his blue
trousers with cuffs and then put on the old-man outfit. He
noticed something else at the bottom of the bag wrapped in
a dried-out washcloth: a small black pistol. It was surprisingly light, like a toy. Franta, who'd never touched a gun before, held the pistol by his fingertips. It felt cold, and he
wanted to check if it was loaded, but was afraid he might ac-
cidentally shoot himself. He hid the gun in the inside pocket
of his suit jacket and then ran to meet Javor, five minutes
late.

"I almost left without you," Javor said and dragged him
onto the tram. "Remember, punctuality is key in the new
workers' paradise."

"Are you a Communist again?"

"We're both Communists," he said. "I'd better explain to
you about pan Novak."

Almost a year before, Javor had been minding his
mother's antique shop on Betlemske namesti after school,
playing with the little Soviet flags they were once obliged
to set in their windows each May Day, a flower-spray tea
set from the Golden Age of the First Republic, a ration book

from the Nazi occupation. An old man with a gray beard and drooping shoulders came in. He was tall and broad like a grizzly bear on its hind legs, and his heavy black eyebrows were streaked gray. "We're not buying any more Soviet or Nazi medals, thank you," Javor said in a tired voice.

"I've got something better," said the old man, and he produced a series of prints from a folder: Stalin reviewing a line of saluting elephants at a zoo; Stalin and Gottwald playing poker on a table shaped like Czechoslovakia; the Defenestration of Prague featuring Stalin in a Rembrandt hat being thrown out of a window of the Castle; Stalin with hot pink lips leaning forward to kiss a figure who'd been obviously and comically airbrushed out of the picture. "You could sell them to tourists. I was hoping to trade for a set of old dishes. You can't find decent Czech china any more, just the crap they palm off on tourists."

Javor told the man that he didn't really think they were worth anything, but his mother would come back soon. She did all the buying.

"Not worth anything," the old man grinned, showing his crooked teeth. "It's only history we're talking about."

Javor leafed through the prints one more time.

"I was banned for sixteen years," the old man said proudly. "At first they liked me, until they realized how my satire directed at Stalin applied to their own regime. They could have sent me to jail. I had friends who went. I could have gone too if they'd forced me."

"Oh, yes, we all *could* have gone." He handed back the prints.

"Shut your big mouth." The man glared at Javor like he wanted to hit him. "We believed in certain principles, not like today where it's all money. They placed me under surveillance. You know when Havel met with Wałesa at the Polish border? I was supposed to have been there."

"What happened?" Javor asked skeptically. "Did you catch cold?"

"Soft," the man sneered. "You had to be strong in those times. May you live someday to understand what it means for a grown man to be under surveillance, with someone watching you all the time, drinking too much, taking a piss, fucking."

"You liked it, didn't you?"

"Oh, sure. Like a prisoner loves his cell."

"Don't prisoners love their cells?" Javor said, flipping through the prints once more. "Wait a minute. Now I know who you are. I read about you in some of the old newspapers we have here. You really got under their skin."

"You have the old newspapers?"

"Of course."

So Javor took him in back where they kept the old copies of *Svobodne slovo* (The Free Word) bundled and tied with twine.

"My God." Pan Novak shed a few tears as he turned the fragile pages, like he was seeing an old friend. "Are these for sale?"

Actually, Javor and his mother used them as wrapping paper, but Javor said, "Yeah. One hundred crowns per bundle."

"Give me five, then," said the man and peeled off five one-hundred-crown bills.

He came back the next week, and soon he was dropping in every few days to buy bundles of newspapers, more than he could ever read, Javor was certain.

"What do you do with them all?" he asked, but the old man wouldn't say. Once, when pan Novak really did catch cold, he phoned Javor's mother and asked if she could send her boy over with a few newspapers.

The furniture in his apartment was arranged in neat lines, nothing out of place. A maid came once a week. Framed prints hung in even rows along the walls. Stalin taking tea, Stalin wearing the Castle as a crown, lime-green Stalin French-kissing a German shepherd. The mahogany end tables were covered with tiny clay models of Stalin dancing the tango with Hitler, Stalin balancing a bottle of vodka on his head.

Pan Novak greeted Javor in his bathrobe and served him tea and chocolate pastries. "They used to come in here and upset everything, like so!" He picked up a clay figurine and kicked over one of his end tables. "Or sometimes they sat in my chairs like you are now and simply stared, trying to make me uncomfortable. Because I knew things and I didn't try to hide it. I wasn't one of those morally sick people who became used to saying one thing while thinking another." He took a bite of pastry and then continued with his mouth full of chocolate cream. "I believe each of us affects history in his own way. I'd rather have rotted in jail than compromise with them."

"But you didn't rot," Javor said. "In fact, you're amazingly well preserved."

"So soft," the old man said. "You young people have plenty to learn. You've no idea how it was to be a man then. Even you, smarty-pants, in your costumes."

After that, pan Novak stopped coming to the shop altogether and depended on Javor to deliver the newspapers. Also, the old man began acting "funny."

"Funny, how?" Franta wanted to know.

"He asked if I didn't want to search his apartment."

"What were you looking for?"

"Me? Nothing. But he pulled open the drawers, declaring he had nothing to hide. After a time or two, I began opening the drawers myself without even asking, which was what he wanted. So then I really got into the part, did it up right, checking the cupboards, the refrigerator, knocking books off his shelves, pulling up his sheets.

" 'And what is this for?' I'd ask.

" 'Nothing at all,' he'd say. 'Why do you keep tormenting an old man?'

"I searched the bathroom, the kitchen, his bedroom, and all the closets, but there was one room he kept locked which he wouldn't let me into. 'You will have to break down the door,' he said. Lord knows, I tried, but it isn't like in the movies. It's a very difficult thing to break a door down, and I was afraid of really doing some damage there, though I really don't think he'd have minded.

"At the end of each visit, he gave me one hundred crowns, like a tip. Once he asked when I'd be coming by next, but then he said, 'Oh no. Please don't tell me.'

"I kept coming every few weeks, always on a different day to keep him guessing. Sometimes I interrogated him and he'd tell me how he was planning his escape, only he said the escape wasn't a real escape, but an escape into the mind.

"Then last fall, Maminka received a letter notifying her I'd been transferred to this school, a much better one than where I was. She didn't understand it because she'd been trying to get me into a different school for years, but my teachers always reported that I was 'undesirable.' Now all of a sudden here I am. Of course I didn't tell her about pan Novak. I wasn't about to share the money he gave me for those worthless newspapers.

"I tried to think of new ways to search his apartment. Sometimes I waited outside his building for him to come out and followed him while he did errands, keeping in plain sight so it was perfectly clear I was there. And then last month, I strip-searched him.

" 'No, not that!' he begged, on his knees.

" 'Shut up!' I barked and took out a gun, a little pistol, a silver lady-thing that celebrities of the First Republic used to carry around for style, not good for much except shooting blanks at sick puppies. But pan Novak didn't know that. He started blubbering and carrying on. I ordered him to stop crying but he wouldn't."

"Disgusting!" Franta said and covered his mouth.

"Get this, when he pulled down his pants, he had a hard-on."

Franta turned red. "Did he ask you to touch it or anything?"

"No way. He's crazy, but no pervert. He just kneeled beside the window in his underwear while I searched his clothes and took seven hundred crowns out of his wallet. I left him the change. But he must have really liked it because the next time I was over there, he told me in an excited voice that he had something special to show me, and then finally unlocked the door to that room I was telling you about. And that's where I saw it."

"You mean Stalin's head?" Franta asked.

"You'll see."

■

THEY GOT OFF at Zelivskeho, next to the New Jewish Cemetery, where Kafka was buried, and Hotel Mozart, a newly built pink cement fortress that looked like it had been transplanted from some seaside resort in Croatia. A crowd of construction workers in blue uniforms huddled next to a shed selling newspapers, M&M's, and hamburgers made out of ground chicken. Javor led Franta over the tram tracks to an alley that ran between two tower blocks of apartments, each with a grid of slate-gray windows. The front door to Novak's building had a dent in it. After Javor jabbed three times at a buzzer marked with the name Jelinek, the door buzzed back and Javor pushed it in.

A metal plaque with Russian writing hung above the control panel in the elevator, which was lined in wood. They rode to the second floor. At the end of the hall a bald man with a white beard and faint wisps of hair over his yellow eyes stood in an open doorway, his back curved like an umbrella handle. "You have no right to disturb an old man," he snarled and pressed himself against his door to let them in. His skin was red and cracked, and he wore a bathrobe flecked with white and yellow streaks of paint. Franta shuddered as he passed under the old man's breath, which smelled like sour milk.

The shades in the living room were drawn. Their edges glowed yellow from the light outside. The chairs stood at crooked angles next to a low table covered with dirty plates and a pair of stretched-out underwear. A radio on the windowsill played static.

Javor sneered, "Why don't you show my colleague here, comrade, what you showed me the last time. In the small room. Desecration of a sacred monument. Theft of public property. The list of charges goes on . . ."

"But I dredged it up from the river. No one wanted it."

Franta mopped his forehead with his sleeve. The apartment was as hot as a greenhouse.

"The people's government wanted it!" Javor insisted. "For the preservation of history. You should have realized."

The old man took a dull gold key from his pocket. He hobbled in his torn slippers down the hall to a narrow door with a frosted-glass window. "I know you've been watching me," he said, his voice rising. "I'm no cretin." With an unsteady hand, he turned the key in the brown lock and let them inside.

The room was dark and smelled like wet clay. And there he was: Joseph Stalin, or his head anyway, golden brown and filling up almost the entire room, his windswept forelocks, his proud nose, his bushy mustache growing out of his nostrils, his ears broken off (or maybe not yet attached), his eyes blank, his chin cracked, his smile calm and wide. Then Franta noticed a plastic bucket of newspaper strips swimming in a gruel of thin paste and a stack of newspapers on the floor. Photos of Stalin were tacked up on the walls and taped to the windows. When Franta looked closer at the head, he saw newsprint through the watery layers of golden-brown paint.

The old man stood in the doorway with his head bowed and muttered to himself.

"He made this?" Franta wondered aloud. "What does he do with it? I thought you were going to show me the real thing."

Javor coughed. "Of course it's the real thing," he said and jabbed Franta's elbow. "This man is a thief! This time we really have to punish him, comrade!"

As Franta walked around the sculpture, he took care to step over newspapers and pots of brushes and paint spread out over the floor. He tried to maintain his distance, but he kept bumping against the walls of the narrow studio. The heavy picture windows at the other end of the room had been flung open, and a frigid wind fluttered through the strips of newspaper that hung off the unfinished back of Stalin's head, hollow except for a nest of metal wires that supported the papier-mâché.

"What's it for?" Franta asked, his voice rusty as an old nail. He stood behind the head and gazed out, past Javor and the meek old bear in the speckled bathrobe, through the slender door to the dark cramped hall with the shabby

mustard-striped wallpaper. He imagined he could see farther, that he was looking down at his entire city, and also
that the little people scurrying below his feet, each one
busy with his own insignificant life, suddenly looked up
to him. His penis stiffened a little and he straightened his
spine. The blank expression he usually wore became rigid
as if intentional. He felt he could reach out with his foot
and crush all the ants below, creeping across the sodden
earth.

"Take out the pistol," Javor whispered behind him.
Slightly dazed by the icy breeze on his neck and the smell of
rotting paste, Franta followed orders.

"Wait," the old man said. "I'm not ready. It takes me a
second." He tiptoed over a bucket of paste and squeezed past
Stalin's head until he stood there with Franta and Javor.
Then he kneeled next to the window and prayed silently.

"It's part of the choice game," Javor whispered. "Like
they played with Jan Masaryk. Say to him, 'Tell us what you
know, or we give you the choice to commit suicide by jumping out the window.' That's his favorite. It has sentimental
value for him if you understand what I mean."

"They actually gave him this choice?" Franta asked. "So
what did he choose?"

"He's still alive, isn't he?" Javor said.

"You mean he collaborated?"

"You're ruining the game! Order him to stand up! Wave
your gun at him!"

"On your feet!" Franta said in a deep voice that didn't
sound like his own. The old man dragged himself to his

feet, puffing and sweating, grasping the walls for balance. Javor reached forward to lend a hand and lift him up, but the old man quickly found his strength and stiffened his spine.

"Tell him to stand next to the window."

"Stand next to the window!"

The artist grabbed the windowsill, his eyes closed.

"And to tell us everything he knows, or else he has the choice to jump out."

"Tell us everything you know, or else you have the choice to jump out!" Franta said and brandished his pistol a bit.

The artist drew in a noisy mouthful of cold air and opened his eyes wide. "It's no use threatening even an old man like me with this little wimp," he growled. "You've been terrorizing me for years. Every week these mindless appa-ratchiks come here wanting to know what I know. I'll tell you one thing. I know we're men, not slaves."

"What's he saying?" Franta whispered. "It sounds like a film."

"He's never done this before," Javor whispered back. "Just play along."

"I told you already everything I know and still you keep coming with your old threats. But this time, it's going to be you who has the choice. Either leave these premises at once or you're going to get it. It's your decision. Watch out now!"

"What do I do?" Franta asked as the old man came shuf-fling toward him.

"Let him threaten you," Javor said. "Let's see what he

does." So Franta, not wanting to disappoint his new friend, clenched his eyes shut as the old man grabbed his arms with a surprisingly steely grip. And then suddenly he felt his feet lift off the floor as the old man grabbed him and hoisted him over the windowsill.

Before Franta could cry out, he crashed into a row of high, thick evergreen bushes that saved his life, or at least saved him the annoyance of wearing a cast or two for a few weeks. Almost half a minute went by while the head of the Communist Party lay there tangled in the bushes as if paralyzed, only vaguely aware of the wind whistling in his ears, Javor laughing at him from the window one story above (the old man had disappeared), as well as the curious neighbors on the sidewalk who'd set down their shopping bags to watch.

A needle from the bush pricked the inside of his thumb. Franta jerked his hand back and stared at the red bubble slowly expanding on his skin. With a sudden fortitude he didn't know he possessed, Franta grabbed hold of two thorny branches and thrashed his way to the ground. His cheeks and hands scratched red and stinging with sap, he yanked himself out of the jacket Javor had lent him, still caught on one of the bushes. Then he ran.

■

FRANTA'S MOTHER HELD her son's quivering form against her breast and wondered where he'd found his strange clothes and how he'd scraped up his poor hands. For a second she was going to ask him about it, but then he pushed her away and looked up with a stubborn, unfamiliar expression, as if he blamed her for whatever had happened. "When's my father coming home?" he demanded.

She didn't know why he had to be so awful all of a sudden, just because of a girl. "Not until late," she replied in a curt voice, and with that legendary firmness of which only mothers are capable, she ordered him to bed.

THIS GROUND YOU ARE STANDING ON

J UST OUTSIDE THE BAGGAGE claim in Prague's Ruzyne Airport, Sarah Schroeder was admiring the foreign stamp in her passport when a native approached her to ask, "You need place to stay?" He looked handsome in a slick, Aryan way, with blond hair gelled into stiff spikes and a sharp nose. She guessed he was about seventeen, her daughter's age.

Sarah grabbed the handles to her and her husband's suitcases more tightly. They were old suitcases with creaky wheels that kept twisting around. "That's very kind of you, but we've reserved a hotel," she said, unable to take her eyes off the boy, whose pretty smile almost charmed her into saying yes when she meant no. "We need a taxi."

"What's the coincidence! I offer a private taxi service. I am called Vitek."

Her husband Carl hobbled up beside her. His left leg had been amputated a year ago; even a small walk left him short of breath and with his forehead dripping. "I don't think so," he said.

They'd planned to go to Europe for her fiftieth birthday, but now it didn't look like Carl could hold out that long, so they went a year early. London, Paris, and Rome were out of their budget, and Sarah had heard Prague was the Paris of the East. A friend had recommended a hotel. Their guidebook described the rooms as "cheerless but serviceable."

"He looks like a nice kid," said Sarah. "Where's your sense of adventure?"

Sensing an opening, the young man held out his arm. "Please, my friends, my car waits for you." He nodded at Carl's crutches. "You need help with bags, maybe?"

"No thanks," Carl said, swinging himself forward. "She'll take our bags."

There was just enough room for them in the young man's red mini-car, with Sarah and Vitek in front, Carl and his crutches spread out in back, and their two bags crammed into the trunk. "Tell me all about the changes here," Sarah asked Vitek, who seemed more interested in flipping between pop stations on the radio. At one point, he yanked the car around a hairpin turn so sharply that Sarah was afraid their vehicle might tip over.

So here was the Old Country. In 1939, her parents had fled to the States from just such a land, a land of herring, dark bread, and Slavic women who drove geese. It was a place Sarah had never been nor believed herself likely to go, thanks to Stalin and the rest.

Prague struck her as depressing, even for a city recently liberated from the throes of Communism. Stark black trees without leaves languished by the sides of the bumpy roads, where the asphalt was coming off in craggy plates. Endless rows of gray cement apartment buildings flashed past like an unbroken monotone, a single note held for fifty years.

But then they crossed a green ridge and the city opened

up like a flower. The dark-green river, crested with white foam, bent like an elbow between two banks packed with crooked red roofs and narrow towers. Sarah stared transfixed at the Castle, a pink-and-lime-green fortress crowned by a jagged brown Gothic cathedral. Vitek said there were no kings anymore, not even remnants of the royal family hiding out in Switzerland.

■

BY THE TIME they crossed the river, Vitek had convinced the Schroeders to forget their reservation at the Hotel Europa and rent a room for a mere fifteen dollars a night from an elderly friend of his, a Mrs. Hubova. "You'll be comfortable there," he said as their car lurched onto the sidewalk in front of Mrs. Hubova's building. Carl, who hadn't slept since they'd left San Francisco, clutched his head in the backseat. "She is gentle-lady in reduced circumstances. And she can do your laundry for fifty crowns."

"As long as she has an elevator," said Sarah, already impressed by the money they were saving. "We're not so good with stairs."

The building had an elevator, just as Vitek promised. And Mrs. Hubova appeared every inch the gentle-lady, with hair the color and texture of banana cream pudding and swept into a smooth wave across her forehead. Her eyes were blue and sedate, her nose regal, her round cheeks like a pair of ripe peaches. She wore a blue bathrobe with a crown stitched to the front pocket, the kind of soft, elegant robe Sarah's mother used to wear.

Mrs. Hubova had given up her largest room, the salon, for visitors. Their thin bed was wrapped tight as a mummy in a brown cotton blanket, with sheets so dry they crackled. "Isn't this great?" Sarah told a dubious-looking Carl as Vitek gave them a tour. She remained in good spirits until they visited the cramped bathroom, which had a washing machine, a small toilet, and a modified birdbath with a showerhead you picked up like a microphone. Carl demonstrated by singing the opening lines to "California Dreamin.' "

After they paid Vitek, Mrs. Hubova wished them a terse good night and disappeared into her bedroom. Carl went to the bathroom to wash up. A bit nervous to be alone in a strange apartment, Sarah opened her bag and frowned at her clothes: a lemon-yellow sweater, a red-and-white-striped shirt that made her look like a barber pole, and a sequined sweatshirt from J.C. Penney's that said "Paris!"

How did she get stuck with some of these outfits? In the stores they seemed completely different, as if she were looking with another pair of eyes.

They had an armoire and one drawer for their things. Sarah couldn't resist a peek into the other drawers, which Mrs. Hubova had reserved for herself with two strips of tape stretched into an X. In the bottom drawer, Sarah found three silver spoons hidden in a stack of towels, just the way Sarah's mother used to hide her pearl necklace and diamond earrings in her piles of sheets, or else stuffed into her father's old socks.

Before digging any further, she pressed her ear to the door to make sure no one was coming and noticed an iron wedge decorated with Hebrew letters nailed to the doorpost. Sarah stretched out her hand to touch the metal.

There were three sharp knocks, and then Mrs. Hubova opened up.

"I brought some things maybe you can use," she said, staring at the carpet as Sarah closed the drawer with her foot. Mrs. Hubova set a map and a dog-eared guidebook on the dresser. "If you need something, you call me. I am in next room."

They studied each other awkwardly. Sarah felt tempted to plant a kiss good night on the old woman's plump cheek, but she only said, "Thank you."

"*Bitte,*" Mrs. Hubova said with a shadowy smile and closed the door.

A few minutes later, Carl came back from the bathroom in a pair of white briefs with the waistband torn on one side. He gripped the edge of the desk, where his medications were spread out like a feast, and licked his dry lips. In public he usually wore a San Francisco Giants baseball cap to hide his bald head.

"Listen to this old Commie propaganda," said Sarah, her eyes fixed on the yellow guidebook Mrs. Hubova had left them. " 'The old city is a huge pile of gloomy, crowded houses, a cheerless world of stone walls and pavement. But on the outskirts of Prague we have built white house-communes radiating in all directions. Each dwelling turns toward the sun to get as much light as possible and is surrounded with flower beds. By every door you are greeted by green giants, oaks, pines, linden trees, the happy singing of birds and the calm, sustained, refreshing voices of trees . . .' "

She looked up from her reading. "Carl, you're almost naked! What if she sees?"

"Am I?" he asked, hopping a bit more to balance himself. He'd been perspiring hard, which partly accounted for his sour, yeasty smell. "I need help with that darned shower-head. You'll have to hose me down."

Sarah came over and offered an obliging shoulder. "It's an adventure," she reminded him. "I found out our landlady is Jewish. She's got a mezuzah on the door."

"Does that make you feel better?" Carl asked.

"Don't be silly," she said. "You know I'm not like that."

∎

MRS. HUBOVA, WHO'D left early for work, set out a plate of rolls for their breakfast. Sarah threw the ones they hadn't eaten into her purse along with an orange she'd found at the back of the fridge, behind a bottle of plum wine and a carton of sour cream.

The apartment was a five-minute walk from the town center, not bad on a warm fall day. After a self-guided tour of Kafka's birthplace, two rooms with a time line on the wall and a few first editions in glass cases, Sarah and Carl visited the Jewish Cemetery. The sky was the color of steel wool, and the crooked headstones were laced with dead leaves.

Sarah, who'd covered her dark curls in a batik-printed scarf that clashed with her skirt, tried to read a few of the names on the stones. A few weeks ago, Sarah had stood with the same vacant expression at the unveiling of her mother's headstone, which took place eleven months after the death as per Jewish law.

"There's a few more synagogues to hit," she told Carl at the exit. He rolled his eyes, so she explained, "I'm not being a super-Jew. We're only here because the guide says the Jewish Quarter is a must-see. We can go to an art museum if you'd rather."

"No, no. It's an interesting place even for us pseudo-Jews, or whatever I am."

What was he exactly? Sarah was never quite sure, even though Carl had consented to a quickie conversion from the rabbi who'd married them, a Reconstructionist with long black hair down to her butt and a falsetto like Joan Baez. Minutes before the ceremony, he'd simply signed a piece of paper that even most Reform rabbis considered invalid.

As she held the cemetery gate for her husband, a pair of old men stopped their conversation to watch. Carl bent his head and kept pulling himself forward.

"No one even cares about your crutches," said Sarah, who never referred to the missing leg, just the crutches. "They take one look and then go about their business." But she'd noticed too; people stared everywhere here, even worse than at home.

"All these cobblestones are giving me sea leg," he complained. "These streets must have been designed by Jewish podiatrists."

"This synagogue looks nice," she said, hoping there was a place to sit inside.

A yawning attendant handed out blue yarmulkes at the door. The walls had been plastered over, and the pews replaced with display cases of menorahs, spice boxes, and Torah pointers. Sarah, who preferred straight history with clearly marked labels and informative wall text, wasn't sure what she was supposed to look at. Even with all the lessons her parents had put her through, she still didn't understand why anyone should repeat words and rituals because someone else had performed them hundreds of years ago.

She examined one of the menorahs for a while, silver, very plain, no interlace or gold filigree like in those garish Judaica shops at home. Carl wanted to buy her one, even after she said no, but there weren't any replicas for sale in the gift shop.

"What does this one say?" Carl asked, picking up a wooden menorah with an inscription in Hebrew.

She blushed as she read it: *If I should forget thee, O Jerusalem, let me cut off my right hand.* "I haven't spoken Hebrew in years," she said. "I hardly remember anything."

"Yes, you do. Why don't you tell me?"

"I really don't remember."

In the next synagogue they visited, the walls had been painted with the names of Czech Jews killed in the Holocaust, all in bright red. Sarah tried to read a few of the foreign names and then let the crowds push her on and out the door.

Your life hasn't turned out so bad, she thought under the clouds. You're lucky.

Before she was born, her parents used to get letters from Poland filled with dried mushrooms that her mother made into soup. Her mother said the whole house smelled warm like those mushrooms. But then the letters stopped coming and there was no more soup. After the war, they found out the Nazis had wiped out all the Jews in their village in one day. Every Yom Kippur, Sarah's mother and her stolid father wept for them. Last year she'd gone to synagogue on Yom Kippur for the first time in years to take their place, but she felt like a dummy without its ventriloquist as she tried to make the words of the memorial prayers come out of her mouth.

"I'm sorry I made so many jokes," said Carl as they tried to find a place for lunch. "That must have been hard for you in there."

"No harder than it was for you."

"Hang on," he said, panting behind her, and she waited for him to catch up. "I saw a sign about a day trip to Terezin tomorrow. I figured you might want to go."

Sarah hated the way he kept pushing her like this, but she couldn't let him know he'd gotten her goat. "I thought we were going to the Castle tomorrow."

"So we'll go there on Thursday. There's no rush."

He sounded serious, and maybe he was. "Fine, if you want to." Actually, she was dying to go, even though none of her family had been lucky enough to make it as far as a concentration camp. Her friends who'd been said very solemnly, "It was *unbelievable*," as if they'd seen a film deserving of several Academy Awards. "Really *something*." Their eyes lit up, and a subtle smile flickered over the corners of their mouths.

■

THAT AFTERNOON, SARAH flirted with the idea of opening the front door to the apartment while Carl snored in their room.

She was impatient to go out and see real people, but she didn't feel safe wandering alone in a strange city.

Since Carl was a doctor, she couldn't keep the gravity of his condition a secret. He'd saved almost nothing, so Sarah accepted a job with a dentist friend of Carl's who understood whenever she had to run home or drive Carl to chemo. Prague was cheap, but they couldn't have come without the help of this same dentist.

Sarah had never been pretty, with her fright wig of black curls and hawklike nose. No one expected her to marry, and she followed some hippie friends to San Francisco and found a job as a speech therapist in the public schools. Instead of going to services Saturday mornings, she meditated to Joni Mitchell records with her cat. Then surprise, surprise, at the ripe old age of thirty, she'd gone for a checkup to a handsome dentist named Schroeder. He had a sharp tongue like her father's, except he could be tender. "I can't stay mad at you when you smile at me in that hurt way," he'd say, nuzzling her neck.

Her parents, on the other hand, stayed mad for years, even after Carl's conversion. ("*Sub*version is more like it," her father said.) Even after their daughter read from the Torah at her bat mitzvah. They thought Sarah was helping Hitler finish the job.

Ah, yes, that good old Hitler flyswatter. She knew it well.

"He was the best I could do," Sarah wished she could have told them, but in those days she'd been too angry and now they were gone.

Sarah was tracing the handle of the refrigerator with her

thumb when Mrs. Hubova came out of her room in a pink bathrobe with another gold crown stitched to her pocket. "You don't go out?" she asked, setting a teakettle on the stove.

"My husband's taking a nap. He gets very tired."

"You can go out alone. There is one nice traditional Czech pub on our street. They serve supper. It is safe for you."

"I think I'll just stay here, thank you. I'm not very hungry."

Mrs. Hubova parted the lace curtains above the sink with her pinkie to check the sky, pea green with mist. "You want tea?" She took out two china cups with thin handles. It was green tea, and as she poured the hot water, she asked how long Sarah wanted her bag to steep, two minutes or three. From behind, she looked just like Sarah's mother, who used to serve her a few spoonfuls of tea in hot milk when Sarah was a girl.

"Do you have any children?" Sarah asked hopefully as Mrs. Hubova sat down.

"Two boys. They ran away in 1980 to München, but now one came back here to Prague. For ten years I didn't see them."

Sarah chimed in without thinking, "My daughter Joni just started college and I miss her very much."

"And so you can imagine how I felt not to see my children for ten years."

"No, no, it's true, you can't compare," she admitted.

"Also, I have a sister, but she ran away to South Africa in

'68 before the borders closed. Last year, I went to visit her. She has a big farm, with fences and heavy security. You must always lock the door to your car and you must take gun everywhere. I think now I am free, but she is not anymore."

Embarrassed, Sarah changed the subject to Mrs. Hubova's command of English.

"I listen to BBC," she said. "And I know *Deutsch*, German, because of the war."

"Are most of your guests American?"

"I don't know. I have lived in my flat fifty years and you are my first guests. A few months ago my husband died. Now I need extra money."

"I'm sorry. I hope we're not too intrusive," she said, but Mrs. Hubova didn't appear to understand. "I mean, too much trouble."

"No trouble. You are nice company for an old woman." She smiled and pushed herself up from the table. "I think I will take some rest now. If you need laundry, leave it for me. I can do it. You had a good day today?"

"Yes! We saw Kafka's home. We love Czech writers like Kafka and Kundera."

Mrs. Hubova looked bewildered. "But Kafka wasn't Czech. He was German."

"German? That's funny," she said, then added significantly, "Oh, and we saw the Jewish Quarter." But the look of recognition Sarah expected didn't come.

"They have interesting museum, I hear."

"You've never been?" she asked, glancing at the mezuzah.

Mrs. Hubova shook her head. "It's place for tourists and Jews."

■

CARL STAYED FAST asleep, so Sarah went out to grab something to eat at the pub Mrs. Hubova had suggested, Mrs. Hubova who apparently wasn't a Jew. At least now the blond hair and blue eyes made sense. But then why the mezuzah on the door? And poor Kafka, who'd lived in Prague all his life. He surely didn't deserve to be called a German.

The pub was small and warm and full of wooden picnic tables. Four fat middle-aged men were laughing in front of a row of empty shot glasses. They invited her to join them. "Where you from?" one of them boomed, his voice echoing against the rafters.

"California!" she said. "And you?"

"Polish," said the man, who had kind eyes. The back of his dress shirt was stained with sweat and his thick lips glistened with saliva. "I am Janosh. I buy you beer."

One of them handed her a glass pint with a thick head of foam.

"First I buy you beer and I buy me beer," Janosh said, lighting a cigarette. "Then you buy me beer and you buy you beer. And we drink together!"

"I can't," she laughed. "Americans aren't used to drinking so much."

"You don't understand!" he bellowed and slapped her knee so hard she slipped off the bench. "When you are with Polish, you must drink like Polish!" Janosh helped her back up and squeezed her knee again. She wasn't sure she liked it. "Name, please," he said, and something about her answer prompted him to ask, "You are Jowish?"

"Half," she said and sipped some beer. It tasted strong, almost like syrup.

"I like Jows," he said. "I have no problem with Jows. But why Israel has so much power? Why they get so much money from United States government?"

She shrugged, unsure of what answer he wanted to hear. The waiters and the bartender and the other patrons had all disappeared and she was alone with these strange, strong men with their heavy Slavic brows and biceps, and long, firm legs—each man had a full pair. They were probably the kind of people who used to harass her father back in his village when he was a boy, but Sarah couldn't help finding them attractive in a coarse way.

"Is good question, no?" He held up his glass and they clinked. For some reason, one of Janosh's Polish friends flapped his arms and started crowing like a rooster.

■

SARAH FELL ASLEEP in her clothes. She was so drunk from her three beers and two shots of vodka (one mixed with wine from a plastic carton) she couldn't feel her own teeth.

When the alarm went off, she covered her head with a pillow.

"I thought we were doing the concentration camp today," Carl yelled in her ear after removing the pillow. He was fully dressed and wearing his Giants cap.

In fact, she'd decided to skip it, but Sarah said, "I'm getting up right now."

Perched on a kitchen chair, she was hunting through the

cabinets for something more interesting than rolls for breakfast when Mrs. Hubova, in a handsome cream-colored suit, came running out of her bedroom. The old lady looked very puzzled.

"I'm so glad I caught you," said Sarah, speaking quickly before Mrs. Hubova had a chance to collect her thoughts in English. Her hand remained frozen inside the cabinet. "As your first guests, Carl and I want to take you out somewhere special to say thank you for having us. We were thinking of the Hotel Europa," she said, mentioning the first place that popped into her head.

Mrs. Hubova made a few polite protests and then agreed. "You are looking for something, maybe? Can I help you?"

"No, no. Well, yes. Just a knife for the rolls," which was a stupid excuse, since there was already one sitting by the plate.

After a quick birdbath, Sarah threw on a warm-up suit. Outside, it was the first sunny day she'd seen in Prague, and the city took on a whole new character in the light. The windows and the pavement and the cement buildings gleamed. The men and women they passed smiled to themselves. She imagined her life as one of them, walking to work each morning, then to grocery stores or a movie theater afterward if she felt like it.

"By the way," said Sarah, careful as always to leave him enough space to maneuver beside her. "I told Mrs. Hubova we were taking her out to tea tonight."

"How sweet. You didn't break anything, did you?" He winked.

"Very funny."

Her hangover was still in full force when they arrived at the meeting place, in front of the Lufthansa office on Paris Street, where a small crowd had congregated on the sidewalk. A woman with a hard brown face came up to them and demanded money. Sarah handed her their crowns and wondered where the money went.

Their tour guide, a lanky kid with peach fuzz under his nose, watched them line up for the "bus," a rust-streaked van that looked put together from scrap metal and a hammer and nails. Sarah and Carl sat up front with two grandmothers from New Jersey in warm-up suits like Sarah's and sparkling white gym shoes. They and their husbands had rooms at the Intercontinental Hotel. Apparently Michael Jackson had stayed in one of their suites. "Are you sure you have enough space?" the grandmothers kept asking, their gym shoes suspended a good two feet above Carl's crutches, as if crutches were contagious.

Sarah couldn't remember what you took for a hangover. She seemed to recall Liza Minnelli downing a raw egg in *Cabaret*, but she wasn't sure if it was safe yet to eat raw eggs here. The only thing close to a coffee stand they'd passed was McDonald's, which Sarah had avoided out of principle.

After a few wheezes, the van growled to life, coughing up clouds of black diesel. Their guide, named Thomas, stared at the cracked windshield and said nothing, no brief history, not how long the trip would take, not even when they could expect to use the bathroom. They could have been headed somewhere else entirely, like Switzerland.

Carl fell asleep as soon as they started moving. Sarah stared at brown fields rotting in the muted sun and felt strangely exhilarated by the impression that she was viewing a former farming collective. The lady next to her asked where she was from.

"California," Sarah said, wishing she could go back to her thoughts.

"My grandson's school is in California, at Berkeley. Is that near where you live?"

Show-off, Sarah thought. (Her daughter had barely made it into UC-Santa Cruz.) "We don't live there anymore," she said. "Actually, we're in Poland now."

"What did she say?"

"She said she moved to Poland."

"What does that mean?"

"I don't know," was the hushed reply. "Kind of a funny person."

Sarah didn't remember falling asleep. She closed her eyes to shut out the hammering in her skull and when she opened them, their group was getting off the bus.

They stood in a small muddy town square with green wooden benches stationed along the perimeter. A pack of boys bundled in winter coats screamed and chased each other through the brown leaves. Just looking at them made Sarah tired.

Thomas was asking them questions about the Holocaust to see what they knew, how many children had been killed, how many Jews, how many Gypsies, how many homosexuals. He had dark blond hair parted down the middle, and his mouth was carved into a heart-shaped pout. Only Eastern Europeans had mouths like that, Sarah thought, touching her own clumsy lips. Maybe it was something in their water.

"And what was the purpose of Terezin?" he asked. "Does anyone know?"

Carl nudged Sarah as if she were automatically the Holocaust expert because she was Jewish. The old people all stared stupidly. She wanted to tell Thomas that Americans preferred to be led around like sheep, not quizzed. And why couldn't they hurry it up and get to the camp so they could be confronted with the horrors they'd paid to see? "It was a transfer point to the other camps," Sarah finally blurted out. "Also, the Nazis briefly remodeled it for a Red Cross visit, as a show camp."

"Yes," he said. She thought she detected a frown. "But remember to raise hands."

Carl waved. "How exactly did they know who was Jewish?"

"In many cases, Jews were reported," Thomas said. "For example, if you wanted your neighbor's apartment, you could write to the Nazis and say, 'That Jew Levy above me has a big apartment when I am living in such a small place with my family. Can you do something about it?' They still have letters like these in the archives at Strahov. A reporter for the London *Times* came and wrote an article about it, so now the archives are closed."

"But that was years ago," Sarah said. "Everything's changed."

"Has it?" Thomas said.

One of the men, a furrier from New Jersey, raised his hand. "When do we go to the bathroom?"

While Thomas led a small troop into the local pub to use the bathroom, Carl and Sarah went with the others into a grocery store with a screen door that hung off its hinges and kept flapping against the splintered wood frame. The metal shelves were dusty and half empty. A man behind the counter sat hunched over like a sack of flour.

Sarah bought a bar of chocolate in an unfamiliar light-purple wrapper.

"I wonder how old Hubova survived," Carl thought aloud. "Lucky lady."

"Actually, she's not Jewish," Sarah said, holding the door for him. "She said so."

"I thought you said you saw a mezuzah on the door."

"Well, then I suppose it's not hers."

Thomas leaned against a gray apartment building and frowned at a dog sniffing the ground for bones. When Sarah came closer, she realized the building was white but covered in a light layer of black soot that was flaking off on Thomas's red jacket. He looked so serious, she was almost afraid to ask, "Want some?" He shook his head and went on staring at the dog, which had found something and was digging furiously.

The chocolate tasted stale, but was recognizably chocolate. "Not bad for a Communist chocolate bar," she said.

"It's a German brand," Thomas said. "We have it in Germany."

She coughed on her chocolate. "I knew you were from somewhere." Why did she sound so stupid all of a sudden? "I mean your accent sounds Australian. Maybe Irish."

"My mother is Czech." He folded his arms tightly like he was hugging himself. "My father, with whom I have absolutely no contact because he is a complete asshole, is

German. I live in Prague now because as a Jew I find it impossible to live in Germany." He pronounced it "Pwag" like he was French.

"What about your parents?" Carl asked. "How did they survive?"

"They aren't Jewish. I am a Jew by choice. I was circumcised two years ago."

"No shit," said Carl, pulling on his shortened pant leg. "That must have hurt."

"For a few weeks, yes," Thomas admitted. "I had to stay in the hospital."

"So you're not really Jewish, then?" Sarah asked.

"According to Jewish law, anyone who converts is as if he was born Jewish."

"See," Carl said to Sarah, "that's what I keep telling you."

"When do we get to the camp?" she asked, crumpling her candy-wrapper and looking for the garbage. "Is it a hike?"

Thomas looked stunned, as if she'd punched him. "This is the camp," he said. "This square. This ground you are standing on. The shop where you bought candy."

"You mean this is where the camp was and now people live here?"

"Correct. People live here."

"And they know?"

"I suppose you would have to ask them this question."

"But I can't ask them. I don't speak Czech. That's why I'm asking you."

"You're asking me?" Thomas spat into the dirt. "They know."

■

AFTER THE BATHROOM break, Thomas led them down a gravel road out of the square. Sarah walked carefully, afraid to step on anything of historic value. The center of town was surrounded by a ring of staunch brick walls with weeds running through the cracks and a moat filled with brown, withered flowers. They visited a cemetery with a giant stone menorah, very plain. They viewed a crematorium with lit candles in the clean, empty mouths of the brick ovens. They marched back toward the square to see a museum.

"I can't believe he's German," she told Carl, but he didn't quite get it. He hadn't been raised to look down on Jews who bought from BMW or Mercedes.

She was glad for the museum because she thought it was what she was supposed to see, what she'd paid for, but it turned out to be just like the Jewish Quarter, more artifacts and Hebrew writing. Middle-aged women in polyester uniforms and black hose watched them suspiciously. Sarah looked at a picture of the Nazi invaders laughing over coffee at a hotel fifty years ago. Had Mrs. Hubova played the genteel hostess back then too?

You put yourself on guard to digest these terrible things, and then . . . No barbed wire, no barracks, no searchlights. Not like the movies.

She was waiting for the earth to open its mouth and swallow them all up.

"Are you okay?" Carl asked, prodding her ankle with one of his crutches.

"Fine," she said and felt cold all over.

For lunch, there was nowhere to go except the grocery

store on the square. The cashier, still hunched on his stool, didn't even pretend to recognize them. A pile of Saran-Wrapped sandwiches had magically appeared next to him at the register.

"What's in these?" Sarah asked and held one up, her fingers lubricated by the buttery Saran Wrap.

The guy shrugged. He looked old enough to have met Germans, Russians, and now Jews, hungry for lunch. She imagined him on that same goddamned stool through it all, not lifting a finger except to slap together sandwiches.

"What do you mean, you don't know? You have to know." She shook the slimy sandwich in his face like a piece of evidence. She wanted him to know she was Jewish. "Didn't you make these?"

"He doesn't understand," Carl said, pulling her arm down. "Calm down."

Thomas spoke to the man in Czech. "They're cheese and tomato. And butter."

Sarah wanted to storm out of the store, but she was hungry. She handed two of the sandwiches to the cashier. "And three Cokes."

She couldn't believe they delivered Coke to such a god-forsaken place.

▪

SARAH WAS STILL having trouble fitting their key into the front door when Mrs. Hubova came home from work. "You have to push a bit," she said cheerfully as she let them in. "Before tea, I must make few phone calls and rest. We go after dinner, okay?"

"I'm not sure I want to take someone like her out to tea,"

Sarah said, closing the glass-paned living room door behind them.

"Maybe she has some story," said Carl. He covered his eyes as he sank into bed.

"I certainly hope so, because I'm going to ask for one."

"She might have just moved in here after they left. Someone had to."

"Even if she did nothing directly, she profited from Nazis. Don't you get it?"

"I'm sorry," he said, yawning. "I'm too tired to talk right now."

Sarah scrubbed herself in the birdbath almost an hour, then changed into clothes that didn't smell like Terezin. She couldn't sleep and she couldn't stay in the apartment either, so she ran out to buy chocolate, but it tasted like dirt as it crumbled between her teeth. The orange streetlights came on and cast blue shadows under the sickly, twisted trees. An old man came running out of a doorway, and Sarah sucked in her breath.

She walked to Wenceslas Square and sat on a bench under the equestrian statue. Two students had burned themselves to death there in 1969. The only memorial was two grainy pictures in metal frames with candles and red-and-white ribbons. It was the kind of thing she'd hoped to find here, but now she wasn't interested. Instead she thought of her mother's gray, meaty brisket, a recipe from the Old Country.

Her mother served brisket every Friday night on a set of plates with bluebird borders from Czechoslovakia. Her father drank wine out of a crude silver kiddush cup they kept hidden in the pillowcases. "This cup belonged to your grandfather," her mother said in her heavily accented English. "We brought it from the Old Country. And it belonged to his father. And someday this will all be yours, when you have your own family, so I want you to know these things." It was all a story of beautiful cutlery hauled across the ocean so it could sit in the cabinets of her sister's house. Sarah got nothing because she'd reneged on the promise she'd made by being born: to keep memory alive.

■

IN THE CAFÉ of Hotel Europa, painted vines and flowers snaked up the walls and around a mirror above a polished wood-framed fireplace. The patrons bent over their short, intimate wood tables while waiters twirled by, coldly handsome in gray uniforms trimmed with white piping. Their faces were stiff and gray like their uniforms.

It took Carl a while to navigate the narrow spaces between the tables. The people in the café looked up from their coffees to stare.

"They're not used to seeing people like you," Mrs. Hubova said later, biting into a pink cake. She wore a fine gold chain around her neck and pearl earrings. "The Communists put all deformed people in asylums. When the doors were opened after 1989, no one believed how many there were. It was like at end of the war, when the wounded soldiers came home."

"My brain still tells me the leg is there," Carl said, shifting in his chair. "I feel it sometimes. My doctor says I may never forget."

All around them, waiters cleared dishes and then snapped hot, damp cloths over the tables to erase all traces of departed guests. Sarah, who'd stifled herself during their tea, stared sullenly at the blond woman sitting across from her and stuffing her face with free cake. This stranger was nothing like her mother.

Sarah suddenly cut in, "Mrs. Hubova, do you know we are Jews?"

"I think so," she said, dabbing the crumbs on her plate with her small finger.

"You know, we thought you might be Jewish too."

Mrs. Hubova looked startled. "But how could you possibly?"

"We happened to notice the mezuzahs on the doors. The metal rectangles . . ."

"Aha, yes. The previous people in our flat, they were Jews. They left their metal religious articles on the doors."

"Mezuzahs," Sarah said, wishing they'd honored their reservations at the Europa.

"I thought about giving them to some museum, but my husband said it's bad luck to remove them." She turned to Carl. "Is it true?"

Carl hesitated. His cheeks looked very gray. "I don't think so, but I'm no expert."

"Why didn't the Jews take the mezuzahs with them?" Sarah asked.

"I don't know," Mrs. Hubova replied. "They probably hadn't enough time."

"You moved into your flat about fifty years ago, you said?

That would be in 1945, '44, '43, maybe?" Sarah said. "How exactly did you find your flat?"

"What do you mean?"

Carl touched her arm, but she went on. "Was it listed in the paper? Did you call the super and make an appointment to view it? Did you have to write to anyone to get it?"

Mrs. Hubova furrowed her brow. "I don't understand. What do you want to know?"

"It's a beautiful place. I can't imagine why the previous tenants would have left. Or if they had, I'm sure they would have asked a friend to hold on to it for them. Unless they didn't have a chance because they'd been reported to the police." She hesitated, then added, "Or something."

Mrs. Hubova pushed back her chair and stood up. She touched her hair to make sure it was all still in place, but did not speak. In her cream-colored suit she looked as beautiful as a French painting. Sarah felt a little afraid of her. "When you are guests in my home, you do not accuse me to be Nazi," said the lady, speaking slowly in a low baritone. "Even when you are American."

"Paying guests," Sarah corrected her.

"And it is reason why I don't say go out of my house now and find some hotel. Because I cannot afford to give back your money. This is not polite!"

"Don't worry about your precious money," said Sarah. "We'll be out tonight."

Mrs. Hubova picked up her purse like a book and marched out the door, her jaw perpendicular to her neck, her spine straight as a rifle. Sarah felt miserable, for herself and for them all, stranded in one of the most dismal corners of the universe. Thank God her parents had had the good sense to escape when they could.

She took a bill out of her wallet, and a waiter with a black purse strapped to his belt immediately came by. "I don't need change," she said. The waiter bowed and spun away.

Carl made inquiries at the front desk of the hotel about a room, but they'd all been reserved. All the hotels in Prague were booked because of a trade convention. "They say it's no use," he said when he came back. "We have to stay where we are."

■

MRS. HUBOVA WAS sewing a button onto her sweater in her room. She'd left the door open, just a crack. Carl went right to bed, but Sarah stopped by to explain they had to stay two more nights as planned. There was a mezuzah on Mrs. Hubova's doorpost too, a wooden one. I should take it, Sarah thought. It would be a rescue, not a theft.

"This flat was empty when I moved here with my husband," Mrs. Hubova said.

Sarah guessed anyone might have said that. "So what happened to the Jews?"

"We don't know. They never came back. It happened fifty years ago. The Communists erased all our history. This is my home now. I am an old woman."

"You should have tried, anyway. Didn't you know their names?"

"I am sorry for them. It's terrible, but I don't know where they are." She looked up from the sweater on her lap. "I believe they are with Jesus."

"We don't believe in Jesus," Sarah said.

"No?" Mrs. Hubova seemed surprised. "What do you believe?"

"It's not so simple," she replied. "I think of it as an attitude. I mean, there are things Jews do and don't do. Like Jews don't smoke or drink too much or anything low-class like that. And they take care of their communities, they're very community-oriented. And education and social justice are very, very important." She realized how inadequate her answer sounded. "Why? What do you think a Jew is?"

Mrs. Hubova shrugged. "Your people have no pity."

■

ON THEIR LAST full day in Prague they slept in to avoid Mrs. Hubova, who left them breakfast as usual, which they didn't touch. They visited the Castle and stayed out late.

Sarah decided she wanted to become a better Jew. She went back to the Jewish Quarter and bought a gold chain with a Star of David. After she left the store, she realized the necklace was too ugly and heavy for her neck, but she wore it anyway. She took Carl to eat lunch in a kosher restaurant called A Taste of Honey.

"I'm sorry about all this," he said over their falafel. "Next year let's try Paris."

"That's right," she said, playing along. "Next year."

When they came back, they found Vitek's business card on their pillow.

The next morning, Sarah called for a taxi and then dropped the apartment key on the kitchen table. One thought still haunted her, however, those mezuzahs clinging to Mrs. Hubova's doorposts, a lie. Sarah decided to take one of the mezuzahs down, install it in a proper Jewish home or a museum, where it belonged. But when she checked the door-posts, they were bare, every one. She pressed the naked wood and looked again and again; the mezuzahs had vanished. No one would have known they'd ever been there except for a few oblong patches of discolored wood, each studded with a matching pair of small black holes.

HEN I MOVED TO PRAGUE, my aunt Cassandra gave me two bits of advice: bring toilet paper and watch out for the civil war. Even after I lugged out our atlas, she refused to believe that Czechoslovakia and Yugoslavia were not the same country.

As it turns out, Czech toilet paper is brown, recycled, and only slightly more abrasive than its white American counterpart. Also, civil wars are in short supply. In fact, my life's so peaceful that I could easily forget that I'm alive if it weren't for my Thursday-morning rides to work, when I cram into a public bus with a mob of shrieking pink-cheeked teenage hooligans on their way to high school. I'm the twenty-six-year-old American with a mole on his left cheek, an authentic Parisian beret, a black turtleneck, and a three-quarter-length black trench coat from a vintage store in Boston. (The coat fits tighter across my gut than it used to; I've had the buttons moved.) The American pops a Rolo into his mouth and pretends to read his wrinkled copy of *The Nation* while the teenagers fire volleys of spitballs over his head.

Today, for fun, I'm staring at a girl, the one in the red ski hat. Her coat's unzipped and her tiny breasts are barely visible through her thin pink sweater. In fact, her breasts are smaller than mine. I pretend I'm about to speak to her in my broken Czech.

With a rude jerk, the bus pulls up to my stop, a snowy corrugated metal lean-to papered over with posters for next week's elections for this country's newly created Senate. No one is sure what a senator does, though like in America they serve six years. Most of the posters feature the sagging jowls of Milos Zeman, the fat, charismatic ex-Communist who leads the opposition. This past month, he's been riding a truck up and down the country with a bullhorn and taunting the effeminate prime minister, Vaclav Klaus, a Margaret Thatcher acolyte who speaks in a tiny, polite voice about tightening belts. His bushy white mustache and eyebrows suggest a slimmer Santa Claus.

The wind reeks of coffee and makes my nose run. I break into a brisk jog that leaves me panting against a wire fence after a few feet. More than once, I've been accused of "running like a girl."

After a couple of Rolos and half a cigarette, I feel healthy enough to go on.

DaniCo coffee factory is a block away, next to the Amway headquarters. Across the road, there's an outdoor market where Vietnamese guest workers who came over in the late seventies as part of a Communist trade pact now hawk cheap batteries and duffel bags.

"I think it is Simon!" Katka twitters as I enter the warm gatehouse. She leans over the desk, and her auburn curls tumble loosely over her thin, pointed ears. Her cheeks are wrinkled in a comforting way, like an oatmeal cookie, and she never wears makeup, even in a land where women apply eye shadow and rouge in thick stripes like house paint. I can see her panties through her white cotton dress, much too flimsy for winter.

Katka is a girl's name. A woman in her forties should be Katarina or Katja.

"*S'il vous plaît,* Simon, can I offer you some coffee? Some tea or biscuits?"

Before I can say yes, her long fluttering fingers fly to the white plastic kettle and at the same time the phone, which she picks up on the first ring. "*Dobre rano,* DaniCo!"

I come here on Thursdays, to "enrich" the students' conversation. The rest of the week, my class is taught by Vera, an iron-faced Czech woman who requires me to write down my lesson plans in a pink notebook. If I don't, she'll make a special trip to the factory to scold or quiz me on fine points of grammar. Sometimes she comes anyway and detains me for half an hour so I can nod sorrowfully as she tells me how Communism wrecked her life.

Back in the swinging sixties, when Czech socialism wore a more human face, Vera was a teenager studying English in London. Then in the spring of 1968, the Russians rolled into Prague with tanks and called Premier Dubcek to Moscow. A few weeks later he retired to Bratislava, where he worked as a locksmith and wasn't heard from until 1989.

Vera could have stayed, but she'd promised her fiancé she'd come home. She wasn't sure she still loved him, but a promise was a promise. "Our government wasn't so bad before," she said, "but they became worse than the Soviets. In the time of perestroika, they used to censor the Russian newspapers because they were too liberal." During the years that followed, Vera had no opportunities to use English. If you obeyed the official rules to the letter, when a foreigner stopped you on Wenceslas Square to ask "What time is it?" you had to, without saying a word, run into the local Communist Party headquarters, get permission to answer the question, and then go back to say "Two-fifteen."

Of course, who except Vera obeyed the official rules to the letter?

A sad story, but sad stories grow on trees here. Pretty girls in berets standing tall and straight with flowers in front of tanks, intellectuals arrested for scribbling clandestine independence manifestos. English teachers whose students never show up to class.

"Au revoir!" Katka giggles and removes my teacup. I tutor her privately in the cafeteria after my regular English class, our secret. Vera probably would have me fired if she found out. Private enterprise on DaniCo property—oh, the horror!

Outside, I cross the yard, a patch of frozen mud and loose bricks. DaniCo clings to a steep, icy slope with a view of the factories spewing gray smoke over the valley between us and the city center. Our own smokestack belches more than its share. Shaggy men in blue uniforms dusted with snow loiter next to a tractor parked in the yard. One of them, Hansa (a nickname for "Jan"), is a student of mine. I call his name three times before he runs over to pump my hand and say he's sorry, but he has a big transport from "Dansko."

"Denmark," I correct him. "Remember when we talked about nations?"

"Yes, Denmark," Hansa says with a bright smile as if he knew the right name all along and was just teasing me. "I no class today. Big, big transport . . ."

"Okay, Hansa," I say. "But please, can you try to come next week? I'm lonely."

"Next week," he says emphatically, just like last week, and pumps my hand again.

Our classroom is a corner of the cafeteria sectioned off by an accordion door. Two women with their hair in plastic nets guard the lunch counter and serve fried pork, fried cauliflower, fried cheese by the gram. They watch eagle-eyed as they pour drinks into glasses marked at 0,3 liters with a white line. You are not entitled to a free napkin.

The accordion door is always locked, even though our stuffy, overheated room contains only a table, plastic chairs, and a flip chart. A mural on the back wall depicts four giant bags of DaniCo coffee on the summit of a snowcapped mountain.

I prop the window open with an old board so I can breathe. I wait. My "lessons" are mostly games, "to promote a free flow of conversation," an hour of treading water. Katka approves. "It's no good to be firm like Vera," she says. "It's not way of Buddha."

"They are so simpleminded," Vera complains. "The most basic concepts, I drill them for an entire hour and I ask, do they understand? They nod their heads yes and then the next week, poof! Every word has flown out of their heads."

She despises them, but how can I despise them? I'm treading water too. Maybe that's why the students like me more than Vera, whom they fear. Still, they go to her classes.

Czech Esquire lured me to Prague by offering me a job as their photo editor. After a mere three weeks, they let me go. I still think it was really a matter of staff reductions and not my supposed sin, calling in sick and going to the zoo, which by the way was a very dirty zoo with mangy, miserable-looking bears. While I was gone, a sickness inspector rang my bell and found me not at home. All illnesses have to be certified in Prague, and these inspectors are very thorough. If you're out buying medicine or even in the bathroom, you need a timed note. Anyway, there was a lot of sympathy for me, but I still got the ax.

I didn't see any use in going home to the States with my tail between my legs, so I picked up an English class. There's always room for an extra warm body, particularly a native speaker.

Twenty minutes after the official start of class, two of my students drop by, Olena and Ivo. I greet them like long-lost relatives and try to draw a map of Europe on the flip chart. The markers don't work, as usual. I press harder, hoping to squeeze out a few drops of ink. Olena watches impatiently for a minute, then mumbles "Sorry," and disappears to a sales conference. I try reading aloud from the text with Ivo, an eager but spasmodic English speaker who has trouble focusing today because he's worried about renewing his residency permit. Ivo is Slovak and thanks to the bungled parliamentary maneuver that caused Czechoslovakia's accidental divorce in 1993, he's as foreign as I am. It was a clean break, very unlike my aunt Cassandra's Yugoslavian nightmares. They simply chopped the country in half. Even the national anthem was split right down the middle.

I let Ivo go ten minutes early with a wink. ("Don't tell Vera!") On the way out, his duffel bag splits open and worksheets fly everywhere. "Stupid Vietnamese bag," he says as we crawl on the floor together. "These are foreigners, not honest people."

As I wait for Katka, I smoke a cigarette out the window and watch the men driving their tractors in the yard. I'm about to open up *The Nation* when I glance through the accordion door and spot a familiar head of stiff blond hair, the color and texture of a corn husk. It's Vera, furiously correcting papers in red pen. We're not allowed to give homework, but Vera does it anyway. She's waited all her life to correct the homework spread out beside the bowl of brown tripe soup sitting at her elbow.

Vera looks up from her papers and slowly removes her iron-framed reading glasses. "Ah, Simon," she says. "I stopped by to ask you about the past perfect . . ." She tilts her head and notices the empty room behind me. "Where is your class?"

I squeeze my magazine and try to think of something to say.

She stands up, pressing her bony knuckles into the table. "Do you mean to tell me all four of them missed today?" Vera hangs her head, as if she's embarrassed for me. The cafeteria ladies nudge each other and fold their flabby white arms to watch.

"Hansa had a big transport and Olena left early. I don't know about Eva but Ivo . . . I try to make the lessons interesting, to promote a free flow of conversation . . ."

"Do not blame yourself," she says. "I shall have a talk with them."

"I wouldn't. I mean, they're all so busy. It's not their fault . . ."

"You are doing your job, but they are not doing theirs. This is no joke. We need English. Our country has fallen behind the rest of the world fifty years. We must to catch up . . ." Vera turns red as she shuffles her papers together against the table, rubber bands them, and then files the bundle in her vinyl briefcase. "Correction: 'We have to catch up.' " She slams her chair against the table and bumps into Katka on her way out.

"Vera is hurrying," Katka remarks and swings her purse, a beige knit bag that looks like a net, over her shoulder. "Such hardness is not becoming in females." She presses my arm. "Please, Simon, today I have half-day holiday. Please, is it possible we can go elsewhere to have our lesson? Here is no atmosphere for learning with stupid kitchen ladies screaming and brutal smell from unhealthy *cuisine*."

As we cross the main yard, Katka chirps hello to everyone we pass, then confides to me what she really thinks: "This man is too ambitious." "She is extravagant." "I don't believe in money, money, money. Please, Simon, what do you think? I think in new era of liberty people care only for money. Young people have no manners."

Katka pays me one hundred fifty crowns an hour (five bucks). The going rate's two-fifty, but she doesn't have much money. She doesn't seem to want much instruction. If I try to correct her, she nods *"No, no!"* (Czech for "Yes, yes!"), then goes on making the same mistakes. She brings art books, dried leaves, an opened box of dusty chocolates, an article about a Baryshnikov show at the National Theater ("Imagine, he dances without music. He is true genius." I smile, remembering when I used to think I was a true genius), a brochure from her New Age club. "Do you know what it is aura?"

"Aura," I said. "It's the same word in English."

"Perfect!" she exclaimed. "Every man has aura, and when we sit in circle with this spiritual man I described to you he can say when I am no so well, *pardon*, not so well from aura. It's true. For nine hundred crowns he can take Polaroid photo of aura. I see with my own eyes. It is very beautiful, like *arc de soleil.* How do you say *arc de soleil*?"

Her older daughter is mentally retarded and makes arts and crafts at a special school. Once, Katka brought the other daughter, the healthy one. Supposedly the girl spoke English, but when I met her, she sat sullenly in her long olive-green coat and black boots. Occasionally she fiddled with an eyebrow ring.

"You want stop at Vietnamese market?" Katka asks. "They are hospitable people."

I shake my head. "Where are we going?" I ask as we take

shelter at the bus stop. The wind, icier than usual, whips the branches of a bare tree against the metal shed.

"It is surprise for you!" She stamps her red pointy boots in the snow to keep warm, then makes a face at Zeman's photo. "I prefer political party of Klaus. He is polite man, highly intelligent, not like loud fear-monster Zeman. Zeman is not credible opposition."

Vera also thinks Zeman is a bully, but she's voting for his party because the country needs a strong leader, not some pansy aristocrat like Klaus.

"It's terrible," I say absently. "You don't even have a real choice."

Katka misunderstands me. "We have choice now. Before we had elections, but only one party and everyone must vote or lose his job. Also, it wasn't secret so if you write nothing on your paper, every man knows it. As government used to say, 'White vote—Black intentions.' But now we have real choices, you and me."

We take the subway seven stops to Narodni trida, then walk five blocks. Katka's red scarf dances with the snow-flakes in the icy wind. She uses a frilly white hankie to dab her nose, which rolls down from her forehead and swells like a teardrop.

"Here we are," Katka says finally. We walk single file through a tight alley with loose planks over the slush. Above the green door, a sign says GOVINDA in curved pink letters. As we wipe our feet on an Astroturf mat, a bald man carrying a bag of trash edges past us. He wears a pink smock and a smudge of yellow paint above his nose.

Inside, Katka pauses to tap on an aquarium by the entrance. The room is paved in green tile that flickers under a domed skylight. There's a framed picture of a fat Indian man decked out with garlands of flowers. He sits cross-legged in front of a crowd of shaved heads. Behind a pastry case, a fairly cute girl with her hair pulled back smiles shyly at us. Her turquoise robe matches the petits fours, which also come in pink and mint green.

"It's pleasant here, no?" Katka says, ducking under the wayward frond of a fake palm. "Hare Krishna people are *charmant.*" Instead of choosing one of the green tables, she steps up to a platform carpeted with more Astroturf. "Please, Simon, remove shoes."

I feel vulnerable and exposed in my socks, but in this country you're asked to remove your shoes so often I've learned to wear socks without holes in them. I sit on the platform and tuck my feet under my knees, out of sight. While Katka goes to the counter, I discreetly undo the top button of my pants, which have been pinching me all day.

Katka brings back a dull metal tray with a pot of green tea, two gold cups, and "Japanese Mix," a bowl of puffed rice crackers and dried peas. I can't help staring at the lines of Katka's bra through her dress.

"Today, I celebrate," Katka says, tossing a dried pea in the air and catching it in her mouth. "I have been married twenty-three years, but in all this time of marriage, only few years in beginning was real marriage." She's never mentioned a father for her two daughters before. I assumed the man had left her. "When love was gone, we stayed together because of children, especially this retard daughter who is specially abled. Also it's terrible to find inexpensive flats just now. Imagine it, Simon, my husband and I must sleep together in one room all these years. Imagine."

"It's terrible," I say, trying to imagine Katka young and in love. My part in our conversations usually consists of "It's terrible" or "That's wonderful."

"No more." Katka puts her hands on her hips. "Youngest daughter will live in university *dortoir* and I say to husband yesterday that when she leaves I must have my own room and he has said yes. For first time since marriage I have my own room."

"That's wonderful" slips out before I can stop myself, but it really is wonderful.

"Yes, it's wonderful. Simon, I have many ideas for decoration of this room. I will have many flowers and I will paint one wall white and one wall purple. And my aura teacher has given to me as special gift plastic stars for ceiling which, when there is no light, will shine like real stars. It's true." She bites her lip to keep from laughing.

"That's wonderful," I say. For some reason, the girl in the turquoise robe smiles at me as she wipes down a table nearby.

Katka points at me. "I must thank you. It is because of you I have strength to ask for my room." I shake my head, but she insists, "Yes, our conversations give me strength to ask for independent life. You are only person who listens me.

When I talk with you, Simon, I feel like I am *très importante*. Thank you." She grabs my hand and kisses it before I can yank it away. "Thank you. Thank you." After a final kiss, she lets my hand go and refills my cup of tea. "And you, Simon? What of your heart?"

"I am not beautiful," I say. "I have no heart."

"Even one who has no external beauty can love. But you have external beauty."

I pat my stomach.

"It's nothing. I know men who have more fat than you. I have theory." Katka puts a finger to her temple. "You have damage to self-image, yes? May I be bold?" She leans forward. "Someone in USA has hurt you, yes?"

I shrug. I don't feel like playing this game.

"And this someone is man or woman?"

Now I see what she's getting at. "I'm not gay. You have the wrong idea."

"Be not afraid to show love. Weakness is strength. It is the way of Buddha."

"I'm not gay," I repeat. "Really."

"Simon, you have choice to be happy and brave or sad and afraid. I am example for you. I thought it was not possible to have my own room. Now, thank you to Simon, I have had the *encouragement* to ask for what I want. Your life too can change. You must not be afraid to show weakness. You must love freely. Man, woman, it's not important."

"You're right," I say. "There's nothing wrong with being gay. But I'm not gay."

"Be not afraid," she commands me.

I pay for our tea and refuse to accept my usual fee. One of the bald men, in Adidas sandals and a pink sarong, holds the door for us as we leave and wishes us a good day.

"Be not afraid, Simon," she says very seriously when we part on the sidewalk.

All right. Enough. I check over my shoulder to make sure she's not following me.

■

THE WOMEN IN my life fall into two distinct categories: ones I can bamboozle into sleeping with me and ones who find me adorable but not in the right way. "You're not gay?" they coo. "But I know a guy who's perfect for you." Even my mom bought into it. While helping me pack to come here, she stared at my sock drawer and said, "We'd love you no matter what, even if you went to jail or if you were, you know, gay."

"I'm not gay, Mom," I said.

She looked up from the drawer, smiling and crying. "I know, but even if you are we'll always love you."

At home, the apartment is as quiet as a tomb. My roommate left for the weekend. A Czech friend of his, a pornographer, has hired him to lie naked on the sets so the photographers can check their lights against his body.

I'm too tired to pick up my *Ulysses* (I've been on page sixty-three for a month), and the thought of heating up tripe soup from a mix depresses the fuck out of me. This empty apartment shouldn't be wasted. Katka is right; I have to love freely. So I muster up the courage to call this girl from *Es-*

quire I used to have lunch with, a girl about whom I've even fantasized a few times. When I was fired, she gave me her number and said to keep in touch, but at the time I didn't think she'd meant it. To be safe, I try her work number, and by some unlucky quirk of fate, she's there and I have to think of something to say.

Be not afraid.

"I'm experiencing an overwhelming and unaccountable craving for dried pork neck stuffed with spinach and drowned in a brown gravy, or beef stewed to the consistency of shoe leather with cabbage sour enough to pickle your tongue, and maybe a side of tough, spongy dumplings. In other words, I'm inviting you out to dinner in Prague."

An hour later, the girl and I sit across from each other at a narrow table covered by a starchy white cloth lit up like a body in a morgue. I like her laugh, pure, without an ounce of affectation. Her nose is straight, her jaw sharp, her eyes black and shiny. Although her name is Shireen, she goes by Charlene. She was born in Syria (it's marked on her American passport) and is constantly detained for questioning at borders.

"At least you can always count on the bear," I say with a crooked smile. Then I realize from her knitted brow that I've misspoken and said "bear" and not "beer." "Beer!" I correct myself. " 'Bear'? Can you imagine? Like one of their local delicacies? Roast bear claw with potato pancakes and cabbage and dumplings?"

Charlene laughs and my heart swells. It's taken years to develop my distinctive blend of wry snobbism and self-mockery. I'm quite proud of it.

I pull my chair closer to her and point at our waiter, smoking a cigarette and sneering at the election coverage on a black-and-white TV above the bar. The screen flashes between Zeman at a roadside rally and Klaus clamoring for order in Parliament. The waiter's bow tie hangs loose and his dress shirt has a brown stain above his heart.

"Look at him," I say. "Czech elegance."

She laughs again, and I feel dizzy. This is a bona fide seduction.

The man sitting behind me taps my shoulder and asks if I speak Czech. "It is not polite to speak this way when you are a guest in our country. It is *americanismus.*"

"Thank you for your opinions," I reply in my best Czech, though as I turn back to my girl, I realize I've actually said "Thank you for your pancakes."

"What's his problem?" asks Charlene, who seems disappointed in me when I suggest we change tables. "You're too nice, you know that?" she says and I sit there in glum silence because I've mucked up everything as usual. Luckily, I manage to brighten a little with the arrival of our chicken covered with cheese and tangerines, and a side of potato croquettes. I've grown very fond of potato croquettes.

Between bites, Charlene tells me about her family, a clan of wealthy Syrian Jews in Deal, New Jersey, who have paired her up with a wealthy Syrian Jewish boyfriend, still back home. He sends desperately pleading letters and e-mails. "I keep saying I want my independence," she says, "but he doesn't seem to get the meaning of the word."

Independence sounds good for my prospects. I nod sympathetically and invite her home to have a glass of one of the cheaper local red wines, sweet, thick Frankovka. The best thing you can say about Frankovka is that if you drink a lot of it and no other kind of wine for a few months you can almost swallow a glassful without noticing the taste. We sit on my bed because there are no chairs. (Earlier, I'd moved my guest chair into the other bedroom.) Charlene straddles a corner of my mattress and thumbs through *The Nation.*

"You don't get *Cosmo* or anything?" She tosses the magazine on my table, next to *Ulysses* and a letter from Aunt Cassandra enclosed with a review of Madonna in *Evita.*

"Not presently," I say.

"Well, I guess you wouldn't. You're not a girl."

"No, I'm not a girl." She laughs again. I move my foot a few inches closer to hers and say, "You know, you look like you're about to fall off the mattress."

"Oh," she says, staring at her hands. "I guess I'm tired. Maybe I should go."

She laughs again and punches my arm. It actually hurts. I think I feel a bruise.

I lean forward for my hug—how many women have I fucking hugged? But as I rest my head on her shoulder with my hand buried in her thick and winding black hair, I think of Katka's impish grin and I kiss Charlene and leave my lips on her mouth. She doesn't move. I pull back, my arm still around her shoulders and my fingers entwined in her black curls. My left eyebrow starts twitching uncontrollably. I put my lips on hers again and then I feel a tight pressure on my nipple. "Nice tits," Charlene murmurs, breathing hot on my chin, then leans forward for another kiss.

Almost any other night I might have let that remark slide, but not now.

"What's wrong?" she asks, looking slightly dazed.

"You should go."

"I like your tits, really," she says, but I hold up my hand. Enough. "Oh, all right." I walk her to the door and we stand next to each other, not sure what to do with our hands. "You're a really nice guy," she says softly with a mocking smile. She gives a little wave and squeezes past me. "See you."

I peel off my pants and throw them across the room. They knock over Charlene's wineglass. As I fall into bed, I watch the carpet soak up the blood-colored stain.

■

THE NEXT THURSDAY morning, Election Day, I put on a shirt and tie instead of my usual black turtleneck. One of the Christian Democrat candidates for the Senate hands out flyers at my subway station. The platform is littered with them.

I push past the teenagers on the bus from Palmovka and get a seat. At the bus shelter, I rip one of the stupid Milos Zeman posters across his big fat mouth.

"No tea, Katka," I say while inscribing my plan neatly with a black pen into Vera's ruled notebook. "Also, I'm afraid we're going to have to stop our tutoring sessions."

"Why?" she asks, with her thin white hands glued to the plastic kettle. She blows an unruly curl out of her face. "Because of homosexual conversation?"

"Don't be ridiculous. You know why. It's not right. It's not ethical."

Katka shuts off the kettle. "I cannot understand your meaning."

I finish the last letter of my lesson plan, dot a period, and close the book. Vera will be thrilled with me. She'll be fucking in love with me.

"Where can I find such a sympathetic conversationalist as yourself?" she asks.

"I'm an English teacher, not a paid escort. You should join my class or find a private tutor off DaniCo property. Those are the rules. Now excuse me, please." She's waiting for me to say it's all a joke, but I turn away and march out the door.

The smell of burnt coffee in the air doesn't bother me for a change. It tickles my nostrils. Hansa is driving a tractor across the yard. I wave my arms and step in front of the tractor, as big and noisy as a tank. Hansa slams on the brakes and shuts off the motor.

"Get down from there, Hansa. It's time for class."

"Sorry," he says, waving for me to move. "Big, big transport is coming today."

"Hansa," I repeat. "It's time for English. Climb down at once and come to class."

"Okay," Hansa says with a shrug and hops to earth. He follows me to the cafeteria where Ivo and Eva are waiting. Ivo is eating fried cheese and French fries.

"Please, Simon," Eva says, "I have sales conference and I cannot attend class."

"No," I say.

"Sorry?" Eva cups her ear as if she didn't hear. She's short and squat, with cropped black hair. In America, she'd be mistaken for a lesbian.

"You have class every Thursday from nine to ten-thirty and I expect you to be here. You'll have to find another time for your sales conference. Where is Olena?"

"I think she have much work," Ivo says with his mouth full. The aroma of bread crumbs in oil makes my nose twitch. He lifts his fork. "You want?"

"No thank you." I pick up a phone on the wall and dial Katka. "Katka, this is Simon from the cafeteria. Can you give me Olena Sverakova?"

Fifteen minutes later all four students sit around the table as I drill them on the past perfect. They sit up straight in their seats, eyes glued to their yellow *Headway* textbooks, which teach proper stilted British English that no one would ever use, not even in England.

In the middle of our lesson, a short, stout man with red eyes appears next to the open accordion door and shakes it in its track. Katka stands a few feet behind him.

"Excuse me, Simon," she says, looking over his shoulder. "Mr. Novotny, head of transport, wants to know why Hansa has left his vehicle to run in the yard."

The man sees Hansa and the two of them begin yelling at once.

"Quiet!" I yell. *"Tichy!"* Then I tell Katka, "Explain to this gentleman that English class is from nine to ten-thirty on Thursdays, and I expect my students to be here."

Novotny ignores her translation and says something to Hansa, who jumps up and runs out of the room. Eva, Olena, and Ivo cap their pens and close their books.

"What's happening?" I ask. "I can't understand him. He's speaking too fast."

"Maybe I don't want to say," Katka replies. "It's not ethical."

Novotny glares at me and says something that I think means stupid faggot. Actually, I know it means stupid faggot. Then Katka follows him downstairs.

Three pairs of eyes stare at the stupid American faggot in his wrinkled dress shirt and ugly tie. They're all waiting for him to open his mouth.

"Well," I say to the students. "We have to go on without Hansa."

Ivo sighs. Eva and Olena stare at their laps.

"Turn to page eighty-six."

No one moves.

"Or how about a game," I say. "Does anyone have a game they'd like to play?"

Nothing.

"Hangman?" I suggest.

"Yes," Ivo says, arms folded like a Roman emperor. "Hangman."

"Okay," I say and loosen the knot of my tie. "Hangman."

I start to sketch a gallows on the flip chart, but the black marker has finally run dry. I keep pressing as hard as I can and finally I slice a gash through the paper. None of them are paying attention, anyway, because there's some ruckus going on outside.

Olena removes her sunglasses. "Look at Hansa!"

We run to the window. At the other end of the yard, four men in blue uniforms are shouting and chasing a runaway tractor rolling downhill, although from our vantage point, it looks like it's already too far gone. Still, Hansa's out in front, running for his life. And I'm just standing there, gripping the snowy ledge as I wait for the inevitable crash.

DEBRA LOOKED READY FOR a fight. She stood on the corner of Revolution Avenue and Dlouha trida wearing a red bandana around her neck, a pair of old jeans, and a red T-shirt with a Nike symbol and the caption CHILD LABOR: JUST DO IT. Her skin was dry and cracked from the cold because she didn't have time for creams and lotions and potions. Debra knew she was ruining her skin—she was ruining it anyway.

She spotted the Pressmans standing across the tram tracks and studying their guidebook. They looked very lost.

"Sorry we're late!" Linda laughed as they crossed Revolution Avenue. (Unlike Lenin Avenue, "Revolution" had proved ambiguous enough to survive the post-1989 street renaming frenzy.) Linda had a starved, waifish figure. She looked like a reed in her blue T-shirt, which she'd tucked into purple jogging pants. Her face came to a point at her chin, like a modern vase, and was framed by a wreath of golden curls that fell loosely around her ears. "Jake's usually good with maps, but the streets are funny here."

"I had just determined where we were," Jake said, shutting his *Fodor's*. He'd recently made full partner in Debra's father's law firm at the tender age of thirty-five.

Debra had little patience for people with no sense of direction. Whenever she traveled to a strange city, she spent at least an hour studying the maps.

Jake gripped Debra's fingers firmly like the handle of a briefcase and planted a kiss somewhere in the air near her cheek. He had darting, gemlike eyes and a narrow nose, and his thin black hair was brushed into seven strands that spanned the top of his chalky scalp. "Good to see you, Debbie," he said, passing her an envelope. "Your father wishes he could be here to give you this himself."

"Is that what he says?" She blushed as she stuffed the sealed envelope, fat with cash, into the waistband of her underwear. "And the name's Debra now, not Debbie."

Linda peered at the bandana around Debra's neck. "What an original idea for a scarf! I haven't worn a bandana since I was a kid."

"Everyone wears these scarves in Prague," Debra said. "It isn't original here."

The restaurant Jake chose, Bohemian Rhapsody, had once been an authentic Czech pub, not this faux-imperial monstrosity with a gold-striped awning, lace tablecloths, and waitresses in traditional black-and-white servant uniforms, like ladies in waiting. Who needed servants to bring your food to you on a tray? In a truly egalitarian society, all restaurants would be self-service buffets.

The three of them were the only customers. Debra hoped no one had seen her go inside. "Sit down," she whispered, nudging them to a table. "You don't wait to be seated like in America." The menus, printed in English, French, German, and Italian, were laminated in plastic that was already peeling off. Wiener schnitzel, renamed "King Rudolf II Plate," cost one hundred crowns when it should have cost thirty.

"I'm not sure this is an authentic place," Linda said, crinkling her nose.

"It's not New York," replied her husband. "That's authentic enough for us." His gold bracelet clanked on the table as he slid his menu to Debra. "What's the difference between 'meat in spicy sauce' and then on the next page, 'meat in piquant sauce'?"

"It's written the same in the Czech version of the menu," said Debra, who'd learned to speak fluent Czech. "They must have mistranslated."

"Maybe they use paprika," Linda said. "I hate too much paprika."

"She doesn't like anything that has any flavor," Jake explained.

"I like healthy flavors. If it were up to him, we'd eat French fries every night." Linda laughed, a long, fluttery laugh that sounded too loud in the empty room. "Any romantic news? Are you still seeing that guy who doesn't use deodorant to save the eels?"

Debra merely shook her head, though the night before she'd stayed up late thinking up witty retorts, like "I don't go into my private affairs at the table" or "These days I prefer casual sex." She got the impression the Pressmans considered her an old maid because at the ripe old age of twenty-eight she still hadn't found a husband. "Just what I need, a husband," Debra thought. Sometimes to scare herself she pictured herself with a life like the one these two clowns led, imprisoned in a colonial on Long Island. She'd even picked out an imaginary husband named Dr. Herbert M. Schwartz, and two brats, a boy and a girl. The girl was a math genius and the boy wanted to be a ballet dancer.

When it was time to order, Debra asked for a lamb joint in perfect Czech. The waitress replied in English: "And for your parents?" They all laughed uncomfortably.

It made perfect sense to Debra that the Pressmans, now anxiously studying their menus to find a compromise between what they wanted to eat and how they wanted to look, appeared so much older than she did. Capitalism had ravaged their bodies. This potbellied lawyer and his shrunken homemaker were the direct result of the millions spent each year (in a world where children were starving) to persuade you to stuff your face and at the same time slim down to impossible measurements if you wanted to be happy and loved.

After confirming that "meat in piquant sauce" and "meat in spicy sauce" were the same thing, Jake ordered the potato pancakes. Linda tried to ask for spaghetti, but Jake pressed her hand and said, "Honey, try something Czech. Get the vegetarian goulash."

"Goulash is Hungarian, not Czech," Debra said, hoping that Linda would stand up to him and get the spaghetti, but no one seemed to hear her.

A Viennese waltz suddenly blared from the bar as the waitress came back with a plastic dish of celery, carrots, and wizened pickles. "You have to pay for each vegetable you eat," Debra warned. "Fifteen crowns each. They don't write it on the menu."

"That's like what, fifty cents?" said Jake, and Debra remembered when she too used to convert prices into dollars. "Take as many as you want. I'm paying." He waved a pickle at her like a baton. "So, Deb. You've been here, what, a couple months?"

"A year," Debra said, though it was just shy of nine months. "With all my work, it's gone by like a shot. Democracy isn't all sweetness and light, you know. First off, who defines democracy? And who benefits? The factory worker barely earning a living wage or the multinational corporation exploiting her?"

"I don't see these people complaining," Jake said. "Reagan told them to tear down the Berlin Wall and that's what they did."

Trying to explain the hazards of privatization to bozos like Jake was like trying to drive a car stuck in neutral. It was like a lot of things in her life.

"Hey, you two," Linda interjected with a knowing smile. "Before you get carried away with politics, I want to ask Debra which museums are worth our time?"

Debra recommended the Decorative Arts Museum because she didn't believe in masterpieces and maestros. They pressed her to join them, but Debra said she didn't have time for museums. "Tomorrow my group and I have an important meeting with a grassroots organization of Czechs who share our ideals." She handed them a purple flyer.

"At least you haven't lost your sense of color," said Jake as Linda held the paper up to the light. "You're studying something, right? Or what is it you're doing here?"

Why did he insist on treating her as if she were still a

gawky fourteen-year-old who spoke too fast and had no breasts or hips? "I'm studying the lives of Czech factory workers before and after Communism for my doctoral thesis." She pictured her thesis, a pile of paper that had been sitting untouched next to her narrow bed for months. Debra preferred the thrills of distributing flyers and placards, channeling muddy discontent into rivers and tributaries of regional meetings and marches. Not that the marches or regional meetings had happened yet. They were the future of her movement, which she'd temporarily christened the "New Socialists." It was one of those things that would have sounded better in Spanish.

"I can tell you right now what their lives are like," Jake said. "Crap. Pure crap."

"I'm on a fellowship," she said, but they stared blankly at her. Debra didn't mention that her fellowship had run out a couple of months before, and she was surviving on odd jobs, cheap prices, and American savings. She felt good living that way, dangling.

"This country is divided," she explained like she was talking to a pair of children, "into those who see market forces as a means to prosperity and greater democracy, and those who view these forces as inherently undemocratic, providing increased freedom for corporations, not people. That's why this meeting tomorrow is so historic."

"Aren't corporations made up of people?" Jake asked.

"Yeah, rich people," Debra shot back.

"And middle management and secretaries and janitors . . ."

"The point is, yes, there are jobs, but what about the quality of those jobs? Would you like to be stuck in a dingy factory or office all day? What kind of life is that?"

"Hey, it sucks," he said, pulling on one of his strands of hair. "That's why I drink. Some nights I fall into bed after midnight. But you can't play around forever. Everyone has to work, even slimeball lawyers. Even you someday."

Their meals arrived. The potato pancakes were served on an oil-stained paper doily, while the goulash came in an orange crock. Debra's lamb joint, dumplings, and cabbage were drowned in a creamy brown gravy. She sampled a bit of the goulash and pancakes, which were delicious. The lamb was tough and the dumplings were overdone and chewy.

"Corporations only serve shareholders," said Debra, sawing bravely into her joint.

"I could never bring myself to order lamb," Linda interjected.

"Because of its nutritional value?" Debra asked. Linda worked part-time as a nutritionist and occasionally led tours of grocery stores. Her motto was, "If I've said it once, I've said it a thousand times: muffins *are* cake!"

"Oh, no. It's just that I think it's inhuman the way they treat those animals."

"It's the food of the people," Debra said. "I mean, this is a typical Czech dish."

Jake asked her, "Don't you ever get scared here, all alone?"

"Never," Debra lied, swallowing a particularly tough

morsel of lamb. On her first day in Prague, a teenage boy had lifted her wallet in the metro. "It's in your underwear! Give it back!" she'd screamed, her backpack with all her posses- sions swinging off her shoulders as she chased him up two sets of escalators. "Police! Police!" Debra kept yelling, but no one did anything. Finally she caught up with the kid and shoved him against a wall. "Is this what you want?" he asked, flinging the wallet at her breasts before he ran. She'd had trouble forgiving him, even when she reminded herself that the little urchin was only a victim fighting to survive in a corrupt system that debased his humanity.

The Viennese waltz faded into a Muzak version of "Yes- terday" by the Beatles.

Linda said, "Young people are brave."

"I'm almost thirty," Debra corrected her. "Only a few years younger than you." She felt tired, even though the digi- tal clock above the bar said it was only 19:30.

"You're a child," Jake said, and the way he said it, she felt like one again. "Still in that idealistic phase. I was like you. I was going to drop out of law school and become a jazz pi- anist. Every Friday night, I'd play in a band at a little smoke- free dive bar up on 106th." He was looking out the window at a blonde in a tight-fitting white blouse.

Debra looked too. "I know her," she said. "We volunteer for this charity that integrates Gypsies, I mean the Romani, into Czech society. The discrimination they face is shameful. In one town, they built a cement wall around their neigh- borhood, like a ghetto."

Jake asked if she knew any Gypsies.

"No, but I've read about them. Their kids get put into special ed classes because they don't speak Czech. How would you feel if you were told that you were retarded because you couldn't pass a test written in Czech? I couldn't pass a test like that."

They nodded politely, but she could tell they were bored. Everything that seemed obvious to her struck them as odd. And now she seemed odd to herself too, too old to be a student still, with a funny hankie tied around her neck.

"She's beautiful," Jake said in a sad voice. He was still looking at the blond woman.

Yeah, asshole, she has big tits, Debra thought. She felt sorry for Linda, who stared at her plate and picked at the bits left over from the potato pancakes she'd shared with her husband. When the bill arrived, he put it all on his firm's gold card.

■

THE NEXT AFTERNOON, Debra waited for her New Socialists in a teahouse off a side street called Michalska. The wooden floor was uneven and scarred, and none of the chairs matched. Flyers tacked to a bulletin board advertised English lessons, used guitars, a vibrational bodywork circle for women, and Debra's meetings. Her flyers and e-mails were printed in English and Czech, but only Americans came, usually three or four, like Maria, a lonely diplomat's wife who also went to synagogue and Hare Krishna gatherings.

The New Socialists had agreed to meet at the teahouse as usual and then take the subway together out to Opatov, to meet the Czechs. However, forty minutes had gone by and no one had come, not even Maria. Each time Debra faced that stupid purple sign on the bulletin board she wanted to guzzle some arsenic. People knew her here. She'd even fucked the waiter, though only a few times, never on any regular basis.

The door squeaked open. Debra didn't see anyone at first, not until Linda took a cautious step across the threshold. Jake came in behind her and paused to pet a knee-high ceramic frog. "Sorry we're late," she said. "We got lost again."

"What are you doing here?" Debra asked, horrified.

"We wanted to wish you well on your big day, since your dad couldn't be here."

"So you could tell him no one showed up and what a loser I am."

"No, no, not at all!" protested Linda, then added, "Mind if we wait here with you?"

"It's a free country," said Debra, secretly glad for the distraction.

Linda settled into a worn chair, its cushion leaking curls of cotton stuffing onto the floor. Jake was still poking at the frog, as if it could jump. "We bought puppets for the kids," she sighed. "There are toys everywhere. It's a city of toys and music."

Debra was about to say, "I live here, I know it's beautiful," but stopped herself.

"A second honeymoon," said Jake. "Honey, do you have our passports?"

"And guess who we saw at the Castle getting out of a limo? The president! What's his name? Pavel? Can you believe it? Just like an ordinary guy going to work."

"You ought to like him," Jake said and pulled up a chair. "He was in jail."

"No, it's great," said Debra, who'd seen Havel dozens of times in Velryba Café and a couple of jazz clubs. You could see him every week if you knew where to go. "I'm happy for you." Strangely, she did feel happy for them just then, happy they were happy.

Debra pointed to her watch. "I should go. No one else is coming."

"You can't go alone," Linda protested. "That would be a disaster."

"The Czech Republic becoming the fifty-first state of America would be a disaster. This is a minor blip, one which I am perfectly capable of handling."

Linda leaned forward. "I was thinking, maybe we could come with you. We could be expatriates, for all these people know. That way we could see what it is you do. And it wouldn't be a lie. Your group does have other members, right?"

Not exactly members. More like a mailing list. Despite what Debra had said, she was embarrassed to show up at Opatov completely alone. "What's the catch?" she asked, sure her father had put them up to it.

"We're just trying to be supportive," said Linda, who looked a little hurt.

"When someone offers to do you a favor, the polite thing to say is thank you," Jake reminded her. " 'What do you have

to lose but your chains?' I could be a Marxist, no problem."
He snapped his fingers for the waiter and mimed the word
"check." "I tell you, there is something about this city that
makes you feel young again!"

"Well, it's not like I need you," Debra said cautiously,
"but if you come, it's my show. I'm the leader."

Linda brightened immediately. *"Achtung!"* she said and
saluted. "Yes, ma'am!"

Jake paid for Debra's tea. She wanted him to, but she
didn't want to want him to.

Outside, a gust of wind blew up the top of Jake's hair, and
Linda struggled for a minute to tap it down. Her husband
thanked her with a peck on the cheek, and as it started to
rain, they held hands. Just then Debra envied them, wasteful, irresponsible, armed with gold cards and air tickets
with the date of their imminent return to the States clearly
marked.

During the subway ride to Opatov, Debra hung from a
metal strap and heard voices, like her older brother, who
once asked, "Does it ever bother you that you'll never make
a lot of money?" Or Jake's eloquent, "I know what their lives
are like. Pure crap."

It wasn't far from the truth. Wages remained stagnant
while prices surged, fueled by tourism and expatriates, even
well-intentioned ones like her. The factories were mis-
managed by ex-Communists who'd conspired to buy up
all the heavy industry just after privatization and had no
idea about budgets, marketing, long-term planning. Most
workers lived in crowded, shoddily built high-rises on the
edge of town. The walls were so thin you could hear the

neighbors' conversations as plainly as if you were in the same room.

The train dropped them off down the hill from a planned community of cement tower-block apartments called Garden City. The brown buildings, which looked even browner when wet, stood in a rigid grid of streets named after different types of fruit. Debra was looking for Unit Four, Pomegranate Avenue.

The sidewalks were streaked with mud, and the gutters overflowed with gurgling brown water. Debra's feet were soaked. A boy kneeling in the dirt imprisoned a croaking toad in his long fingers and then let it go.

"Brown, brown, brown," Linda said. "How wretched to stare at this all the time."

Debra smiled for the first time that day. "Now you see what I'm fighting against."

"It's awful," Jake agreed. "Who's this group we're meeting with, anyway?"

"I don't know too much about them. Does it matter?"

The organization, named the Illustrious Order of the Golden Fleece, had as its vague-sounding mission statement: "To promote the virtues of magnanimity, justice, prudence, fidelity, patience, and clemency." Debra assumed they were a local version of the Kiwanis Club. The woman at the Municipality Office who'd given her the contact sheet of community groups and political parties didn't seem to know much about them and wasn't interested in finding out. The other clubs on the list had brushed off Debra's phone calls, but the director of the Golden Fleece had responded very affably to her on the phone, especially when she talked about decaying social values.

Jake said, "Of course it matters. You have to tailor your message to your client."

"My message is the same for everyone," Debra insisted. "Look, I'm just going to let it flow naturally. I can handle this. I'm in charge, remember?"

"Hey, hey, it's your show," he said. "We're just tagging along."

No, they were spies, Debra thought, here to report every detail back to her father.

They stood confused for a minute in the overheated lobby of Unit Four. A giant rust-colored star on one of the cinder block walls had been thinly painted over with a royal Czech lion. The building caretaker sat on a low stool and picked mud off his old boots with a stick. He pointed the way without looking up from his boots.

The meeting room was a dark, hot, gloomy square with a stage lit by a powerful fluorescent lamp. The windows were covered in black curtains. A small crowd, mostly older men wearing dark coats and gray neckties, promenaded in twos and threes up and down the room and lifted their top hats as they passed each other. The crisp black silhouettes of their wet coats stood out sharply against the light from the stage as well as a few candlesticks set up in the corners. Wrinkled women in long dresses sat very still, as if embalmed, in small circles of orange plastic chairs and cradled Styrofoam cups of tea in their gray hands. Debra had never been in such a silent room with so many people in it.

"Are we in the wrong place?" Linda whispered. "It looks like a funeral."

Debra stopped an old lady in a pink ball dress with a high lace collar and asked in her most polite Czech if she knew Walter. They were looking for Walter.

"Certainly," the old lady replied in Czech, picking at her lace. Under her dress, she wore brown orthopedic shoes. "I can't find my maid. You aren't a maid, by any chance?"

Debra said no and looked down in shame at her shabby jeans and moccasins.

"Oh, well, then. I suppose I'll have to take you to Walter." The old lady, who had a charming old-fashioned accent, bit crisply into each syllable of her words like they were expensive chocolates. She clutched Debra's arm as she led them to the front of the room.

Walter stood at the edge of the stage, looking out at the crowd like a captain in the prow of his ship. Behind him, the red, white, and blue national flag drooped listlessly from a pole. He was a heavy man, about forty, with a swollen neck and a long mustache with the tips glued into points. "Honored to make your acquaintance in the flesh," he said, kissing the rough white hand Debra held up for him to shake. "I find telephones so impersonal, though a necessary evil, like most other modernities. But where is your group?" His Czech was sweetly perfumed with an old-fashioned accent like the old lady's.

"The others couldn't come," Debra lied. "There's a protest at the Castle."

"It's a crime what's going on up there," Walter said, huffing as he climbed down the steps. His breath smelled like hazelnut. "Do you know that upstart peasant-playwright plans to move into the royal chambers!" He bowed to Jake and Linda, his eyes twinkling in the light of a candle dripping down a brass stick. "Would you care for some ginger tea?"

They smiled blankly. *"Nerozumeji cesky,"* Debra explained, dismissing the bewildered Pressmans with the back of her hand.

"But I speak quite exquisite English," he replied to Jake and Linda's apparent relief. "I also speak excellent German and Spanish. My French is merely passable."

"And you must have learned Russian in school," Jake said.

Walter bowed again, stiffly. "Yes, of course, but it isn't considered polite to mention." He invited them to sit on a long piano bench beside a boxy upright with a few keys missing. "Would you like your tea now?" he asked with a bewitching smile. "Bozena will take care of you. Ladies and gentlemen, my wife Bozena."

He motioned toward a heavy, slovenly maid in a flaccid cloth tiara and an apron wheeling a metal cart with a samovar, a stack of Styrofoam cups, and a plate of sugar-coated biscuits. She'd tried unsuccessfully to disguise her mustache with pink powder.

"Ooh, can I see the box of cookies?" Linda asked.

"Linda, give it a rest with the fat content," Jake said. "You're on vacation."

"I'm going to have one," she said. "I was just wondering how they list nutritional information here."

While Bozena served them tea, Walter slung a red-and-white banner over his shoulder. He lowered the Czech tricolor flag from the pole onstage and hoisted a new one in its place. The new flag had a shield adorned with a roaring black lion, red and white stripes, three eagles, and the initials *A.E.I.O.U.* A golden sheep dangled from the shield by a chain. Its eyes were closed and its still face wore a striking haunted expression.

"A. E. I. O. U. Austriae Est Imperare Orbi Universo," Walter explained from the stage. "It's the Habsburg motto, and it means 'Austria is destined to lead the world.' Frederick II, one of those rascal Hohenzollerns of Prussia, rather snidely changed it to *'Austria Erit In Orbe Ultima,'* or 'Austria will one day be last in the world.' Unfortunately, this alteration turned out to be quite prophetic."

"I'm not sure I get it," said Linda. "Is this a masquerade ball fund-raiser?"

"It is not a fund-raiser and it is not strictly speaking a masquerade either since everyone here is not dressing up as something they want to be, but as who they really are. For example, I work as a history teacher. However, by rights I should be a full professor. Unfortunately, because of my political views, I've been rejected for posts at five major universities in the so-called Czech Republic."

Walter went on to explain that the Order of the Golden Fleece was a grassroots movement with chapters in Brno and Bratislava. "Our country has attempted without success three forms of government: democracy, fascism, and Communism. Independent Czechoslovakia was a noble experiment, but it has failed. Hence, our Order proposes a return to the more civilized age of the Austro-Hungarian Empire and the Habsburgs."

"The Who's Burgs?" Linda asked.

"Don't be such a tourist," Jake said. "They own that big shoe store downtown."

Walter leaned over the edge of the stage. "Actually, my friend, they are an illustrious imperial dynasty which for five hundred years ruled all the land between Kraków and Yugoslavia."

Debra, who was making an effort not to show the Pressmans the horror and the dread she felt, reminded herself that progressive alliances often made for strange bedfellows. "Are there any Habsburgs still alive?" she asked as casually as she could manage. Unlike most Americans, Debra didn't find kings colorful or quaint. Just recently, Princess Diana had visited Prague, and the city had closed and disinfected its largest public pool so the Royal Freeloader could enjoy her usual morning swim untainted by peasant bodies.

"Several, in fact," Walter said. "Otto, a very young ninety-two years old, is the current paterfamilias. He is a member of the European Parliament from Germany, and his son Georg is also a member, from Hungary. Would you care to see Herr Otto's picture?" He produced an eight-by-ten glossy, signed and stamped with a dead sheep hanging from a blurry shield. A caption at the bottom in Czech, German, and English read:

Behold his Excellency, Otto von Habsburg, often called Hapsburg, the rightful and much wronged Emperor of Austria, King of Jerusalem, Hungary, Bohemia, Dalmatia, Croatia, Slavonia, Galicia, and Ludomiria; Archduke of Austria; Delightful Duke of Lorraine, Salzburg, Wurzburg, Franken, Styria, Carinthia, and Carniola; Clever Duke of Cracow; Proud Prince of Transylvania; Handsome Margrave of Moravia; Distinguished Baron of Sandomir, of Masovia, of Lublin, of Upper and Lower Silesia, Auschwitz, and Zator, to say nothing of Teschen and Friuli; Right Honorable Prince of Berchtesgaden and Mergentheim; Princely Count of Hapsburg, Goritz, and Gradisca; and Magnificent Margrave of Upper and Lower Lausitz, and Istia.

Otto, who looked more like a watchmaker than an emperor to Debra, smiled pleasantly as if he'd just finished a nice lunch. He wore a simple coat and tie and boxy brown glasses that magnified the ruddy bags under his eyes. His mustache was white and bushy, and the top of his head was dotted with freckles. There was no trace of the famous Habsburg protruding lip and jaw, which, as Debra recalled from her World History class, had proved so painful to Charles the Bewitched that he was unable to chew solid foods.

"What does good old Otto say about all this?" Jake asked, slipping off one of his loafers to adjust his dress sock.

Walter sighed. "We believe Herr Otto is willing. But you see, after the unfortunate result of the First World War, the government of Austria banned the Habsburgs from their native soil unless they should renounce all claims to former greatness. Therefore, in 1961, on the occasion of the birth of his elder son, Karl von Habsburg-Lothringen, Otto made his sacrifice. He is now a modern, enlightened Habsburger. And now, if you'll pray excuse me, I must call the meeting to order."

Linda and Jake applauded like at the end of a performance. Debra bit her tongue.

"Are we helping?" Linda asked her. "I hope we're helping, not in your way."

"You're fine," Debra replied, though actually they were in her way. If they hadn't been there, she could have made a run for it.

Walter motioned with his hands for everyone to stand up. Their backs stiff and their hands on their hearts, the crowd sang a rollicking chorus of a song in German that Debra didn't recognize or understand. Afterward, the women sat down again and Walter clapped for attention.

"Today we have a presentation," he announced in his most regal accent, "from American visitors." Everyone stretched their necks to catch a glimpse of the three Americans in modern dress.

"Not really a presentation," Debra said, trying to laugh. "More like a greeting."

"Tut-tut," Walter said, clicking his tongue. "She has a message about values."

For a moment, Debra stood frozen, her throat dry, her face contorted into an uncertain smile. A glance at Jake and Linda stiffened her resolve. She squared her shoulders and mounted the stage. Here was her chance not to preach to the converted for once, but to the convertible. These people had tirelessly marched and waved homemade placards to earn their newly won freedom, and now they were being swindled into forfeiting that freedom to some blue-blooded phantom. The loquacious charmer to her left suddenly sprouted a pair of horns to match the finely tweaked tips of his handlebar mustache. But Debra could break his spell.

Eyes flaming, hands trembling with indignation, she stood before them, rigid and proud. With all the dignity of Subcomandante Marcos speaking on behalf of the indigenous peoples of Chiapas, she delivered a fiery speech in Czech about substandard safety inspections and the declining value of real wages. She explained the need for a greater understanding of ergonomics and crippling nationwide strikes, the people taking back the streets. A strange feeling stirred in her chest as she spoke. She felt like an artist.

The crowd regarded her coldly. Debra was staring at a collection of waxworks, not real people, with flat, painted smiles and glass eyes that registered nothing. Occasionally they lifted their cigars or Styrofoam cups to their lips like windup soldiers. Jake whispered behind his hand to Linda and nodded at the exit.

"You've finally liberated yourselves thanks to a popular movement for and by the people, and you want to go back to your chains?" Debra called out.

A gentleman with a row of medals pinned to his left

breast raised an elegantly cupped hand and stepped forward. "Forgive the contradiction, but we did not liberate
ourselves. We were liberated by His Excellency, Otto von
Habsburg."

Debra couldn't help laughing, but no one else seemed to
think the notion was ridiculous. "Fine, have it your way. I
give up," she announced.

"Is it going well?" Linda asked in a stage whisper.
"Should we leave?"

"It's fine," Debra hissed, climbing down from the stage.
"It's going great."

The gentleman with the medals stepped forward to lend
Debra his arm, but she made it back to the floor on her own.
The rest of the crowd began milling around the room again,
or lining up in front of Bozena's tea cart.

"To understand us, you have to understand history," the
gentleman explained in Czech. "The Iron Curtain began its
fall in the autumn of 1989. But in the summer of 1989, Otto
von Habsburg hosted a picnic on the Austro-Hungarian border. Coincidence?"

"Yeah, sure," Debra said. "Whatever."

The gentleman chortled a bit and said, "This was a very
significant picnic. At this picnic, Austrians and Hungarians
openly defied Soviet guards by crossing back and forth for
the first time in fifty years. Because law or no law, no one
says no to a Habsburg."

"The Habsburgs were rich but they cared about the people," added a young man whose top hat was too big for him
and kept falling into his eyes. "They used to disguise them-

selves in peasant clothing and mingle with the people to find out their concerns."

Debra was just about to mount a counterattack when she was abruptly cut off by a few familiar chords chiming from the box piano. Jake was playing the chorus from "Love Me Do." "This old thing's all right," he said, his fingers fluttering over the keys.

"Kind sir," a lady with a gold paper fan said in English, addressing Jake, "perhaps do you know 'Hey Jude'?"

"No sweat," Jake said and plunked out the tune. A small circle of Czechs gathered around him and hummed all the lyrics, except for "Hey Jude," the only words they knew. "I didn't know you guys were allowed to listen to the Beatles," Jake said.

"Oh, yes," Walter assured him, tapping a gloved hand on the piano. "The Communists were quite fond of the Beatles. As are Archduke Karl-Lothringen and Prince Georg, the sons of Otto von Habsburg."

Linda was holding up the box of biscuits and talking animatedly with Bozena, who said she wanted to lose a stone or two. "I don't know how much a stone is, but anything's possible," Linda said. "As long as you look at your diet as a liberation instead of a burden. It's a way to free yourself from habits you don't need anymore."

Look at these people, Debra thought, frittering away their chance for true freedom to sing an old Beatles song. They're as sluggish as the sheep on their flag. They deserve their misery.

But what if they weren't miserable? Maybe there was a

fundamental failure in the way she saw the universe, not they. Maybe there were no revolutions worth waging anymore, just people who enjoyed revolutions. But then how could that be right as long as one person suffered? If everyone acted in her own interest, the world would be a horrible, selfish place.

She was picturing Jake and Linda having a good laugh at her expense back at their hotel when the old lady in the pink dress grasped her arm. "You need to speak more clearly, young lady. You have such a strange accent, but I approve of you."

"Really?" Debra said and began searching through her bag for some literature.

"Certainly." She patted Debra's hand. "You know, I was personally acquainted with the Habsburgs."

"Great, great. What were the old bats like?"

The old lady smiled shyly. "One of them was very handsome. He promised to marry me, but then he ran away from the Nazis, to Switzerland, because he was part Jewish, and then he had to stay there when the Communists came because he was an aristocrat. His family recently got their castle back from the state. I read it in the papers."

You could always go home and get married, Debra thought. There was always someone to marry. But she didn't want a family, not the traditional kind. She didn't want diapers and graham crackers and apple juice, and then a part-time job she didn't care about just to get out of the colonial, away from Herbert M. Schwartz and the two brats crying. She hated cooking and ate out every chance she got. She refused to clean—that was what men were for. Sponges disgusted her. She felt trapped just thinking about them.

Jake suddenly began howling the chorus of "Hey Jude," ridiculously off-key as if drunk. Debra was so angry and ashamed she could have murdered him. She marched over to Jake, seething. "Since when did this meeting become your personal coming-out party?"

"What are you talking about?" he asked. "We're having a good time here."

"Play, play," said the old man who'd lost his cigar. "Why do you stop?"

"You capitalists, you're so big on ownership," Debra went on. "Products, people, it's all the same. You think you can just take over this meeting whenever you feel like it? Maybe your wife puts up with that kind of oppression, but as a family friend, a woman, an intellectual, I demand more respect." In a flash of inspiration, she added, "You know, I could have you fired."

Jake went very red. "Hey, Deb, don't talk like that. Even to kid around."

"Who's kidding around?" she said, highly gratified by her ruthlessness.

"You think you can talk that way because of who your father is? Like I'm one of your goddamned servants?"

Debra pretended to be absorbed in grinding someone else's cigarette butt into the floor. She knew she owed him an apology and she'd make one in time, but for now he deserved to quake under her thumb, to get back a bit of what he'd been dishing out.

"I couldn't help overhearing," Walter said in Czech. "Your father has some sort of elevated station in America?"

"Yeah, he's rich," Debra said. "In America, that's even better than royalty."

Walter beamed. "But why didn't you tell us? We can use you!" He grabbed her hand and led her back to the stage, into the light. "It's the world's oldest alliance," he said, "the aristocracy and the poor united against their natural enemy."

"Who's that?" she asked, a bit dizzy.

"The bourgeoisie." Walter wrinkled his nose. "Right now, they're selling off this entire country to their fellow merchants in the West, those fat, comfortable cosmopolitans, the usurers and the moneylenders . . ."

"IMF, WTO, the World Bank," Debra thought aloud as Walter exhorted the crowd to treat her to a round of applause that tickled her ears.

"What's happening?" asked Linda. "What's going on?"

"She's nuts," Jake marveled. "And all this time we thought she was just eccentric."

Bathed in the hot, blinding spotlight, she could see her regional meetings clearer than ever, and her marches, her surging masses waving lit candles and flags with limp, golden sheep to symbolize the plight of the people. Let them call her a Don Quixote, or a rich girl in revolutionary's clothing. The world needed people like her who could afford to speak truth to power instead of wasting all day in a hospital or a law firm.

"My friends . . ." she began, still blinded by the spotlight. "My friends . . ." But she was drowned out by deafening applause from an audience she couldn't see. "My friends, my friends," she repeated, trying to shut them up so she could go on.

THEY'D STUCK THE PRAGUE Stock Exchange at the back of a renovated shopping arcade with polished faux marble floors and glass walls. The state-run department stores had been replaced by Marks & Spencer, Pretzel Time, and Eyeglasses Unlimited.

While Donald waited by the entrance, he glanced at a newsstand tacked with a column of porno magazines, a ladder of tits in full color. His eyelids kept drooping because he'd been out late the night before with a Spanish kid he'd picked up. Evidently, the only English this boy knew was "Hot dog!" All evening he'd been silent until they got into bed and then he'd grabbed Donald's erection and exclaimed, "Hot dog!"

Donald was about to knock when a scrawny teenager with a bad case of acne and dressed in a green security guard uniform that was too big for him opened the door. The toes of his patent leather shoes peeked out of the hems of his pant cuffs. His gun belt, anchored by a real gun, kept sliding down his hips.

"I'm the English teacher," Donald said with a bright smile. "It's my first day."

A receptionist in a green vest squeezed past them and

knocked the oversize guard hat off the boy's head. "*Ahoj,* Schwejk!" he called out.

The young guard scowled and pointed to a green vinyl couch next to the reception desk. "Thank you, Schwejk," Donald said. The guard scowled again and then retreated into a corner to pick at one of his pimples.

While he waited, Donald thumbed through his worn copy of *Maurice.* He'd been plugging away at the book for four months now, and even though he found it boring, he was determined to get to the end because he believed serious reading would improve his mind. As soon as he'd finished *Maurice,* he planned to take up *The Picture of Dorian Gray* and after that, the rest of the gay classics, if there were any other ones.

Donald thought of himself as a gun for hire, like a cowboy in the Old West. One day he was teaching at an English-owned manufacturer of household cleaners, the next at a Swiss candy company that sold ordinary chocolates in shiny red or silver wrappers, as gifts for lovers. The Stock Exchange was his first Czech-owned concern. Two of his colleagues, both women, had tried their hands at an intermediate English class there and faced a revolt. The students told Donald's boss they could only learn from a man.

Donald tried to imagine what his students might expect from a man. In high school, when he'd been the sole male cheerleader for the football team ("W-E-S-T!" Chest-thrust and simultaneous grunt! "M-A-P-L-E!" Chest-thrust and simultaneous grunt! "West Maple! West Maple! Yay! West Maple!"), his nickname had been Miss Donaldine.

"Cheerleading's a manly sport!" he'd protested. "It's a form of gymnastics!"

He was about to nod off for real when an old man waved from the reception desk. The man had a pinched face, slits for eyes, and a frighteningly skeletal body, as if he'd been starving himself all his life in order to slip through cracks. "Morning," Donald said in a deliberately gruff voice. He almost added, "How's the score in the big game?"

The old man punched a code into the wall next to the electric gate, which refused to budge. "It never work," he said, jumping over it instead. Donald shrugged and jumped too. They rode the elevator to the sixth floor without speaking. Reasonable, Donald thought. A real man didn't bother making pleasant chitchat to set his companions at ease.

The class met in a boardroom with no windows and a polished wooden table that smelled like pinesap and stuck to the back of Donald's roster. He had five frowning students: three young, one middle-aged, and the old man. They watched him struggle to pull out his heavy gray chair, which, embarrassingly, he needed both hands to move.

Donald cleared his throat. "My name is Donald and I'm from Canada." He paused and took a deep breath. "Also, so you know, I'm a homosexual and I don't expect you to have any problems with me."

The students smiled uncomfortably and then looked to the old man, who fixed Donald with a hard stare before his papery cheeks relaxed into a smile. "Yes, you are for us. We are ready for your," he waved his long blue hand in the air, "enlightenment."

Another student raised his hand. "Can you explain me the future conditional?"

Donald, who had no idea what the future conditional was, replied, "Oh, I never bother with grammar. It's too basic."

Afterward, he felt so elated at his success that he wanted to share his good news with someone. He went out that night and picked up a young go-go dancer named Martin, who sold tickets at the main train station when he wasn't stripping. Martin spoke halting English, which was all right by Donald because his body was a poem. The next day, Donald called up the train station to say what a good time he'd had the night before.

"Yes, I remember who you are," Martin said. In the background, a loud, garbled voice in Czech announced the next train departures over the p.a. "Long line of customers wait to buy tickets. I can telephone you later?"

Donald read *Maurice* at home and waited all evening for the call that never came. He felt a bit disappointed, even though the boy was only a dancer.

■

DONALD LOOKED FORWARD to arriving at the Stock Exchange each morning and hopping over the electronic gate with the men in business suits. The guard continued to scowl, even though Donald always greeted him with a hearty, "Hi, Schwejk!" Donald figured maybe he was upset about his acne, which only seemed to get worse each week.

He wasn't supposed to have favorites, but he couldn't help a tender spot for Roman, who always ran in late with his tie hanging loose around his open collar because he was taking care of his wife, now six months pregnant. "I must boil her one cup of milk every day," Roman said with a bashful smile.

The students were computer programmers, not stock-brokers. They spoke in fits and starts, and it was hard for Donald not to think of them as his "kids." Whenever Donald called on them, they smiled into their hands, even after he told them, "Don't worry if it's not perfect English. I *like* when you make mistakes." He coaxed them through four rounds of a game called "Garage Sale" to loosen their tongues. ("Pretend you're trying to sell me an item you have on you. Make me want to buy it from you. That's capitalism.")

Every couple of weeks, the kids took Donald for dinner at a pub behind the Kotva department store. They ordered his meal for him: dumplings, cabbage, a delicious pork cutlet, and a beer, which they encouraged him to drink right out of the bottle. Also, they taught him Czech slang like *kurva sopa.*

Roman said, "It is for real hot, you say 'hot,' yes? For hot slut! Now you say it."

They laughed at his pronunciation and slapped him on the back. Roman pleaded, "Donald, find some nice Czech girl, get married, and be our teacher forever."

"But I'm gay, remember?" The thought of "forever" gave him a chill.

"It's no matter," said Roman. "There are husbands with worse problems."

"I'm sorry, but America is my home. I couldn't live anywhere else," he lied.

Roman looked confused. "But I have impression you are from Canada."

■

THE FOLLOWING WEEK Roman stayed a few minutes after class and invited Donald to dinner with one of his shy smiles. It sounded almost like a date. Donald had never dated a student before, but he couldn't resist a man who boiled milk.

He checked himself in the window before entering their usual pub, where Roman sat at a table for two with a young woman. Her hair was dyed the color of raspberries and brushed into a pompadour like Ronald Reagan's. She didn't look pregnant.

Roman stood up. "Excuse me, friend. My wife feels pregnancy sickness and I must go home now. But my sister speaks good English. Please stay and enjoy supper."

He ran out the door.

"I'm sorry," Donald said, standing over the woman. "But I think I know what this is all about, and your brother has made the hugest mistake."

"No mistake," the woman said in a British accent. Her skin was fair and her lips were painted brown. She wore a black dress with a square-cut neck and she was fiddling with the wooden handle of her square black purse. "I believe it goes something like this. You're Roman's English teacher. He likes you and wants you to stay in our country, and to that end he's enlisted me to marry you. The only problem is you're a homosexual."

"Being gay isn't a problem," he said and turned to leave, but she held his wrist.

"I was only joking, silly. Sit down. I was joking." He glared at her hand, which she removed from his wrist and thrust forward at him. "My name is Jana and believe it or not, I didn't come to ensnare you, and I've told my brother so. It's just that I don't often have the opportunity to have a conversation in English these days, and I'd so enjoy just talking." Her British accent was flawless, a dead ringer for Emma Thompson.

"You people . . ." he began, then checked himself as he grudgingly shook her hand.

"We're . . . what? Backward? Obliging? Simple, yet generous in such a peasant-hearted way? Devious? Stubborn? We've got a reputation, you know. Napoleon called us a city of men without courage and women without morals."

"You guys just wear me out," he said and finally sat down.

She laughed and passed him a menu.

Jana was the creative one in her family. "I can't help it. It's my nature." She'd studied British and Russian literature at Charles University for almost three years before she'd been kicked out for cheating. Her former boyfriend, an Irishman, had written a paper for her on D. H. Lawrence. "I could have done it on my own but I simply didn't have the time because I'd taken on too many English lessons and translations. I needed the extra money, you see, and now because of economics, my career is ruined."

"You could have asked for a . . ." said Donald, snapping his fingers to think of the word. "You know, more time."

"You mean an extension? This professor never grants extensions."

"But isn't there some kind of higher-up you could have talked to?"

"I suppose," Jana sighed. She dug in her purse until she found a lipstick without a cap and painted her lips a rich cakey brown, like mud. "You don't understand our culture. Big fights are for big countries that march through our territory on their way to invade each other. We bend with the wind to survive. We don't always follow rules. Understand?"

"But look where it got you. Was it worth it? I mean, cheating is wrong."

"Thanks a lot." She blotted her lips with a tissue. "As if I needed reminding."

He blushed. "I didn't mean to judge. I'm sorry."

"As well you should be. Haven't you ever done anything dishonest in your life?"

"I'm sure I have, though if so, I'm a man more sinned against than sinning."

"*King Lear*. My favorite play by Shakespeare."

The way Jana said "favorite" made him imagine it "spelt" with a *u*.

"I didn't know it was Shakespeare," he said. "You read Shakespeare?"

"Only in the original. You can't expect me to abide these so-called 'translations.' 'Perversions' is more like it. That was my dream, to translate Shakespeare decently. Not all of it, of course. A few plays, some of the sonnets. I'm in love with the sonnets. My favorite is, well, I forget the number now, but it goes something like, 'Let me not to the marriage of true minds admit impediments.' There's something gloriously English about those lines, the rolling rhythm of that word 'impediments.' It's a lovely word, isn't it?"

They lived in the same direction and rode the tram together after dinner. As they crossed the river, Jana pointed out the swans, now returning to Prague with the melting of the snow. The Communists had made it a crime to waste bread by feeding it to swans, but the people of Prague, risking arrest, fed them anyway, often in the middle of the night.

"Thanks to them, the birds continued to return year after year," she said, and it seemed to him that her eyes looked a little wet.

"I'm really sorry for what I said before about your paper," Donald said as their tram ticked its way to his stop, which came first. "And, if you wouldn't mind, I'd like to see you some other time, for tea or something. It's really hard meeting people here, people I can really communicate with. This isn't like a date, obviously."

"Obviously." When she crossed her legs, he noticed she was wearing black-and-white-striped stockings.

"And I could help you with your translations," he offered.

"It's a deal," Jana agreed. "But here we are. You'd better not miss your stop."

"That's right." He stood up and held out his hand.

She laughed. "Donald, you're such an American. Haven't you learned yet that in Europe it's customary to *kiss* a woman good-bye?"

"Oh, right." He kissed her cheek and then jumped down

from the tram before he remembered that he was really a Canadian.

■

"DO YOU MEAN you've *never* experienced intercourse with a woman?"

"Why? Did you ever do it with a woman?"

"Yes," she shot back immediately.

"You really slept with a woman?" Donald asked. "So how was she?"

"A pill," she said. "It was after I got dumped by the Irishman because of the essay incident. I needed comfort. But who knows? I might do it again with someone nicer."

They were wandering through a rambling wooded park on the edge of town called Divoka Sarka. The forest was named for a wild woman named Sarka who'd led an unsuccessful women's revolt. Rather than surrender to men, she and her band of amazons had jumped off a cliff. But that day there was little evidence of battle, only spring: small bursts of green buds gleaming and white starflowers pushing through the mud. A man by the entrance sold sticks with brightly colored ribbons tied to their ends. Every Easter, said Jana, men bought the sticks to beat their wives in order to make them fertile.

"Doesn't that make you mad?" Donald asked.

"Nonsense," Jana said. "I'd be embarrassed if I didn't have a man to beat me."

"So who's going to beat you this year?" he asked. She didn't seem to hear.

They'd been seeing each other regularly for a month.

Jana started it. She had an extra ticket to the Philharmonic. In return, he invited her to see *The Remains of the Day* at an international film festival in Mala Strana. She laughed at his description of the garage sale and explained that "Schwejk" wasn't the real name of the young guard with acne at the Stock Exchange. Rather, he was a hero from Czech folklore, a bumbling soldier and idiot savant more likely to attack pints of beer than invading armies.

In class, Roman made wisecracks about their friendship, which Donald ignored. Obviously, Roman had never heard of a "fag hag" before.

"Any interesting men in your life lately?" asked Jana, gently tucking a daisy behind her ear. The effect was most becoming.

"They're never interesting," he said bitterly. "Their English isn't good enough for us to have a real conversation like the one we're having."

"Then why don't you try to meet ones who speak decent English?"

"I am trying," he insisted. "They're not out there."

"You're exaggerating now. Plenty of young men speak English. If you can't seem to meet them, it's either because you don't try, or else you're not looking hard enough." Two policemen crossed their path and Jana asked, "Which one do you fancy?"

"Do you have to keep bringing up this stuff?"

"It's not *keeping* bringing it up," Jana said, making a rare mistake in English. She picked another flower and tucked it behind her ear. "I've always got on with gay people and native English speakers, though you're the first one I've met who's both. Anyway, why shouldn't I bring it up? Should I pretend you are who you're not?"

"Who I have sex with has nothing to do with who I am," he told her.

"Oh, hell. Give me your hand. Give it to me, I said."

He obliged and was surprised by the strength of her grip.

"Friends, right?"

"Friends," he said. "If you have to know, I like guys with dark hair."

Jana smiled in triumph. "I'll take the blonds, then. Let's walk for a while."

She didn't let go of his hand as they strolled past a skating rink now closed for spring. The air smelled fresh, clean. A pair of old women gave them approving smiles.

■

WHEN HIS PHONE rang that evening, Donald guessed it was Jana inviting him to the Rudolfinum to see an exhibition about Charles IV, whom Jana had described as the Czech version of Henry VIII. He'd had four wives, two Annas, an Elizabeth, and a Blanche, but the second Anna was the only one he'd married for love.

"Here is Martin," said the voice on the other end. Here I am. Here is the penis.

"Martin," Donald repeated, trying to recall who Martin was. He closed his eyes and saw a pair of black-and-white-striped briefs sliding down a thick leg. "Is this Martin the dancer?" Donald realized he hadn't been with a penis since right around the time he'd met Jana. He'd been taking a break to focus on his work. "I've missed you," said Donald and felt himself get hard.

"It's reason for my call, my pretty friend."

At Martin's suggestion, they met in a dim, overheated restaurant behind the train station. The walls were lined with slot machines. Donald sat at a table in the back covered in a coffee-stained wax tablecloth. He tried plugging away at *Maurice*, which he was still reading, but it was too dark to concentrate.

Martin breezed into the room half an hour late and blew Donald an air kiss. He wore plaid pants, a white scarf, and suspenders. "Hello, good friend!" He put his hand over his heart, opened his mouth, and made a tragic face. "I sing American pop song. Is good joke, no?" Martin laughed and then choked on his cigarette smoke as he sat down. Donald would much rather have listened to Jana lecture about the whims of Czech royalty.

The waitress shuffled over and rolled her eyes as Martin ordered a "Viennese coffee," espresso with whipped cream and chocolate powder, served in a tea glass.

"I have many American boyfriends. *Americany* love Martin, always." He poured in three packets of sugar and churned his coffee with a teaspoon, splattering espresso all over his fingers. After licking them clean, Martin told a story in half English and half Czech, which Donald only half understood. It concerned a rich American whom Martin had met while selling the guy a first-class to Munich. The American lived in a Miami beach house where there was always food, sun, and gold necklaces like the one Martin had on.

"He is old. Ugly. Stupid. No like you." Martin slipped off his shoe and rubbed his foot against Donald's ankle. "He say me before I go back to Prague if I have problem, phone him. So now I need money for my problem and I phone him. But no answer."

"What problem?"

"Stupid hotel now where I live, I must pay . . ." He snapped his fingers for help.

"Rent?"

"Yes." Martin pressed his foot into the toe of Donald's shoe. "I will be have no money when I give rent. No coffee." He lifted his pack of cigarettes. "No good cigarettes like Marlboro. Expensive. Sparta, Gauloise is shit, shit, shit." Donald reached out to pat his arm, but Martin took his hand and pressed it into his thigh.

The yawning waitress came over to say the restaurant was closing and stood over them until Donald paid the bill. Outside, Martin looked around before taking Donald's arm in his for a few seconds.

On their way to the train station, they passed the old Communist Parliament, now home to Radio Free Europe. "Did you know that's Radio Free Europe?" Donald said.

Martin shrugged. "Is ugly. Why they don't make into nice boutique like Versace?"

At the train station, a circle of Gypsies smoked and talked on a bench outside the main doors. "Garbage," Martin said loud enough for them to hear. "I am very hungry. Excuse me." He bought a quarter chicken with a slice of bread from the only vendor still open. Donald took out some coins, but Martin slapped his hand away. "I don't want your money," he said. He ate the whole thing in a few bites and sopped up the juice on his paper plate with the slice of wheat bread. "I have plan for us," Martin said, smacking his lips. "My friend is good drag queen with show at L-Club."

"Not there." Donald pulled the young man close. "I want to be romantic."

"I must be in L-Club tonight, but it costs three hundred crowns." He held up three fingers with a helpless smile like he'd wet his pants. Ten dollars, Donald calculated, counting them off on his fingers. Or maybe fifteen. Something like that. "Please. Only one time I ask for money." Martin clasped his hands and sniffled.

"You don't understand. I'm a teacher. Not rich like the American in Miami."

"I phone him!" Martin's voice broke. "He say when I am in Miami, I love you, I love you. Now I am here and he don't answer phone. I leave message. I say, answer me. I have no money, no food." He slapped his own cheek. "Martin is stupid."

Donald breathed on his neck. "I have food at home. I'm an excellent cook."

"What you want?" He pulled out his carton of Marlboros. "Good American cigarettes? I buy only yesterday. Three hundred crowns."

"I don't smoke."

Martin took off his plastic watch. "Here is watch. You don't want? What you want? Cigarettes, watch?" He leaned over and licked Donald's ear. "Me?"

Until then Donald had imagined telling Jana the story as

a bawdy joke, the way they laughed at German tourists who came in for the weekend to shop for boys.

"No," Martin laughed. His eyes crinkled so that Donald couldn't see into them. "Is only joke, my friend."

I want you, Donald thought as the blood rushed into his heart and his penis.

"No," the young man said. "Not three hundred. One thousand. I am expensive."

Martin laughed again, kissed Donald's cheek, then headed toward L-Club. "I see you some other night. Bye-bye!"

Donald calculated the balance in his bank account. He could have afforded the requisite thousand crowns. Suddenly he felt old.

■

JANA PREFACED HER request with, "It's so absolutely boring I hesitate to ask you this, but I have no one else to call. Where were you last night? The phone rang and rang."

Her grandmother had invited Jana and the Irishman to her village for Sunday luncheon. Roman had been invited too, but his wife was expecting any day now.

"It's a complete pose," Jana said. "I just couldn't tell her the disgraceful truth. She's so very old. It would be a significant disappointment."

"I'm happy to help you out," Donald said, "but I don't have an Irish accent."

"She'd never know the difference. You see, she can't speak a word of English. Please. It would be so interesting for you. It's a very quaint, very dear little town."

Sunday morning they took the train to Tabor. While Jana bought the tickets, Donald hid behind a post and peeked at the ticket windows. He wondered which might be Martin's. At Tabor, they switched to a special one-car train the size of a living room. Pages from the color tabloid *Blesk!* (*Lightning!*) were taped over the middle windows as curtains. A rectangular bit of brown cardboard the size of Donald's thumb served as their tickets instead of the computer printouts they'd bought in Prague.

Slabce was a bright-yellow country station three stops and forty minutes from Tabor. They were the only passengers left besides the conductor, who climbed down to greet an old man in a striped shirt and blue pillbox hat coming out of the station.

In her emerald silk dress and black platform shoes, Jana looked as out of place as he did in his tweed jacket and tie. Though she hadn't said so explicitly, Donald had guessed their visit was a formal occasion.

The streets were wide and quiet. They passed a handful of single-story stucco houses as plain as cake boxes and a marshy stream fringed with tall bunches of bright green grass. Their path forked around a war memorial, an obelisk with a wreath of red, white, and blue ribbons and roses at its base, though Donald found it hard to believe war or empire had ever touched such a still, empty place.

"It's to commemorate the Czechs who got killed as they shot at the retreating Germans when the war ended," Jana said, pulling his arm. "We used to throw rocks at it when we were younger." She skipped ahead to a pink house with a

fenced-in yard. As she unlatched the gate, two German shepherds came bounding at her. *"Ahoj, Cesnek! Ahoj, Kocku!"*
Jana played with their tufted ears and then slapped their
snouts when they slobbered over her face. Donald stared at
a gray cat stretching in the shade of the porch and was suddenly filled with a crazy, intense longing to become the cat:
sleepy, settled, a lazy native of the place where he stood.

"There's chickens and rabbits in back," Jana said. "We'll
see them after lunch."

Jana's grandmother opened the door and quickly shrank
back from the light. Her potato-colored cheeks hung limp
from her reddened eyelids, and her head, permanently bent
forward, was wrapped in a green kerchief. After Jana bowed
for a kiss, Donald shook the grandmother's fingers. They felt
thin and cold, almost like nothing at all. He was shocked to
learn she was only sixty-eight years old. She pretended not
to understand when he told her in Czech how nice everything looked.

Suddenly she pointed at him and erupted, "James Joyce!"

They sat at a card table set with a lace-fringed cloth and
four heavy brown plates. A shamrock had been carved into
the butter. Jana's bachelor uncle came tottering downstairs.
He had a fat, red, splotchy face and by Jana's whispered es-
timation was nearly always drunk, though no one bothered
him about it anymore.

As they were about to start, the village priest dropped by
and Jana's grandmother insisted he stay. The priest wore
dark glasses and tapped his way into the room with a white
cane. Donald rushed forward to take his arm, though Jana
said to leave him alone.

The grandmother served them bread and bowls of meatball soup with her shaking hands, then hovered over them to watch how they ate. Donald flaked off a morsel of his craggy meatball, which was as big as a plum. The meat tasted spicy but satisfying in a deep, hearty way. He smiled up at the grandmother, who was staring at the priest. He really was quite a good-looking priest, with thick dark hair that grew into his eyes.

After complimenting the grandmother on her soup, the priest told Donald in fluent English that he lived in the city and commuted to Slabce and another village on weekends. "You have a nice, clear voice," he told Donald. "Your English is easy to understand."

Jana heaved a loud, theatrical sigh. Her shoe tapped loudly against the floor.

"The church here is a landmark. Jana will show you later," the priest said, and his cane fell to the floor. As Donald picked it up and set it against the table, his hand met the priest's searching fingers. "My home monastery is in Prague, near Strahov stadium. It's convenient for attending sporting events and concerts like the U2 concert 'Pop Mart.' "

"Do you wear your collar to U2 concerts?" Jana interrupted.

"For such events it's permissible to remove it, my dear child."

"And tell me, Father," she said, "is it true what they say about priests and homosexuality?" Donald kicked her leg under the table, but Jana ignored him.

"It's not a big problem," the priest said in a quiet voice. His ears turned red.

The grandmother pressed him to accept another meatball. She said that if he'd really enjoyed the first two as he'd claimed he would have asked for another. He replied that if he ate like that everywhere he came calling he'd be as big as an elephant. "They think if you have a priest over you have to stuff the poor man."

Jana piped up, "Maybe they think the poor fellow isn't getting any sex so we must render unto him some substitute for his sacrifice. Donald, would you stop kicking me under the table? The Father and I have an understanding. Isn't that right, Father?"

"Exactly," he said. "Jana mocks me and I pray for her soul, if I think of it."

The uncle picked up his bowl of soup and tilted it into his mouth.

After the meal, Donald insisted, so Jana led him up a path overgrown with wild clover to the church, an octagonal sanctuary the color of warm sand, topped by a blue onion dome. The entrance was covered in rusty scaffolding. Chinks of plaster had flaked off the walls and dandelions dotted the lawn.

"Hardly anyone among the young people goes regularly," Jana explained and took Donald's hand as she led him inside. It had become their habit to walk hand in hand.

The ceiling was painted with a blue sky and clouds of pink and gray smoke. At the end of the sanctuary, an embossed gold-and-silver altar glittered in the light that passed through a bank of windows above the side chapels. Donald stared at the altar and imagined the good-looking priest draped in white robes and railing against hellfire and free love.

"Every night I used to dream of getting out of this town," Jana said.

"Jana, that was very disrespectful back there," he said. "I mean, wasn't it?"

"What's the good of this freedom of speech you Americans are so proud of if you can't use it?" Her voice echoed against the cold floor and the walls.

"I'm Canadian," he reminded her, but Jana moved on.

"You all gloss over anything that might be considered indelicate. For example, if I were American, I'd never admit to having had an affair with another woman, just as you never tell me about your romances with men."

"But I haven't had any since I've met you." He hoped Martin didn't count.

"That's awfully sweet, if it's true. But if you had, I'd hope you could tell me. Even if we were romantically involved, I'd understand if you needed to relieve yourself at times. Like Vaclav Havel and his first wife, Olga. She was hideous. But she was his partner, only not in that way. You see?"

"I guess." He winced. "Shouldn't we get back? We'll miss our train."

Donald was afraid the brittle grandmother would crack when he leaned over to kiss her good-bye. He spoke to her in Czech, but she still refused to understand his accent.

They caught the early train home, crowded with families returning from the countryside as well as sleepy-looking soldiers at the end of their weekend leave. Donald and Jana had to stand the whole way, but for some reason he liked it. Everyone squeezed over to make room for the soldiers to sit, lifted their bags for them onto the metal racks above, and shared their bread and cheese and beer. A troop of children in olive-green scout uniforms sang a birthday song about counting years. Outside, the sun touched the black crest of trees on the horizon. It was warm and crowded and close inside their car.

The train arrived in the main station a little after nine-thirty. Donald didn't see Martin working, but he hurried Jana out of the station just in case. They rode the tram together as always, and just before his stop he said, "Thank you for this day."

"Don't be stupid. I should thank you because . . ."

Donald interrupted, "Do you want to come over for some tea?"

He didn't have any tea.

"Water, then?" he asked and peered sheepishly out of his kitchen.

"I was just admiring how clean you keep this place." She was leafing through his copy of *Maurice*. "The Irishman was a complete pig. Even worse, he expected me to clean up after him. One of the many disadvantages of relationships with heterosexual males."

"Homosexuals are just as bad, I can tell you. So how about that water?"

She raised an eyebrow. "Yes, water sounds nice. You know, we have very good water here. It comes from the mountains."

Donald was about to fetch it for her when the phone rang.

"Hello, good, good friend," breathed the raspy voice on the other end. "Please can you meet me? I have some big problem. Please, I need help."

"Who was it?" Jana trilled as Donald came in without water. He looked stricken.

"An ex-boyfriend of mine," he said to make it simpler. "He says he's in trouble."

She straightened her posture. "Then you should go to him."

"How can you say that?"

"Isn't that what you're asking permission to do?" she asked. He stood gaping at her. "Weren't you listening before, at the church?"

Donald realized he'd made a horrible mistake. He'd been confused about everything and he was offending her.

"So aren't you going to meet him?" she asked.

"I guess."

"You guess? Don't you know it?"

"I guess I know it." His tongue felt clumsy. "I haven't really decided because it doesn't matter to me one way or the other. He's stupid, really."

"And I'm smart." She picked up her purse and walked out. He tried to squeeze her white hand, but she yanked it from him.

■

MARTIN HAD SAID he'd wait for Donald in the sex shop next to the train station. The shop was painted black and served coffee, beer, and Coke. Old men smoked in the corners, alone. Donald sat by one of the smudged glass vitrines with videos with bare-breasted women, dildos wrapped in plastic, handcuffs, oils, and condoms locked inside.

He waited for two hours, breathing in stale smoke until his eyes hurt like they were bleeding. The fresh air outside hit him with a jolt.

Feeling a bit horny, Donald stopped in at Muzika and then ordered a beer at L-Club, which looked a little seedier than he'd remembered. A young, good-looking British tourist approached him. Donald, feeling nervous, replied curtly to his leading questions and focused instead on his friend, who was old and almost bald except for a few furry curls around his ears. They worked as secretaries in the same office in London and usually went to Portugal for boys, but they'd heard good things about Prague. Their verdict? Colder than Lisbon but cheap. And the boys were good.

The good-looking Brit gave Donald a sorrowful look and then abandoned him for a drunken Czech kid in a black jacket. After a minute, they strolled off to the bathroom, arm in arm. Gun for hire, I'm a gun for hire, Donald kept thinking. At least I'm not some stupid secretary. For now, anyway. But what about when I get old, like when I turn thirty?

At the end of the night the two Brits dragged out the drunken young man by his arms. "Where we go, boss?" the boy mumbled and nuzzled the bald man's neck.

They invited Donald to whisk away with them in their taxi, but Donald couldn't. What if he lost his head and said something stupid? He had class the next morning, anyway. Besides, what would Jana think?

"Can't get it up?" grinned the good-looking one. "Machinery out of whack?"

"I can always count on the machinery," Donald said. "That's the problem."

■

THEY DECIDED ON a September wedding in Canada, even though Donald had hoped for the run-down church in Slabce, the blind priest, and then lunch at the grandmother's. A honeymoon in the Sumava Mountains, not a quick weekend at Niagara Falls.

"We can always go back next summer and do it your way," said Jana, eager to start literature classes at the University of Toronto. "The church isn't going anywhere. In fact, it hasn't for centuries."

His aunt picked them up at the airport. Donald had been raised by her and his uncle since the age of fourteen, after his parents died in a car accident. When Donald called to announce the engagement, they'd been more than a little surprised but very pleased.

"You wonderful, wonderful girl!" his aunt cried. She kissed Jana on both cheeks and hugged her tightly. As they walked down the terminal, Jana began talking about how beautiful Canada looked from the plane, how it reminded her of the English countryside.

Donald yawned. Maybe it was just jet lag, but he was starting to get seriously annoyed with her regal queen act. Also, why was everyone talking in such loud voices? It was harder to block out all the chatter here at home. He felt it pressing in on him from all sides.

"This is so much fun!" his aunt was saying. "We can't wait to show her around."

Show her off is more like it, Donald thought as they walked through a tunnel of glass to claim their baggage. He felt the old teenage resentment creep in, but his fiancée squeezed his wrist. Just then, a pair of male pilots jabbering in Spanish wheeled their overnight cases past them toward the gates. Donald followed their reflections moving in the window and caught one of the pilots looking over his shoulder, as if to check him out. The image in the glass was a bit hazy, but Donald was fairly sure the pilot had turned around.

ERE IS MY LIFE.
        I dress in plain clothes. I station my-
self with a partner in one of the neglected elbows of the
Prague metro. Our favorite is the bend in the corridor between the "C" and "A" lines at Muzeum station. When we've
found our targets, my partner and I flash our metal badges,
nestled lovingly inside our extended palms.

"*Kontrol,*" I murmur slowly, softly, like a seduction.

The badges are red with a gold eagle and gold trim. We
polish them with spit each morning.

The passengers try to look bored as they show us their
tickets. But really, who isn't afraid at a checkpoint, the security guards at the entrance to a department store, the custom
officials at the border, your local priest? Who among us has
not sinned? Who among us does not secretly yearn to be
caught, to accept the punishment we deserve?

Hourly tickets must be stamped in the machines by the
station entrance at most one hour before riding. Otherwise
they're expired.

Weekly and daily passes must be stamped in front and
signed on the back.

The laminated monthly passes are mostly in order except when the picture's been doctored, or a twenty-year-old masquerades as a student, or a fifty-year-old as a pensioner.

All transgressors get slapped with a fine, which varies. Sometimes eight hundred, sometimes two-fifty. It's up to us. Because my regular salary is so pitiful, I often move numbers around. When I collect eight hundred crowns I write it down as five twenty-five and pocket the remainder. For six hundred I write four, and so on.

There's been talk of replacing us with machines, but nothing's happened yet.

Tourists are easy to intimidate, even with my imperfect English. Most of my encounters go like the one I had last week with a backpacker. (Why do they think they can fool us? Oh, yes, you with your two-kilo neon pink backpack, you must be a local!)

"Here is control. Ticket, please."

"Hey, I'm really sorry, dude. I totally didn't realize you needed a ticket."

"You must pay fine of eight hundred crowns."

"Oh, man. I have, like, no money on me at all. No dinero. I'm really sorry."

"You are American? Can I see passport?" While holding the passport, I said, "We go to police or you pay eight hundred crowns now."

Americans are sniveling cowards in deathly fear of Czech police. They imagine gruesome scenes with KGB agents in fur caps and black leather coats. Most of them pay on the spot in dollars or German marks. Or if they're not cowards, they make a fuss before paying up, a big show like their movie stars. I remember one specimen in a leopard-print silk scarf scented with some expensive Western perfume who failed to sign the back of her tourist pass. Her excuse was no one told her to sign it.

"This is not how a democracy works," she said, searching through her dainty black leather handbag for the money to pay me. "How are you going to attract tourism if you treat people this way? What would Vaclav Havel think?"

"Eight hundred fifty crowns," I repeated until she opened her purse.

On my way home from work, I collect newspapers, magazines, and, on lucky days, even a few pornos left behind on the seats. I read them in my apartment with the lights low, over bread and margarine with a bottle of beer. Our people didn't use to be so wasteful before, but now everything is changing and not all for the better. People who obey the rules are a dying breed. My own wife divorced me seven months after our wedding because she was fucking a waiter who plays piano with a chamber music group for tourists on weekends. That's what women are like. She said she couldn't stand being married to a "subway Nazi," which is how she refers to a person doing his job. We have a small son and on Sundays I take him to the country to hunt for mushrooms. I'd like him to remember me in a better way than I remember my parents, but my ex-wife keeps poisoning the kid's mind with all kinds of lies behind my back.

My colleagues and I frequent a pub out in Opatov where the beer is still normally priced. It helps relieve the stress that comes naturally from our job. We've traded all kinds of work stories over pints, but there's one I've never shared with a soul. It's too strange.

This is something that happened to me almost exactly one year ago, last summer. On Saturdays, I had nothing else to do and I needed the money, so I worked alone at the Jir-iho z Podebrad station. (Now I always work with a partner.) It just so happened that I stopped a flat-chested woman with sort of fascinating eyes and a wild mop of long dirty curls like a rag doll. This hair was the color of a maple leaf in late September, and it had what you could call a sheen. I re-member thinking it almost looked alive.

The woman wore a white cotton dress with sparkling beads sewn into the cloth, and her plastic bag overflowed with ruffled vegetable leaves. She claimed to have no money on her and no identification either. Supposedly she'd left her purse at home and only brought enough money for vegeta-bles.

There was something in her eyes, which I now recognize as the mark of a gremlin toying with a regular guy doing his job. But at the time I thought she was another passenger laughing at how helpless I seemed before her superior logic. Go on, she seemed to dare, the corners of her mouth twitch-ing. Just try to collect. There was nothing sexual implied at first, or maybe a small something, but I wasn't sure.

I straightened my blazer. It was very hot to stand for hours under the ground, and I decided to take a break. "You will lead me to your home," I said. "I will wait at the door while you find your purse."

The woman lived a block away from the modern cathedral on the square there, a real eyesore if you ask me but no one ever has. This area is named for the royal vineyards which used to bloom right here before they paved over the soil so we can build such modern conveniences as apartment buildings, trams, and now a Mexican restaurant.

My new friend didn't seem in the least bit nervous, as if she believed she was above all earthly jurisdiction. In fact, she made a few attempts at chitchat, the generic kind. Wasn't it perfectly beautiful out? Wasn't it a shame the government was doing nothing about inflation, especially for the poor, old people? What did I think of her vegetables? Look inside her bag—hadn't she picked out some beauties?

"Is it much farther?" I asked as I stared at her wild hair, bouncing with each step.

"No, no," she giggled. I should have known then she was sent by the devil. But I thought she was just one more of these satiric Czechs, always snickering at something.

Her apartment was on the third floor of a red building decorated with horned satyrs. There were stairs but we had to wait for the elevator because she said it was "more fun." The two of us crammed into a tiny creaking cage, that wasn't what I would have called fun. And on the way up, one of her frizzy red curls tickled my nose and made me sneeze.

The woman had left her door unlocked. She asked me to leave my shoes just inside the door, on a clean rag printed with pink and red flowers.

"I prefer to wait here at the doorstep," I said. "This shouldn't take long."

She looked me over with a thoughtful expression. I checked my tie but it was wound tightly around my neck. And I knew my jacket and pants were spotless.

"I have something to show you," she said seriously.

"I am a very busy person." I was starting to be suspicious, but then she squeezed my arm. Her fingers were strong, or maybe they weren't strong, but it had been a while since a woman had touched me with such a purposeful grip.

I took off my shoes, embarrassed that I was wearing Tweety Bird socks. They were the cheapest ones at the Vietnamese market. Such are the rewards of capitalism.

Still clutching my arm, the redheaded imp set her groceries in the sink and then dragged me down the hallway, which was dark even with the lights shining from her kitchen. I made out a few black-and-white photos of the desert hanging on the walls. "My father was a diplomat," she explained. "Our family lived in Iraq when I was a child. Isn't it a beautiful country? My daughters are not at home. Over there is my husband's room." She sighed. "We're separated but we still live together."

If she'd meant that as a ploy for sympathy, I found her strategy a bit obvious. Plenty of other couples I knew lived in similar conditions because of the housing shortage. My own wife stayed with me an entire month after I learned about her little fling because the artistic piano player lived with his parents. I used to come home late and find her sleeping on the couch. Even worse were the nights when I came home and she wasn't sleeping on the couch. Sometimes I sniffed through her clothes, opened her letters, that kind of thing, but I never found any clues. One night I jerked off into a pair of her panties and left them on her pillow. When I came home the next evening, she and all of her things were gone.

"And here is my room," the woman said and opened the door.

At first I saw nothing. Darkness. But then hundreds of stars and quarter moons glowed from the ceiling, like a night I haven't seen since I was very young and my family stayed at a cottage in the Krkonose Mountains. When the woman turned on the light, I saw the stars were cut out of orange plastic. She'd painted the walls purple and green, and hung pink curtains with silver threads over the windows. In the corners, plastic pots of ivy suspended from silver hooks drooped leaves down to the floor. There were scattered overstuffed pillows instead of chairs and a mattress covered in a faded pink sheet against the wall. Over the mattress hung a portrait of the goddess Diana aiming her bow at the moon.

The purse, a battered maroon leather sack, slumped on its side against the closet.

"Your purse," I reminded her. I wanted no more of that spooky room.

She shut off the light. "Are you hungry? These days I eat alone mostly, even though I have such a small appetite. So there's always extra. Would you join me?"

I never shared meals with anyone except my son, but I was hungry. I told her, "Only on the understanding this meal is not a substitute for the fine you owe."

"I'm not stupid enough to try to bribe someone like you." She winked.

Her name was Katerijna. "Katka," she said as if we were already old friends. I sat at her kitchen table and sipped a shot of Becherovka while Katka chopped mushrooms into a soup. She asked if I wouldn't mind some music while she prepared dinner. I didn't mind. We listened to the radio, one of Smetana's operas. I can never distinguish between them, but I like them all, even though they're a bit heavy and overly sweet.

In a few minutes we were slurping soup across from each other. A perfect little domestic scene. "You're not Czech," she said as I crumbled gray bread into my bowl.

"Why do you say that? Because of my profession?"

"I can tell from your aura. Every person has an aura. I have a teacher who is very spiritual. I go to him every week for spiritual and physical healing and he has taught me how to read these auras. I'm not Czech either. I'm from Moravia."

"So that's Czech too. Moravia, Bohemia, Czech, it's all one."

"Not at all, sir. The people in my village are friendly, not like those cold Bohemians. They make wine."

"My father was in the Foreign Service too, which accounts for my accent," I confessed. The Becherovka was loosening my tongue. "We lived in East Berlin until I was twenty, and then we were recalled when everything changed."

"So you're still a young man," she exclaimed.

"Not so young," I replied. "Why? How old are you?" I guessed about forty.

She ignored my question. "Can't you find some other work? To feed the soul?"

"Why do you all think we're soulless? My work feeds my soul. What do you do, anyway? Play piano for tourists? Water plants in a nursery?"

"I used to answer telephones in a coffee company, but I'm not feeling well lately."

"You see? It's all the same."

Her jaw trembled. "No. I refuse to believe you, in your anger and fear."

I pushed away my soup. It wasn't very good anyway. Too much curry powder and I detest curry powder. "Enough." I stood up. She was nothing, so thin I could have cracked one of her arms as easily as a pencil. I crossed to her side of the table, put my hands on her shoulders, and squeezed. She looked up at me, blinking hard, breathing fast. "What's wrong?" I asked. "Isn't this what you wanted when you invited me here?"

She turned, raised her hands while fixing her eyes on mine.

"Now what are you going to do, hit me?"

She set her hands on her head. And then—and this is almost too strange for me to describe—her head moved but her hair stayed in place. She took off her hair.

The skin underneath was smooth and white and speckled with gray dots like a duck egg. Her face, angular and hollow, looked shrunken below her strangely tall and blank brow. I stepped back in disgust, my hands still curved to fit her narrow shoulders.

How long did she have left to live, anyway?

"I see you've changed your mind," Katerijna said, toying with the wig in her lap.

I swallowed a lump of bile rising in my throat. I had to think fast but I couldn't think as I stared into that face I'd almost touched, only now coming into focus: the gaunt, shriveled neck, the crow's-feet stamped around her eyes, the sallow skin. "I don't want any trouble," I said. "I'll knock the fine down to three hundred and then I'm gone."

"No." The naked lightbulb over the table glared down on her white scalp.

"Two hundred fifty, then. That's as low as I'll go," and then I added, "Katka."

She shook her head. "Not that either."

"You said when I agreed to dine with you, this wouldn't affect your fine."

"It has had no effect. I was never going to pay you anything."

I slammed my fist on the wooden table, rattling my half-finished bowl of soup. "You've got to pay me something."

After setting her wig on the table, next to her spoon, Katerijna marched out and returned with a ten-haler coin. She slid it to me across the table. You used to be able to buy something with a ten-haler coin. Nowadays most people throw them into the sewer, but not me. Ten ten-haler coins make one crown, and that's a crown you didn't have.

She thought she'd won against me, but I pocketed the coin and then I told her, "It's because of people like you that the government's in crisis, that inflation's out of control, that our children grow up with no morality." I tried not to look at her wig all sprawled out next to the soup like an octopus. "Typical Czech cheaters like you, always looking to cut an extra corner, taking from their neighbors instead of paying their fair share. In a modern country like England or Germany, everyone obeys the rules. Believe me."

"Do you want dessert?" she asked calmly. "I have ice cream."

That was when I knew she wasn't human. How could she have been, to offer me ice cream without at least putting her wig back on? Why didn't she throw me out of her home at once, me the subway Nazi, the mole, the low-life creep who didn't deserve to collect his fines because she was so morally superior to such a type of person? Never mind that I was only doing a job, a job that protected her right to go to the market and back for fresh vegetables in clean, smooth-running, and frequent trains. "I'll be leaving," I said.

"Go, go," she said, petting the wig like a small dog and pulling out the strands. "If you've got what you came here for, then you should go."

I didn't wait for the elevator. I marched down the stairs.

Can you imagine sex with that plucked chicken? It would be like fucking death.

Still, I kept seeing her face as I stood on the corner and waited to cross the street. The traffic signal changed, but I went on standing there for a few seconds, or maybe twenty or twenty-five. I was sure I'd forgotten something up in that apartment. In fact, I almost went back to look. But when I searched all my pockets nothing was missing, not even the ten-haler coin. The light began blinking white, yes, you can walk. And yet I stood there frozen like my feet had grown roots into the sidewalk.

Finally, I composed myself and crossed the street. Katka's worthless haler coin clinked dully against the badge in my pocket.

On the subway ride home, I spotted a pornographic magazine someone had left behind, full of young women with luscious blond hair and big tits and mouths stretched wide, gaping with pleasure. There was no one else in the car, so I made sure the magazine wasn't too dirty or wet and then sat down to glance through the pictures. And I know this sounds crazy, but for a few seconds, as the train hurtled through that dark hole under the ground, I imagined that everyone else in the world had disappeared and I was the only one left, the savior of humanity, with just the trashy tart on the magazine cover for company. It's not entirely impossible. I mean, when the Soviets built the metro system, they dug the tunnels deep enough to withstand a nuclear attack, to double as fallout shelters. In the end I came to my senses quickly enough. But for a brief dizzy moment, as I stared into that hot black mouth, my stomach tightened like a fist and I felt certain I was about to die.

I lowered my take by fifty crowns for a while. Then I went back to normal.

Now, a year later, I'll sometimes get drunk and stroll around the neighborhood. I never dare to walk on her street, but I stand on the corner and check her windows. If I see a light on, I feel at peace. I'll stand there and wait a bit for the light and wonder if she's still alive or if she was ever really alive and not some kind of bald demon. When I'm too tired to wait any more, I sit on one of the green chairs opposite the ugly cathedral that should never have been built. But no one asked me.

I glued the ten-haler coin to a square of black paper, which I keep in my wallet for luck.

1.

THE RUSSIAN TAXI DRIVER took the two Americans to a suburb thirty minutes north of Tel Aviv. He dropped them off in front of a white stucco home surrounded by a wall of black hedges. They heard the hiss of a neighbor's sprinkler, strangely sinister, and farther off, a truck grinding its way up the main road. It was almost three in the morning.

Still groggy from the flight from Prague, Michael hoisted his monogrammed backpack off the sandy sidewalk and stumbled forward. He was a head taller than Becky, his traveling companion, best friend, and temporary heterosexual cover.

"Into the lion's den," he said, checking the address on his Palm Pilot a third time.

"Don't be so dramatic," Becky whispered. "They're your family."

Michael rang the doorbell. "Yeah, but they're so Israeli."

His aunt opened the door and frowned. She wore a pink robe and a pair of thin wire-framed glasses with narrow lenses, as if all she needed to see of the world could fit within those two rectangles. "I told you on the phone to knock, don't ring the bell."

"I'm sorry, Aunt Sarah. And I'm sorry the flight came so late. There was a bomb scare in Ruzyne Airport. It's the latest trend in Prague. They're always fake, but . . ."

"Please speak more quietly. You're waking the whole house. And who is Aunt Sarah? Call me Sarah." She closed the top of her cotton robe, perfumed with the fabric softener Michael's mother sent from the States. "You will stay in separate rooms," she went on as she led them upstairs. "Here is Becky's room." She flicked on the light and stood back from the door. "And this one is for you, Michael. It's Eli's room. He wanted you to have it. He's staying now with a friend from the army."

"He's not here?" Michael asked.

"You'll see him tomorrow. He's coming to dinner with his girlfriend."

Eli's room smelled musky, like boy. The walls were tacked with photos from a trip to Europe, including a shot of himself standing by the Vltava River in Prague. A pile of folded laundry sat beside the bed, with a pair of red briefs resting on top like a jewel.

Sarah shut the glass door to the balcony, which someone had left open, then drew the curtains. "Cold," she said, rubbing her arms. "It's all okay? So good night."

"Wait, Sarah," Michael said. Standing before her, he was surprised how small she was, coming up only to his chin. "I mean, it's wonderful to be here, to see you."

She extended her cheek to give him permission, and then he kissed her.

A few minutes later, he crept next door and knocked softly. "Are you naked?"

Becky let him in and went back to unpacking her camera equipment. She was checking her lenses for scratches. "And if I was naked? It's not like you'd get off on it."

He slumped on her bed and sighed, but with a smile. "My aunt hates me."

Becky sat next to him and kissed the top of his hair, thick, dark, and tangled from the trip. "Sarah doesn't hate you. She's just Israeli." She ruffled his curls and whispered in his ear, "Who could hate you, Michael? You're irresistible."

Confused by something sad, even hopeful, in her voice, Michael kissed her forehead and then jumped to his feet. "You're the best," he said.

"I'm the best," she echoed, "until your next boyfriend comes along."

■

BACK IN ELI'S room, Michael slid the balcony door open and then threw himself on the mattress facedown without taking off his clothes.

He dozed for a few minutes and woke up to his lover coming through the curtains and squeezing a bright red flower in his left hand.

Their plan had seemed simple when Michael phoned at the end of November, even though they were only supposed to write. In response to Michael's weekly fat profusions, bursting out of their airmail envelopes, Eli had sent a grand total of one postcard.

"They give me vacation for Christmas," Michael said. "Please let me come. I won't tell a soul."

"Israel is too small to hide," Eli objected. "Everyone knows everyone's cousin."

"Then I'll be your cousin," Michael replied.

He recruited a girlfriend (Eli already had one from the army) and invited himself and Becky to stay at his aunt Sarah's house (the prerogative of all American Jews with relatives in Israel). And now his Eli stood before him, passing a flower back and forth in his hands. He looked awkward and thin, with pointy elbows and knees, and jutting ears. His black hair had grown out of his army buzz cut.

"*Shalom,*" Michael said, slightly afraid of him. "I remember this house now, when my parents used to take me to Israel with them. You were five. You were very quiet."

"I don't remember you. I tried." Eli stepped out of his shoes. His feet were slender, sharp. "You didn't take off your shoes. My mother always asks to take off your shoes."

"Can I have a kiss?"

Eli pressed his ear to the door to listen for his parents. "No, it's okay. I hear nothing. Did you meet my father? You must speak to him tomorrow."

Michael leaned back on the mattress. "Are you going to give me that flower or stand there holding it all night?"

"It's from my mother's garden. I thought you must have some present." He tossed the flower to Michael, who twirled the stem like a pencil. It smelled sweet, simple. One of its petals was bruised. "Did you see? I put some of our photos on my wall."

"But no pictures of me."

"I don't need for you." He shuffled across the room and

crumpled into Michael's lap like a rag doll, but the effort of the gesture struck them both as strained. Michael's hands felt big and clumsy. He was glad the lights were off; his fingernails were dirty.

"You're glad I'm here, right?" he asked. "I mean, I know you are, but are you?"

"Please, we must stay quiet."

Michael's hand wandered down Eli's spine and into the back of his pants, but Eli pulled the hand away. "Not here," he whispered. "I must go, before they find me. My girlfriend and I will come tomorrow for supper. My mother is the best cook in the world."

"Does your girlfriend know?"

"Yes, but we don't talk about it."

"Then how do you know she knows?"

"We are not Americans. It is not necessary to talk about everything to know it." Eli slipped into his shoes. "We will see each other." He kissed his cousin quickly on both cheeks and grabbed the flower, "so my mother will not ask who gave you it."

The balcony door closed behind him with a muffled thud.

■

WHEN MICHAEL WOKE up, his first instinct was to check his voice mail, but his cell didn't work in Israel. He grabbed Eli's phone and began punching in the Sprint access number until Sarah picked up and said in Hebrew, "Who is on the phone?"

"Sorry, Aunt Sarah, I knocked it over with my foot," he

said, feeling flustered and temporarily incapable of explaining about phone cards. He quickly hung up.

The room was too stuffy for him to fall back to sleep. Instead he put on a polo shirt and khaki shorts and rubbed on extra-strength sunblock. He'd lost so much weight the past few months, the shorts kept riding down his hips, even with a belt on. After clapping on his metal watch, shoving his Palm Pilot into his pocket, and hooking his cell to his belt because it made him feel safe, Michael trotted down the stairs two at a time.

Appiah, the servant from Nigeria, was mopping the kitchen tile. The front door had been left wide open and the hot white light outside hurt Michael's eyes. "Good morning, sir," Appiah said in an English accent. "Breakfast will be in the garden."

Michael walked around to the backyard, where the wet blades of grass poked through his sandals. He looked for the flower Eli had brought him among the severely trimmed rhododendrons that stood at attention along the garden wall. Their waxy green leaves flapped in the warm wind. On a plastic table covered in a pink cloth, Sarah had set out a light breakfast: black grapes, cucumbers, bowls of marinated salads, glistening olives with a light sheen of oil, slices of Swiss cheese, individual cartons of blueberry and strawberry yogurt, a basket of rolls wrapped in a pink napkin that matched the tablecloth, and two glasses of fresh orange juice, thick with pulp.

A young orange tree stood tied to a stake in the middle of the yard.

Sarah, in dark slacks and a white silk blouse, slid open the screen door. "You're hungry?" He realized in a different world she might have been his mother-in-law.

"This is wonderful, Sarah. A feast for a king. I'm sorry to put you out like this."

"It's only food. You have to eat. What's missing? What do you want?"

"Nothing. It's all perfect. Maybe some tea, if you have it, but if not, fine."

"If you want tea, ask. No one is allowed to be afraid in my house."

Michael clapped his forehead. "Oh, wait! I forgot!" He dashed upstairs, where Becky was coming out of the shower in a striped towel that had once hung in his mother's bathroom.

"After all this time in Prague, I feel like we've finally stepped back into civilization," she said. "Screw liberty. Give me fluffy towels or give me death."

Michael ran back down with a box of tea cookies. For weeks, he'd been searching for the right gift. He was terrible at this, and he knew it. His secretary (a native) suggested a vase. For anyone else he'd have bought a vase, but for Eli's parents, he wanted something unusual, authentically Czech and memorable. He chose a box of delicate tea cookies shaped like moons and stars, glued together with jam and powdered lightly in sugar, each one a work of art and a taste of the culture. These he offered to his aunt, packed in a plain white box that suddenly struck him as too informal.

Sarah opened the box and sniffed. Several of the cookies

had crumbled during the trip, and Michael wished he'd bought a vase. She bit into a cookie, then threw it back into the box. "Nice," she said. "I'll bring your tea."

"Yummy oranges! I feel like I've never eaten an orange before!" Becky exclaimed later at the breakfast table, her hunter-green camera pack between her ankles. Michael looked on gloomily as she did her best to fill in the silences between Sarah's frantic cell phone calls. Each one sounded more anxious than the one before, but Sarah said, "It's my friend. She wants to meet for lunch and she can't decide where to go. She is a donkey."

Sarah asked Michael something in Hebrew that he didn't understand, so she repeated herself in English. "You don't want to call your mother to tell her you're safe?"

"No thanks," he said, stirring his yogurt absently. "I'll call her when I'm back."

"Okay. Do it your way," she said. "I would never allow Eli to live so far. He wanted to go for university in Haifa at the Technion, but I said go to Tel Aviv. Why should he live far away and eat falafel? Here I can cook for him. He's sensitive, special."

"He's special to me too," Michael said and caught Becky smirking.

"I was happy last summer when he stayed with you instead of going with his friends to Vienna and Berlin and all these terrible places." She wiped her eyes under her glasses. "So what exactly are you doing there?"

"We work as consultants," he said, brightening a little. "Like doctors for sick companies. We come in, see what's wrong, and give advice."

"How are you qualified to make such a diagnosis? Do you have training?"

Michael swallowed. "It's complicated. See, people in the company might know the actual business, but we know more about process. For example, Becky just led a very well-received seminar on developing website content." Sarah threw her napkin on the table and pushed her chair back. "It's a good living," he added. "I could take care of someone I loved on what I make."

"I don't understand." She grabbed a broom resting against the screen door and began sweeping sand off the concrete porch. "Eat, eat. You'll be hungry later. You want some different kind of tea, maybe? Jasmine? Earl Grey?"

"You don't have mint by any chance?" he asked. "If it's no trouble."

"You want mint? Why didn't you tell me?" Sarah bent over one of the plants in the yard, her expert fingers picking through the leaves until she found the sprig she wanted. She washed it off with a sharp blast of her garden hose, then plunked the fresh mint into Michael's mug. "There's your mint tea."

▪

THE SUN GRILLED the back of Michael's neck and made his eyes water as he waited with Becky for the bus to Tel Aviv. Even the shadows of the trees, shifting in the gusts of hot air that blew down the street, sparkled with yellow-gray light.

"Where does this sand keep coming from?" Becky asked. She held onto his shoulder and shook out her sandal. "We should have rented a car."

"Sarah said to take the bus," he said in a dead voice. He needed sleep.

"Michael, you're almost thirty years old. I think you can rent a car if you want to."

"But Sarah said . . ."

"Sarah thinks we're children. She asked me if we wanted her to pack us a bag lunch." Becky slipped her sandal back on and checked down the road for the bus. "Nothing," she said. "You know, she told me she was twenty when she had her first kid. I'm waiting until thirty-five. If I'm not married by then, I'll have one on my own. You can be the father." He hoped Becky would change the subject, but she said, "I mean it."

"Why? Because I'm the last guy you've gone on a date with?"

"I was paying you a compliment, jerk." She punched his shoulder. "My parents still think we're getting married. My father says, 'It's no one's business what the two of you do in your bedroom.' "

"There's no one else I'd rather pretend to be married to," he said. "How's that?"

"I think you'd better try again," she said, and the bus pulled up.

They sat next to a fat woman with dyed blond hair. She was reading aloud to herself from a Russian newspaper.

"I need to send a fax when we get downtown," he said to steady himself. Becky launched into a story about a friend's wedding back in New York that Michael wasn't listening to. He was thinking of what a boor he'd been to put his hand down Eli's pants on their very first night together after all this time like, like some child molester, and then the bewildered look on the poor kid's face. He blurted out, "I made a mistake!" and the Russian woman looked up from her newspaper. "Sorry," Michael said, wiping his eyes with the backs of his knuckles. "Eli visited me last night," he told Becky in a softer voice.

"You're kidding. And?"

"And nothing. I think I was just a phase."

Her fingers crawled between his. They felt clammy, like women's hands felt. "It was a long shot," she said. "The whole kissing cousins angle, the ten-year age gap . . ."

"Seven and a half," he interrupted her. "I trusted him. You don't know what the men out there are like."

"That's right, I'm pathetic. I never meet men."

"I didn't mean it that way," he tried to explain. "I meant my kind of men."

"Forget it." She pinched his cheek, forcing a smile. "Forget him. Hey, I'm here, remember? We're here in Israel, our Jewish homeland. Don't you feel homey?"

"And to top it off, Sarah hates me," he said, laughing in spite of himself.

"Let's rent a car and take off. We could go to Jerusalem, stay in a hostel like a couple of backpackers, meet Americans. They have Ben and Jerry's in Jerusalem."

"I don't know." He was thinking of summer.

■

SIX MONTHS BEFORE, Deloitte & Touche had sent Michael to Prague to consult for CzOL, a Czech service provider modeled on America Online. His mother passed his phone number to Eli, then traveling through Europe after his stint in the army.

Except in pictures, they hadn't seen each other since Michael turned thirteen. Then, in a fit of teenage rebellion, he announced he would no longer accompany his parents on their annual summer visits to the Holy Land. As an adult, he continued to avoid Israel out of a kind of habit that seemed like principle. Politically, he considered himself pro-Israel the same way he considered himself for capital-gains tax cuts. The only difference was that a warm feeling welled up in his heart whenever he thought of capital-gains tax cuts.

Before Eli's arrival, Michael practiced his speech in front of the rented antique mirror above his desk: "I'm as much of a stranger here as you are and I don't have time to show you around." That was before he met the embarrassed kid shuffling his feet in the doorway.

"A place to sleep, it's all I ask," Eli said in a meek voice beside the air mattress Michael had borrowed for him. He unpacked the meager contents of his duffel bag, lining them up against the wall: a couple of T-shirts, black and red bikini underwear, a folding tin utensil kit, a car magazine, a stash of envelopes pre-addressed by his mother.

Their first night together, Eli curled up on his air mattress and grasped his thin blanket in his long, careful fingers. His head was a black dot above the blanket. Michael, tired of reading report summaries, got up and turned out the light in the living room. He stood in the doorway a few seconds with his hand glued to the light switch. "Feel free if you want to go out later."

"No," was the muffled reply. "It's lonely to go places without friends."

"So why did you leave them?"

"Because they wanted to go to Berlin and my mother said I should see you."

"Aha." Michael snapped the lights back on. "You feel like taking a walk?"

They wandered through Mala Strana. Michael led Eli down a crooked street below the Castle, where crystal animals glittered in the dark souvenir shop windows, and pigeons roosted on black iron railings twisted into vines and flowers. Eli stopped to check his reflection in the side mirror of a Skoda. "I have black circles around my eyes," he said.

"So in the army," Michael said, "did you ever see . . . Did you ever kill anyone?"

"I was in reconnaissance, not the regular army. We went out with a team to look for terrorists, and then we called for help if we found them. Mostly we didn't fight."

"How did you know if someone was a terrorist?" he asked. They sat on a cement ledge outside a closed pub. The air smelled like piss and beer.

"In Lebanon, anyone who goes outside after curfew is a terrorist."

"Everyone? What if there's an emergency or something?"

"Okay, not everyone. I didn't do personal interviews like on the American television, excuse me, Mr. Arab, are you a terrorist? But you can see them moving in lines across the fields. One night, they shot a missile at our tank. It went over our heads and we hit them back. Four were dead. The others ran away."

They stopped talking as a tram rumbled by.

"I guess you have to grow up fast where you live," Michael said.

"First you are afraid, but then it's okay. You are like a machine, to save yourself."

"Is that why you're so quiet?"

"You think I am quiet?"

Michael nodded and dared to squeeze him by the shoulder.

"Maybe I am." Eli's look, alert, mocking, vulnerable in the corners of his trembling flat lips, was an unmistakable invitation. Michael kissed his cheek and then laughed at himself. "I've heard men kiss a lot in your culture," he tried to explain.

Eli hesitated, then kissed him back, on the lips. "I like listening to you," he whispered.

That dizzy night, they kissed against the concrete wall of the Wallenstein Garden and inhaled the perfume of cut grass. A month later, they were crying at the train station.

■

ELI CAME LATE to dinner with his girlfriend, P'ninah, who wore a low-cut fluorescent yellow bikini top, cutoffs, and platform sandals. She had a rose tattoo on her left breast.

"She's gorgeous," Becky marveled.

"Sort of," Michael admitted, wondering if P'ninah really was only a cover like Becky. "But in a kind of up-front frank way, like a porn star."

Sarah kissed P'ninah on both cheeks and seated her next to Eli.

Michael's uncle, Alain (he'd been born in Morocco),

presided over the table, his thick forearms folded over his belly. The Israelis pronounced his name "Élan." He was short and squat, with a face like a bullfrog and thick lips drawn into a pout as if he was continually about to spit. Occasionally he reached over to pat Eli on the back of his head.

P'ninah startled Michael with her American accent. She'd spent a year in a high school in Iowa and hated it. "Do you like the yogurt in Israel?" she asked. "It's much better than American yogurt, right?" She kissed Eli on the cheek.

Michael shoved a forkful of rice into his mouth and tried not to look at her.

"Why are you eating so much?" Sarah asked him. "Didn't you eat in Tel Aviv?"

Eli excused himself to the bathroom, upstairs. Michael went too and waited outside the door until his cousin came out.

"What?" Eli asked, trying to get by. "We can't talk in here!"

Michael buried his nose in Eli's neck. "I have to touch you," he breathed.

"So is that what you want? To fuck with me now?"

"I just want to be with you, you idiot. That's all I'm saying."

"I am no idiot." Eli pushed him off. "Wait one minute before you come after me."

When Michael returned to the table, Becky was trying out a joke about American English teachers in Prague on a bewildered-looking P'ninah.

"We're driving to Jerusalem tonight," Michael announced and sat down.

Eli's head jerked up from a dish of cantaloupe his mother had cut into bites, the way he liked. Everyone stopped talking. Becky smiled triumphantly.

"It's Shabbat," Sarah said. "Everything is closed. How will you find your way?"

"Hotels are always open," he replied. "They gave us maps with our rental car."

"So what's in Jerusalem? Why do you want to go to Jerusalem?"

"Who's going to Jerusalem?"

"They're going to Jerusalem. Tonight!"

"It's Shabbat. They can't go to Jerusalem."

"Jerusalem? What do they want in Jerusalem? With all those crazy Jews?"

"There is nothing in Jerusalem," Alain concluded and they all fell silent. "If you want to see this famous wall I can drive you there and back in one afternoon."

"That's very kind, but we want more time there," Michael said. "I'm sorry."

Alain threw up his hands. One of the hands landed on Eli's neck.

2.

ELI HAD BEEN HIDING in the fingerlike shadows of the vines that crept up the trellis of his mother's house. A garden hose curled up at his feet as if asleep. Moths flitted against the wildflowers that grew between the cracks in the cement path, which threatened to split open. Upstairs, behind the purple windows, Michael was waiting for him. A miracle.

Eli suddenly resented his cousin for transforming his own mother's house into a place as foreign and dangerous as a field in Lebanon.

Still, he enjoyed the climb up the trellis, his sandals scraping the stucco walls, silvery in the moonlight. His mother had caught him at it once and warned him never again. He might hurt himself. She wasn't someone you wanted to argue with.

But tonight he was an explorer, an astronaut heaving thin air. One of his mother's flowers brushed his face, and he choked on its perfume.

The tall and bony American cousin sat up on the bed, his rolled-up shirts and underwear spilling all across the carpet, his backpack in the middle of the floor. Couldn't Michael put away his clothes like a person? But how elegant he looked, perched like a stork on the edge of the bed. He wore an expensive shirt the color of a plum and shiny black shoes, like for a meeting.

"Shalom," Michael said. "I remember when you were five. Can I have a kiss?"

This was the mythical boy whose mother sent his old clothes for Eli to wear: T-shirts and sweaters with American words, and faded jeans.

"So are you going to give me that flower or stand there holding it all night?"

The muscles in Eli's neck went lax under Michael's awkward icy fingers massaging his skin, deliberate and greedy with lust. Eli wished he could speak more English. He wished they could stay in a hotel by the beach and touch for hours with the door locked. Who would have found them? No, it was impossible because they deserved to get caught.

Eli kissed Michael's forearm. Unlike his own, it tasted plain, with no tang of salt.

"You are glad I'm here, right? I mean, I know you are, but, well, are you?"

"Please, we must stay quiet." Eli had never understood why Michael needed to talk so much. He and his American friends all traded intimacies like poker chips: "This scar's from when my stepmother hit me with a brush . . . He fucked me up the ass four months before I told him it hurt . . . No, the *third* time I was hospitalized for depression . . ."

"Does your girlfriend know?" Michael asked. "How do you know she knows?"

His head throbbed remembering it all, especially with his parents in the next room.

"We'll see each other," said Eli, desperate to sneak back down the trellis, away.

■

WHEN ELI TOLD his parents he was going to Jerusalem too, his mother kissed his forehead and said she was proud of him. That was what family was for.

That's just what's wrong, Eli thought. *This* is not what family is for.

Still, it was what he wanted, and during the drive on Highway 1, he didn't resist when Michael rested his hand on his thigh, centimeters from his penis. In back, Becky prattled on about an ice cream shop. At last, five minutes from the city, she fell asleep, and Eli felt free to guide Michael's hand toward his zipper. The hand crawled into Eli's underwear and rocked gently. They rounded a curve and hit the blinking lights and purple hills of the capital. A white banner suspended over the road declared that Peugeot welcomed them to Jerusalem. Becky woke up with a start: "We're here!"

The hotels Michael had phoned were full, so they stayed in the apartment of a friend of Eli's, whose parents had gone to Austria on vacation. It was a small place, with a slender hallway that connected three tight rooms stuffed with pressed-wood shelves and a collection of African masks and sculptures. Becky got the children's room. Eli had never slept in such a big bed as the one he and Michael shared (with a bamboo frame and canvas sheets), like the one his parents had. A wooden figure with a banana-shaped nose and webbed fingers leered over them. He stared up at it as Michael climbed into bed.

"What?" Michael asked as Eli crawled away from him. "Don't you want to?"

"I want," he said, his penis sliding against a wet spot in his underwear, "but I don't want. I came with you here but not for sex."

Michael frowned. "So you are fucking your girlfriend."

"I don't fuck with her!" he insisted. "I tell her I am traditional. I lie to her because of you. Because of you, I'm lying to my parents too, all of the time. I never did that before. And I must think, why am I lying? Why am I so much ashamed?"

"If it wasn't me, you'd be lying to them about some other guy."

"Who? I don't go to these places." He couldn't say "gay

places." "Anyway, you are my cousin. We should not do it, like you should not do it with your brother."

Michael began pacing next to the bed. "If you'd asked me before I met you, is this a good thing, I'd say no. But now I have to look at it differently because . . . Because I can't stop thinking about you, because you have the power to make me miserable, because I need you. And to me it comes down to who am I hurting?"

"If you say it's okay for us, then why not okay for a mother and son?"

"I don't know . . . Forget that. You can't explain why this is wrong. What's wrong with us, with you and me?" Michael offered his hand, but Eli flinched. "That's great. Thanks a lot. So now what? Do you want to be friends?"

There was the dirty word: "friends." If one American knew another for five minutes, suddenly he was his "friend" and required to lay down his life for a stranger. Wait one minute more and they'd forget each other's names.

"I'm tired," Eli said and put his pillow over his head.

Michael tried to pull away the pillow. "What did you expect when I came here?"

And what did *he* expect? Eli thought. To fuck me in the house of my mother?

■

FOR ALL THEIR sunscreen and water bottles and guidebooks and maps, they were helpless. Michael almost brought his Palm Pilot, but Eli said, "You are addicted to this machine like drugs."

Michael stared at the Palm Pilot and then tossed it on the bed.

The guidebooks irritated Eli especially. "What do you need me for?" he sulked. When the girl wanted to go to Mahaneh Yehuda market, he asked, "You need groceries?"

"We don't have markets like yours in the States," she replied, slinging her camera around her neck. "Or in Czech Republic."

"Yes, you have. I was there." He blushed as he thought of the Havelska market, where Michael had bought him a miniature clay bird with its wings folded over its eyes. "Looks just like you," he'd teased, sneaking a kiss when no one was looking.

In the throng of shoppers at Mahaneh Yehuda, Becky aimed her camera in all directions, at an Orthodox woman pressing into a melon, then a pair of brawny young men in blood-soaked aprons at a butcher stall. She took shots of mounds of olives, wheels of cheese in glass cases, trays of smoked fish with their mouths gaping open, oranges as big as grapefruit and grapefruit the size of small melons. "Let me peel you an orange," she said.

For a minute Eli didn't understand, since he'd never heard the word "peel" in English before. In Hebrew, "peel" meant elephant.

"It's okay," he admitted as he chewed his slice.

"You're smiling," she said, and he grinned wider. "You have a beautiful smile! Why don't Israelis smile? Whenever you walk into a store in America, everyone smiles."

Eli turned to look for his cousin, who'd disappeared. It was Michael's first day in Jerusalem and he didn't remember Hebrew so well. Did he even have any shekels? Eli climbed on a wooden crate to get a better view, but it was all a blur of nuts and olives. An ultra-Orthodox fatso in a black bathrobe bumped into his hip. Eli spat on his black hat and looked around the market again. This was Becky's fault, Becky and her stupid oranges.

But there Michael was, sulking next to a banana cart.

"Here, taste," Eli said with a relieved smile and extended a slice of orange.

Michael bit into the orange slice, which sprayed juice all over his face and eyes. He glared as if Eli had planned it. "Let me help," Eli said, digging in his empty pockets, but Michael had already taken out his travel-sized packet of Kleenex. How efficient of him.

Next, they wanted to drive out to Yad Vashem.

Across the valley from the museum, dark clouds sagged over the hills. Eli advised them to tour the gardens first in case of a downpour. Becky walked ahead, taking pictures. Michael paused in front of a bronze sculpture of a woman with her head buried in her hands. "I know how she feels," he said.

Eli laughed. "You are speaking about this statue like it's really some person."

"I suppose that's against the rules too."

"No, it's nice." Eli patted his shoulder. "It makes me like you."

"What else can I do to make you like me?" Michael asked, his eyes wet.

We shouldn't talk about this here, Eli thought, not with all the Nazis and ghosts. "Let's go on before it rains," he said.

They passed through the Avenue of the Righteous Gentiles, a grove of trees with dark coin-shaped leaves, then entered a maze of Jerusalem stone walls engraved with the names of all the towns in Europe where Nazis had killed Jews. Michael found LUNINEC—the shtetl in Poland where their great-grandparents had lived, had been killed.

And instead of continuing the line, we destroy it with our fucking.

"I never saw this before," Eli said.

"Why not?" Michael asked.

"It's the past. My mother's uncle traveled to this town last year. He saw nothing." Eli didn't know how to say in English that their history had been erased, buried in a place with no marker. Now other people lived there. "It's nothing. It's nowhere."

"I know." And Eli knew that Michael really did know.

"Why don't I take a shot of the two of you by the name?" Becky said. When they bent over to touch the engraving, their hands met.

■

ELI WANTED TO start all over again in the bamboo bed, but first they had to drive in the rain and find a place to park, and then where to have dinner on Ben Yehuda Street, the Israel with no relation to Eli or anyone he knew. His father was right: any time of day, you could walk there and see not one Israeli. Instead there were religious fanatics from Brooklyn, tour groups in search of T-shirts, French fries, and frozen yogurt.

Back in the apartment, the Americans washed and brushed, skin, teeth, and hair. Michael took an extra shower, "for the glory of having a hot shower." Eli removed the African sculpture from over the bed and hid it in a closet.

"What?" Michael asked when he came back to their room. He smelled like the seaweed shampoo he'd borrowed from Becky. "Did I do something wrong again?"

Eli pinned him against the door and gnawed on his neck.

"I don't get it. What's happening?"

He kissed Michael on the mouth to shut him up.

They dropped to their knees. Eli tugged at his cousin's towel and kissed the rough points of bone on his narrow shoulders. His tongue trailed down to a pink nipple island in a shallow sea of black hair. He sucked gently, then looked up with his eyebrows raised. Neither of them smiled. Eli stretched his T-shirt over his head and then pulled off his pants and underwear. He dragged Michael to the bed and balanced himself on his cousin's body. The tips of his fingers and ears tingled, like he was angry. Eli grunted and rubbed harder.

"Good, good. Take it out on me." Michael's cool fingers tickled under Eli's balls and then plunged into his anus, which Eli clenched shut. "Relax," Michael whispered. "I'm gentle." So Eli let his cousin pry in there, pull where the skin was wet and sensitive.

"Ay, ay," he breathed, almost crying.

"Shh," Michael whispered, smoothing Eli's face and hair with his free hand. He said in Hebrew, "You're safe with me, right? You're safe."

And then Eli streamed white curls over Michael's stomach.

■

THEY STOOD NAKED at the window together and watched the gray sunrise with regret. Michael said, "You're okay with this? The gay part, the cousin part, all of it?"

"Yes, yes, yes." Eli kissed Michael's neck three times. "I need you with me." Here was love, everything he wanted. He couldn't imagine anything else.

"What about your parents?" Michael said.

Eli shuddered. "My father must never know about these things."

"I guess even if they knew you were gay, it wouldn't do *us* any good."

"I like your body." He stroked his cousin's chest. "Why are you not fat like so many American tourists, like, how do you say . . . 'peel'?" Eli blew up his cheeks, hung his arm from his nose, and made a noise like a trumpet.

"Elephant," Michael laughed.

"Yes, elephant."

"Come here, elephant," Michael whispered and kissed him. "You're not tired?"

"I don't want to sleep," Eli said. "I can sleep any other time."

3.

HER LAST EVENING IN ISRAEL, Becky sat on the couch in Sarah's living room and studied a cooking magazine. She didn't cook, but she might someday in that house in the sub-urbs she and Michael always joked about sharing. Alain, sunk into his brown leather easy chair, watched TV in Hebrew.

The two lovebirds had abandoned her as soon as they'd returned to Tel Aviv that morning. In Jerusalem, they'd become intolerable, inseparable. They wanted to linger all day under the lime-green awning of the café at the top of the street and babble together in Hebrew, their secret language, which Michael suddenly remembered. She tried to persuade the couple, if that's what they were now, to go with her to the Old City, so she could take pictures in the *suk* for friends.

"*Friends,*" Eli sneered. "Americans, always with your friends."

Like she was some flirt, which couldn't have been further from the truth. Though men often asked her out, she rarely went on dates anymore, maybe because she was too picky. The men she met were too awkward or else too smooth, too pretty or too dirty, too ambitious or too dreamy, and she wasn't going to settle for anything less than what she had already with Michael.

They'd tried dating in college a few times until Becky told him she was looking for her knight on a white horse and he wasn't it. They became reacquainted in New York, after he'd come out and become polished. Sunday afternoons he'd tell her about his love life over brunch and then they'd relax in his apartment. She took photos from his terrace, which overlooked the Hudson. The doorman knew her name. (She wanted a doorman! Sometimes she pretended Igor was her doorman.) Michael escorted her to weddings, bar and bat mitzvahs, seders. The extended family didn't know the truth; telling them would have been like exposing a rash. Anyway, the truth was more like a lie since she was the closest thing Michael had to a better half, the way he went through men.

When he went to Europe, she called him and cried about the drudgery of her job at the Joint Distribution Committee. He arranged for his firm to bring her over. Her mother baked brownies, which Becky brought across the ocean in her overnight bag. She sent his mom postcards from the Jewish Quarter, and when Michael was too busy to send his own postcards, he signed his name next to hers.

Every few weeks, he fell in love and forgot she existed, which was all that Jerusalem was. All gay men were like that until they got dumped. Then they came crawling back and cried on your shoulder.

She'd insisted they visit the Western Wall at least, but by the time they showered and had a bite to eat, it was almost dark. Black birds swirled overhead as the falling sun sizzled against the Dome of the Rock, then lit the Wall orange. Dried weeds grew out of the cracks near the top where smaller stones were jammed in together like bad teeth. Below, worshippers in black had crowded up against the base. How strange to pray to a wall, Becky thought. She wished she'd brought color film.

The boys sat on a stone bench while she finished up with her pictures. They held hands under the shelter of Michael's day pack and Becky wanted to scream, *Your kids will have six toes!* But of course she couldn't, since they wouldn't.

Alain suddenly leaned forward in his chair and asked, "Do you like Israel?"

"What? Oh, beautiful," she said. "I'm surprised how many Russians there are." She was going to add that in New York she'd raised money to aid in resettling them.

"They are all robbers," he said. With his accent, Becky thought for a second he'd said "rubbers." "They steal *mezuzot* from our doors to sell on the black market."

"Maybe," she said, the way she would have to a child.

"Sorry my English is *kacha-kacha*." From his gesture, she knew he meant "so-so."

"It's fine. You're doing very well."

The rush of color in his brown cheeks was not unattractive. "You are always welcome here," he said. "Beautiful girls are always welcome in my house."

"Merci, monsieur," she laughed. Just then she could believe he'd been handsome as a young man, like his son.

Eli and Michael came in with P'ninah, who looked skinny enough to be a model in her hot-pink bikini top. Looking at her made Becky feel bloated, often on the verge of exploding. Sarah came downstairs and sent Eli and P'ninah back out to buy pita. Michael stretched out on the couch next to Becky and yawned. Eli had shaved Michael's head, and she thought he looked like a shorn sheep.

"What'll they say at the office?" she asked.

"Does it matter?" Michael giggled. He seemed awfully chipper for a guy who was leaving his "true love" behind the very next morning. But then he was always in "love." What a cheap word, she thought. No one was in love.

"You are packed for your trip home?" Sarah called out on her way to the kitchen.

"Almost." Michael scratched his fuzzy skull. "It's all laundry anyway."

"You have laundry? Where is it? Give it to me. You too." She pointed at Becky.

They each brought a heap of clothes, which Sarah insisted on separating into colors and whites even though they said they never did. "*I* separate them," she said.

Becky felt relieved at the sight of the washing machine. People were supposed to live with washing machines in their homes instead of dropping their clothes off at some harshly lit laundromat manned by bitter Czech grandmothers. She noticed a framed sepia-toned photo above the dryer: a handsome soldier and an elegant woman with thin, delicate hands, also in a uniform. "Is that you and Alain?"

Sarah, about to slam down the lid of the washing machine, smiled. "Yes. It's us."

"How did you meet?" Becky asked.

"We worked in the army together," she said quietly and shut the lid.

"There's much more to it," Michael said after Sarah went downstairs to make dinner. "She's Ashkenazi, from Eastern Europe, and Alain's Sephardi. Back then, that was like a black and a white person getting married. They were Romeo and Juliet."

"I bet Juliet didn't keep Romeo's picture above her washing machine."

"I don't know," he said seriously. "Maybe sometimes you need reminding." From the tone of his voice, she guessed it hadn't worked with Eli, as with all the others. Of course she was glad Michael had found himself, but was he really happy this way?

■

SARAH SERVED A heavy dinner: potatoes fried until they were hard and yellow, green peppers stuffed with ground beef. Becky pointed her pepper away from her face, afraid the hot breath of the meat would make her acne flare up. Alain kept smiling at her. He asked if she wanted hummus and laughed when she pronounced it to rhyme with "pumice."

"CHOO-moos!" He refused to pass the bowl until she pronounced it correctly.

Michael's skin was a feverish shade of orange from too much sun. He wore a red shirt printed with flowers and leaves that Eli had bought from an Arab tailor in the Old City because Michael had said, on a whim, that he liked it. Eli picked at pita and olives. He said nothing except to answer *ken* or *lo* when his mother asked if he wanted anything.

P'ninah asked if Becky wouldn't miss the oranges of Israel.

"We have oranges at home," she retorted. You're just a cover like me, she thought. Don't put on airs.

After dinner, they all drank tea and nibbled on Michael's crumbled tea cookies. Meanwhile, Michael couldn't stop babbling about the wonderful food of Israel, Sarah's beautiful home and gorgeous garden, the sights, smells, tastes of Jerusalem.

"Jerusalem is absolutely a fascinating city, though it surprised me that it wasn't exactly beautiful, not in a strictly aesthetic way, not in the same way as say, Paris."

Alain slammed his fist on the table and pointed at Michael. "You are a beatnik!"

"Why am I a beatnik?"

"Because you speak of beauty and you wear flowers. Do you know how many men have sacrificed their lives for Jerusalem, the most unique, special, beautiful city in all the world?"

"Then I guess I'm a beatnik." Michael winked at Becky and put his arm around the back of Eli's chair.

■

THEY FOUND THEIR laundry on their beds, folded into piles and decorated with plastic bags of kosher candies tied with red, white, and blue ribbons.

"Amazing," Michael marveled, sampling a hard lemon candy. "She's . . ."

Becky closed his door. "I want to talk. I'm mad at you."

"Okay." He sat down on Eli's bed. "What's up?"

"To be honest, I'm a bit tired of playing the supporting character in your boy-toy-of-the-week mini-dramas. You dragged me here, and now we're leaving . . ."

Michael interrupted. "Becky, you should know. I'm moving to Israel."

"Are you crazy?" she yelled out, then lowered her voice. "He's your cousin!"

"Well, it's not like we're going to have kids," he said.

But *we* might have, she thought.

"I found out, I can just show up, prove I'm Jewish, and boom, I'm on the government dole for six months. It's the Law of Return. Eli and I asked about it in town today." Michael touched her arm, but she shuddered and stepped back from him. "I'm realistic. I'm sure it's headed for disaster. Eventually. But now . . . we're right together."

She snorted.

"Maybe you're cold enough to abandon him, but I can't. If I leave him here, he'd be lost. I'm the only gay guy his parents would let near him. Anyway, I've always wanted to move to Israel. The army ought to do wonders for my abs."

"Bull-fucking-shit! You hate Israel! *We* hate Israel."

"I don't *hate* it."

"You're living in a romance novel. What about your job? You love your job."

"You're not listening," he said. "Maybe you don't know me so well, not really."

"Oh, yeah. I've listened to your crap for ten years, but I don't know you."

"Maybe you don't," he said. "It's not like there's anything tying me down. I mean, if I'm so eager to drop my job and everything to do this, then maybe that whole life meant nothing. Maybe this isn't crazy. Or maybe it's just crazy enough to work. I don't know." He scratched behind his ear. "All I know is my head itches from this haircut."

She was hurt, but she didn't want him to know. "So you're not going back at all?"

"No, I am going back, to settle things first. Hey, are you interested in a slightly used Palm Pilot?" He put on an Israeli accent. "I can make you good price."

"Thanks, but if I wanted a Palm Pilot, I could buy a new one."

"I'm kidding, I'm kidding. Of course it's yours for free."

I haven't made a dent on you, Becky thought, no more

than a mosquito landing on your arm for a few seconds. "I guess you have to pack now," she said coldly and left the room. She hated him for what he was about to do to his life.

Becky thought over the whole story as she scraped her face with Noxema until her cheeks burned. She tried to imagine making a sacrifice like this for any of the men she'd dated. There wasn't one she'd have done it for.

On her way back to her room, Becky looked in on Michael, who'd left his door open. With his haircut, and in the silly shirt Eli had bought him, he looked like a stranger. He was leaning against the door frame to the balcony, and from far off, she could hear a child crying, somewhere outside, far away. She watched him standing in the breeze, scratching his freshly shorn head and just breathing, breathing deeply.

N 1994 I MOVED TO PRAGUE to escape the capitalist grind of San Francisco and the swal-
lowing up of all the creativity and intelligence in the world.
An ex-boyfriend hooked me up with a couple of porn magazines and a video company that paid inflated sums for my
HOT HOT HOT sketches of men with men, women, animals,
whatever. I'd dash them off in a day and make enough to
cover my expenses for a month. In a short time my name got
around to a few rich perverts in town who bought my work
for private consumption. Through them I was invited to museum openings and live sex shows. I partied with the pretti-
est people I'd ever met and woke up in their beds. I climbed
up to penthouse apartments and down to dark basements
where I ended up on my knees with my pants around my
ankles. I drank and sniffed and sucked until my lips turned
purple.

I got bored. And then a month later my mother came to
visit me.

We waited behind the Spanish Synagogue, closed for
restorations, to join a walking tour of the Jewish Quarter. I
was the only one with a silver stripe in his hair. Our guide,
Zara, was as tall as a man and wore a suede hunting jacket.

Her withered brown hair was tied up around a pair of chopsticks, and the strap of her leather side bag cut between her tits.

"The community here numbered only about three thousand," said Zara, her fluent English tainted with a slippery Slavic accent. "But now we have enlarged because of these American expatriates. We are estimating two thirds of them are Jewish."

"Do they go to services?" my mother asked with a disapproving glance at me.

"Many Americans attend this community called Bejt Praha, which is quite popular, because they offer lessons for Israeli folk dancing on Thursdays."

"Sounds like a meat market," I said, lifting my orange-tinted sunglasses.

"I prefer to attend a small alternative community with the name of Bejt Ahava," Zara said, rolling her *r*'s. "You should check it out."

"You have a beautiful accent," my mother said. "Where did you learn English?"

Zara seemed startled by the question. "I am from New York City," she replied.

My mother and I stopped for lunch at a pizza place called KGB that offered Lenin and Stalin "plates." Lenin was green pepper and Stalin anchovies. My mother remarked, "Those huge eyes, and that accent. I think she's striking." She picked at a glass bowl of "Bulgarian salad" I'd recommended: shredded cabbage and feta soaked in oil.

"Yeah, like an amazon," I said, wielding an imaginary club in the air. "Wham!"

Her fork froze. "Remember how serious you were as a child?" She knew full well how I made my living these days, but we didn't discuss it. "On Halloween, you used to dress up as your favorite rabbi, whatever his name was."

"I don't remember anymore."

His name was Johanan Ben Zakkai. He'd escaped from Jerusalem in a coffin.

"Why don't you try that synagogue some Friday night?"

"To meet a nice Jewish girl from Eastern Europe?"

As she chased down an intractable morsel of feta, the Hermès scarf around her neck came undone. "Well, if you're interested, I think it'd be a waste if you didn't reproduce."

"Heartwarming." I flashed a monkey grin with all my teeth, even the gums.

"Ha, ha." She pushed away her bowl. "Too much oil. This is not a salad."

■

I FELT LONELY when my mother left, her suitcase loaded with marionettes and T-shirts printed with a puffy gray version of the Pillsbury Doughboy and "I saw the GOLEM!" She'd been the most serious company I'd had in a long while.

If you were looking for Americans you could find them watching *Seinfeld* or *The Simpsons* on tape in Sports Bar, up the street from American Express where I got my mail. Or sometimes they performed at "Beefstew Night," downstairs in an expat lounge called Radost FX. I went there once, alone, and listened to an excerpt from a novel about painter's block and eating disorders. Afterwards the young authoress was saying to everyone who'd listen that she'd moved to Prague to write a novel, and I told her, "Oh, everyone moves to Prague to write a novel."

A Czech woman with flowing blond hair out of a shampoo commercial and leather pants recited a poem about American colonialists invading her country. She gave her number to a reporter from *The Prague Post,* the English language expat-rag. Next came a black man with dreadlocks and a huge gold cross. He wet the tips of his fingers to put out his joint, then threw his head back and sang a pompous rendition of "We Shall Overcome." The crowd gave him a standing ovation like the guy was Paul Robeson, when in reality he wasn't even Cuba Gooding, Jr.

■

ONE FRIDAY NIGHT, I rode in a taxi to Bejt Ahava. I wore a killer black leather coat my mother bought me in Milan, on her way here. And I bleached my hair.

The streets in this neighborhood were named after foreign countries where, for fifty years, none of the residents could actually visit. Bejt Ahava was on a gloomy block named after Uruguay, in a gray cement building with bars over the windows. The synagogue was in the basement with two street-level windows painted over with menorahs and smiling faces. All the lights were off.

A man in a padded gray coat addressed me in Czech. His voice was shaky like old-fashioned handwriting. I asked if he spoke English, but he shrugged and rang the bell.

"Oh? Was I supposed to buzz?" I said, and he looked down at the cracks in his shoes. "Fuck you too," I added with a sweet smile.

We heard a dog barking. The door opened and a woman with a strong nose, thin worn lips like old bits of leather, and two angry black holes for eyes glared at us from the dark vestibule. She pulled up a barking chocolate Lab, which was missing a patch of hair on its back and bared its teeth.

Another woman hid behind her in the shadows, young and pretty, with black hair brushed smooth and a tight button of a mouth painted strawberry red.

I heard *"Ameri-chan,"* and the woman with angry eyes looked me up and down. Her heavy mane of brown hair framed her face like a nun's habit. "Come in, come in," she said in a tired voice, as if we were imposing.

Our breath turned to mist in the dimly lit hall, which stank of cabbage. The plaster walls had been stained a color between olive and aqua not found in nature and otherwise only in Eastern Europe. Straddling the yapping brown Lab, the woman unlocked an iron gate. She led us down a steep flight of narrow stairs to a cramped, freezing basement room where two splintered red benches and a dozen folding chairs had been pushed into a sloppy circle. A plastic lemon hung over the door.

The woman tossed her keys on a brown upright piano wedged in the corner, below a low shelf crammed with Jewish-themed paperbacks in English like *Golda's Story* and *Portnoy's Complaint*. Letters of the Hebrew alphabet, chopped crudely out of construction paper, were Scotch-taped above a silver velveteen Torah cover that sagged on the far wall.

"No Torah," she said, "but a Torah cover, which is very important."

The man in the gray coat climbed upstairs with the young woman and the dog.

"Sit comfortably," commanded the angry woman, leaning against the piano and gnawing on a hangnail. "You're new," she said, pronouncing "new" like it was an adjective of contempt. Clearly I'd made a mistake in coming here. Somehow I'd hoped the experience might fill me with a feeling of history, or at least weight.

I was about to leave when the angry woman said, "I'm Evzha Lorandova. We'll wait, in case anyone comes. And what brings you here?"

"To services or Eastern Europe?" I asked, settling a bit in my chair and rubbing my arms to stop my teeth from chattering.

"I mean here to Central Europe."

"I'm not a tourist," I said, to clarify things. "I live here. I'm an artist."

"Another of these young men fucking teenage girls like Henry Miller in Paris." Just then a bell rang, like at the end of a boxing match, and she ran upstairs to get the door.

Well, at least she put on a good show. At least she wasn't boring.

It was still freezing in there, and I was looking through the books for potential kindling material when a tall man in a peacoat entered alone. He had a high, sloping brow, thick cheeks, and a mane of black wide-curled hair that he kept twisting between his fingers.

"Are you American?" I asked. He looked young, and I hoped he could show me where to find the college students, the political activists, the real artists.

The guy let go of the curl he'd been teasing. "Er, no," he said as if I'd startled him.

"So then, let me take a wild guess . . . you're Czech?"

"Er, yes." He took out a notebook and pen and jotted something down.

We huddled in our coats as several congregants entered at once. They were led by a small boy with a delicate, doll-like face, frighteningly deep blue eyes, and blond forelocks. He wore a long dark coat and a fur-trimmed black top hat like a textbook illustration of a Hasid. A man with a silver beard muttered to himself as he sat between me and a pair of giggling teenage girls, one of whom tried to conceal an overbite by covering her lips. Evzha and her young friend with the button-mouth returned. But no dog.

Then came the foreigners: two doubtful looking middle-aged couples from Indianapolis ("Is this the right place?" "Maybe," Evzha replied. "Sit, sit"), a rabbinical student with a British accent ("Didn't you get my letter?" "Letter? It's probably mixed up with all these papers. Go sit down"), and a woman with a drab bun of hair a shade between brown and gray ("I am sorry I have come late," she mewed in Eastern European–tinged English). She removed a block wrapped in wax paper from a white plastic bag.

"Ah, this spicy zucchini bread," Evzha said. "Put it on the piano, Maria." She stared at us, then mumbled in Czech. "Start, start," she said in English. "Why do you all look at me? It's your service. Sing something. Lenka, give them what to read."

The young woman with the bright red mouth handed out stapled prayer booklets with goldenrod covers. My cover had been scribbled over in black marker. A quote on the first page read: "The boulder that the builders neglected became the cornerstone."

"They don't even have real books," marveled one of the ladies from Indianapolis as we sang "Ma Tovu," printed in Hebrew, English, Czech, and Czech transliteration.

"It's a miracle they have anything at all," said her friend.

We'd used pamphlets like these at Hebrew Day School, where every morning from the age of five to thirteen I attended services in our dusty gym. I carefully mouthed each syllable of the prayers because our rabbi explained it was a sin to mangle a word or miss one. He also told us that God (G-d) chose a prophet every ninety years. The last prophet, Theodor Herzl, had died in 1904, so we were due for a new one in 1994, the year I turned twenty-one. Coincidence? For years I hugged my book to my chest and promised to obey each of G-d's (God's) six hundred thirteen commandments if He'd pick me as His vessel. I kept my end of the bargain, but He didn't.

Sometimes I glanced over my pages at the other boys staring wistfully at the basketball nets. They were powerful, snickering boys in wolf packs, and if they caught you noticing the shape of their eyes or the graceful curves of their

necks, they'd just as soon punch you to death as slice a sandwich in half.

When I graduated from Day School, I was supposed to
worship God at B'nai Tzedek Synagogue, the largest congregation in northern California. We met in a soaring wedge-
shaped tabernacle as enormous as a battleship, but a
battleship that wasn't going anywhere. From our padded
seats in the audience, we would have needed binoculars to
make out the grim face of the rabbi, enthroned onstage in a
high-backed red chair in front of a marble ark. I guess they
wanted to keep him from noticing that we were mostly
asleep while he was up there talking to God for us.

My mother sent me to one of their youth dances when I
turned fourteen because she wanted me to get married. By
then I'd already smoked my first joint.

"Why aren't you dancing?" asked the vice president of
our USY chapter, a cute redhead with freckles. He kept
nudging boys onto the dance floor.

"It's my herpes flaring up again," I said, puckering my
lips. "Come over here."

It was so much fun remembering what a brat I'd been
that I actually felt disappointed when in the middle of the
service, Evzha announced she was bored. "Why don't we
skip to the kiddush and Maria's cake?" With a flick of her
head, she repeated herself in Czech for the regulars. Stop-
ping without finishing had never occurred to me even as an
option. And yet here she and her pretty friend were blithely
passing around plastic cups of wine with Maria's zucchini
bread and wisps of *vanocka,* or "Christmas bread," as the
Czechs called challah.

As I turned in my booklet, I felt a little thrill, like I'd gotten away with something.

The boy in the fur-trimmed top hat continued to rock on his heels with his eyes closed. He had his own book, an antique with crumbled gold edges.

The rabbinical student was telling the American tourists in his British accent how inspired he was to see them here, real Czech Jews rising like a phoenix from the ashes of the Holocaust. His white skin glowed through his newly grown beard.

"Now, hold on," said one of the tourists. "We're from Indiana."

The wind whistled through a gap in the window frame. I chewed Maria's zucchini bread, which stuck to my fingers and turned into a muddy paste in my mouth. No one talked to me. I watched the man with the notebook struggling to chat with the girls and take notes at the same time. He had a bit of a potbelly, but it looked kind of cute on him.

The rabbinical student slipped his square of cake into his pocket and approached Evzha, who'd put her feet up on the arm of an empty chair. She licked zucchini bread off her thumbs while Lenka whispered in her ear. "I've heard so much about you," he said.

"What did you hear and who from?" she shot back.

"Everyone. They say the work you're doing over here is amazing."

"Well, here I am." She stuck her thumbs in her ears and wagged her fingers. "Our group is really quite small. We have about fifty who come regularly, not counting the

Americans—they're impossible to keep track of. And Maria always comes. She's Catholic—I think she goes to church too on Sundays—but she always comes. I don't give blood tests at the door like our beloved chief rabbi, that Nazi Kahn, who asks for official *papieren, Achtung!,* to prove you are one-hundred-percent Jew. This man fathers an illegitimate son at age seventy, but he has his official papers, so he's a Jew."

Though I knew nothing about the case, I was immediately on Evzha's side.

"Then what do you think makes a Jew?" asked the student, and I inched forward in my chair because I was curious to hear the answer myself.

"Ask the goyim. They always figure it out. You know how I knew I was a Jew? I came home one day from school with a report saying I am a Zionist. I thought, okay, you want me to be a Jew? Why not." She picked up the plate of zucchini bread. "More cake?" The student opened his mouth, but Evzha cut him off. "To Rabbi Kahn, being a Jew means obeying a list of six hundred thirteen rules, which you act out from your head, not your heart."

"But I've heard Rabbi Kahn is a good man," said the student.

"He's a good jazz pianist. I'll admit that."

I wanted to hear a few more of her zingers, but the man with the notebook was putting on his coat. I followed him, so we'd happen to leave at the same time.

"That was a good show," I said, holding the door as we went outside. "Is she always this way? And what's the story with this Rabbi Kahn? He's a Nazi?"

"Oh." He rubbed his forehead like an old man. "I have not so much skill in English. Please accept apology for faulty sentence constructions."

"Who is she, this Evzha? Is she some kind of rabbi?"

"Not rabbi. She began Reform seminary in London, but they expunged her for subverting statements. She disapproves this Rabbi Kahn, because he now declares that only Orthodox Jews are legal Jews. However, he himself was not real Jew because his mother wasn't Jewish, only father, and he must convert in absolute Orthodox way."

I asked the man's name and after a bit of eyelid-fluttering and more forehead-rubbing, he admitted it was Lubos. He shook my hand with moist fingers.

"Regrettably, here I must turn for metro to Hradcanska. My maminka expects me at home." Lubos pointed down Belgicka Street toward Namesti Miru station.

"I live that way too," I said, which wasn't exactly true, but I wanted to become his friend. "I'll ride with you."

He seemed surprised that I knew the street names and how to use the metro. As we squeezed in together on the padded orange seats of our subway car, Lubos told me he studied theology at Charles University. He'd been visiting Evzha for a few weeks. "Czech people are traditionally atheists, highly suspicious of religious activity. Many people say rumors that Evzha raises money for drugs or her group engages in illicit liveliness. But you see it is not so." He also planned to sample the services at the Jerusalem Synagogue one day, but not the official Alt-Neu Synagogue, where non-Jews were unwelcome. "You witnessed poor Tomas, this growth-deficient youngster next to piano who looks as Hasidic boy? He had attempted to attend services in official Alt-Neu shul, but Rabbi Kahn expunged him in belief he is trying to mock them."

"So was anyone in that room actually Jewish?" I asked above the roar of the train.

"Evzha, yes. And Tomas thinks he is Jew. He owns video of *Fiddler on Roof.* His parents are rich and have video machine."

"But you don't convert to Judaism because you like *Fiddler on the Roof.*"

"Perhaps." Lubos shrugged. "I am now very intimate with foolish Tomas, who has few friends his age. He asks me often to visit Budapest with him to meet Jewish girls. Germans did not arrive there until 1944 so there still exists sizable Jewish community. But it is foolish idea when we do not speak Hungarian. Beside, I think my maminka would be unhappy if I date some Hungarian girlfriend. Hungary, it's very far away by train."

Before he got off the train I asked if he'd be at Evzha's next week.

"Yes, I will be there," he said with a tight, mysterious smile that looked like gas.

■

IT TOOK A week for the black roots to show under my bleach job. During that time, I looked forward to seeing Evzha in action again. She reminded me of the rough, untrained shepherds who used to rise up from the rabble to save Israel. Sort of like Jesus.

Most afternoons I'd go to cafés and sketch outlines of writhing bodies in ink, then fill them in later at home. I liked Blatouch, Café 14, and Gulu Gulu if it wasn't too smoky. The other patrons, miraculously lean and stylish in tight white pants, puckered their lips through cigarette smoke and coffee steam. They took a European pleasure in lingering.

One afternoon I spotted an American hottie sitting alone in Café 14 and asked to share his table. He had that corn-fed look: soft blond hair and plump pink cheeks with dimples, and he said that God had sent him to Eastern Europe to spread the Good News.

"How about yourself?" asked the evangelist.

"God doesn't talk to me anymore," I said, suddenly feeling a bit jealous.

"I mean, what do you do here?" he asked, and when I told him I was an artist, he actually put his hand on his heart. "I love art. What do you paint?"

"Sex." He looked confused, so I explained it to him. "You know, fucking, sucking, jerking off, orgasms. Men, women, animals. Which do you prefer?"

He answered the question calmly. "Well, women get to wear better clothes."

"How do you mean?" I asked.

"Men can only wear pants, but women get to wear skirts. Much more comfortable. In fact, sometimes when I come home, I put on a skirt, to relax. Not that I'm a cross-dresser or anything." He had a rapt look on his face, not at all ashamed. "My friend at seminary gave mine to me. It's black felt and it used to have all these little mirrors on it, only now they fell off. She used to let me come to her house and put it on, and then for graduation, she gave me this box and the skirt was inside, so it's very dear."

I showed him the drawing I was working on, your standard two guys fucking. It was for a well-off dealer in rare postcards who ransacked the antiquity shops and sold cards he'd bought for a crown or two each for five hundred bucks a pop back home. Jewish themes were especially valuable, even if the postcards were new.

"I'd love to take you to a prayer meeting," he said, bumping his knee into mine.

"I don't think I'd fit in," I said. "But why don't you come to my group?" I added, remembering I had a group.

"Oh, are you Christians?" he asked.

"Actually, we're Hare Krishnas."

The hottie declined my offer politely, though he bought my drink and got my number. Before leaving, he clasped my hand with both hands and promised to call. He never did, which was a real shame because I'd have liked to fuck him with his skirt on.

■

FRIDAY EVENING, I rang the doorbell on Uruguay Street fifteen minutes late. Zara the Amazon answered with a glazed look in her matte-gray eyes.

"Don't you remember me?" I asked. "From the tour?"

"Oh, yes," she said slowly, as if she'd forgotten the words in English, and unlocked the iron gate. She'd woven her hair into a long braid instead of tying it up with chopsticks. "You are late," she whispered. "I hope you will find some free chair."

I wasn't worried, but when we walked in, the room was almost full. Tomas, in the same top hat and black coat, prayed to himself behind the piano. I grabbed a seat next to a guy with gray-blue eyes and the start of a paunch. "What up, dude?" he said. "The name's Jason." As we shook hands, he pressed my fingers with his thumb like a European. His long nails, like almond shavings, were in dire need of a trim. If not for his accent, I'd have guessed he was Czech from the white plastic bag next to his chair. Czechs carried plastic bags everywhere, like security blankets. Not all stores offered them for free.

Jason said he was employed by a charity that worked to integrate Gypsies—he called them "Romany"—into Czech society. He turned out to be half Gypsy himself; the other half was Jewish. He spoke hip-hop accented English, as in, "This one mayor here, he so whack he wants to build a fuckin' wall around the Romany 'hood in his town. That's right, a fuckin' ghetto."

Evzha came in holding hands with pretty Lenka and singing the hymn "Ma Tovu." They were followed by Lubos and Maria, without cake this time. A Hare Krishna pamphlet stuck out of her purse. I moved my coat and waved to Lubos.

"*Sh'ma Yisroel!*" Tomas cried out and pulled the brim of his hat over his eyes.

"Jesus, he scares me," I whispered as Lubos sat next to me. I was glad to see him. "That kid is going to end up a juvie delinquent. You know what that is?"

"No, no." Lubos took out his notebook. "Tomas is very serious. I admire him. He almost eloped to England for con-version in Reform way, but parents uncovered his plans and stopped him in anger."

During the service, Evzha paced by the window as if to watch for saboteurs. There were no yarmulkes because Evzha had left them on her tour bus to Terezin, and it felt strange to pray with nothing on my head. Lubos kept his sailor cap on and the rest of us covered our heads with napkins or not at all. I tore my napkin into a lovely snow-flake.

Evzha had also forgotten the wine for kiddush so we used Becherovka, a Czech liquor that tasted like pumpkin. I downed an extra shot in the hope that I'd get trashed.

"What now?" Evzha asked as Jason nudged me and grinned like we were friends. "How about you, my Gypsy friend? You want to discuss the morality of belly dancing?"

I thought of asking Evzha about prophets, but a tourist from Spain raised his hand. "Excuse me, Teacher. I no understand. You are Reform Jewish?"

"The Reform is the most religious branch of Judaism we have," Evzha said, steamrolling over him. "When a Reform decides to put on a yarmulke or to fast on Yom Kippur, each act is a conscious decision. To me, this is much better than these super-Orthodox *yeshiva bochers* who run around in black and argue if it's permissible to drink a glass of milk five hours after eating a steak instead of six. Black hats are not part of my culture."

Lubos whispered, "Shall we go? There seems small pos-sibility of cake."

I'd been listening so intently, I'd forgotten he was there.

As we left, Jason handed me a crumpled card, still warm from his pocket. His name was spelled the Czech way: Dzej-son. "Yo, call me," he said. "Let's grab brews."

Outside, the top of the snowbanks along the curbs had frozen into a silver crust. I slipped on a black sheet of ice and Lubos held my arm.

The neighborhood was one of those characterless quar-ters every city needs, brightly lit commercial avenues of pharmacies and tobacco shops. The buildings were all caked with soot except for one block they'd cleaned for a movie.

I took him to Meduza, a parlor of plush red chairs lit by candles dripping over empty wine bottles. The walls, papered in gold, were decorated with framed portraits of Greek gods and messages scribbled by art students and literary types. Lubos, who'd never been there before, or-dered an orange juice. I asked for absinthe. There's not too much wrong with a country where you can legally drink ab-sinthe. I was hoping to get addicted like Van Gogh, but the stuff tasted like it came from a sewer. Plus, it gave me a headache.

Our waitress was a tall willowy woman with spiked hair dyed purple-black like a bruise. A silver chain with a Jewish star glittered below her gaunt white neck. I asked in English if she was Jewish too, but she smiled blankly and turned her back on me.

"I guess she didn't understand," I told Lubos.

"I think she understands but is embarrassed to wear fashionable Jewish star, which she has no real right to wear," he said. "All things Jewish are fashionable now."

A new waitress, without a Jewish star this time, brought our drinks.

"For myself, I always felt sympathy to Judaism because Communist regime decried Jews as potential spies for Israel and America." He drank his orange juice in one gulp. "May I ask, what is nature of your religious belief?"

"Art is my religion," I told him. "I'm not a big fan of Judaism. It excludes certain groups, like women." I paused. "And fags." He didn't understand. "I mean, gays."

Lubos thought a minute. "I think if some gay wants to attend service he is able."

"Not openly. Believe me, I've tried."

I thought he'd be shocked or embarrassed, but instead he went on with our argument. "Why is it important openly? One does not discuss sexual life in synagogue."

I forgot what I wanted to say, and suddenly I was the one who felt embarrassed. "The way I see it is that if God's wrong on homosexuality, then what else did He fuck up? I'm not the one who claims He's perfect, remember?" But I was skirting dangerously close to sounding like I gave a fuck, so I wound it up with, "All religions are a lie."

"But not Evzha," he said. "She could not lie."

"You're right," I said. "She's real. I wish I'd had her around when I was growing up." And right then I really admired her.

■

I CALLED HOME and told my mother I was going to a synagogue. She blew me a kiss through the phone, and I liked it. "We went too, on Saturday," she said. "The service dragged on forever. Even the rabbi looked tired."

I fantasized about Evzha hauling our morose rabbi down from the stage at B'nai Tzedek, dragging him through the congregation by the hem of his black robe.

"No one goes to B'nai Tzedek to pray, just to bitch," I said.

"So which is better? To bitch at home or in shul with your fellow Jews?"

■

LUBOS CAME TO pick me up at my apartment on Friday night. "Must I remove shoes?" he asked when I opened the door. I hadn't had time to color my hair, but I wore a tight-fitting silvery gray coat from the new DKNY store on Wenceslas Square. The manager was a client of mine. His store was clean and white with neatly folded clothes in small, incidental piles on the shelves and prices for tourists and overnight Russian millionaires. Televisions showing static hung from the ceiling.

In my bedroom, Lubos ducked under a clothesline of watercolor penises I'd hung to dry and flipped the lights on and off. "All for yourself?" he asked. "And you cook for yourself? And clean toilet? Oh, Maminka would be very impressed."

I held up my copy of *Unbearable Lightness*. "Isn't Kundera a genius?" I asked.

"I have never read his books," Lubos said. "Do you think he is genius?"

"I guess," I said. I'd only made it halfway through the book, but I'd wanted to offer a compliment to his country.

The crowd at Evzha's was the largest yet. The Torah cover was tacked up properly to the wall, and the faded Hebrew letters had been replaced with crisp new ones. Evzha assigned us seats. Tomas propped himself against the piano and looked morose as he muttered prayers out of his antique book.

The service was conducted properly from start to finish. Evzha sat quietly in her chair, and when she stood for the kaddish, she clutched Lenka's elbow and read piously from the prayer booklet they were sharing, like a real rabbi. I hoped she was ill.

After a rousing "Adon Olam," Evzha announced: "Today we are honored by the presence of a special guest, Rabbi Samuel Adler of the Beth Israel Reconstructionist Synagogue in Washington, D.C., a key supporter of our work here. Welcome."

As Evzha translated her introduction into Czech, I thought, well, of course, it was money. Whenever something doesn't make sense, the answer's always money.

Rabbi Adler leapt to his feet as his plump wife beamed at his elbow. His hair was lush and dark like a carpet, and his cheeks gleamed as if he'd scrubbed them with Brillo.

"My friends, after two visits, I feel at home," he said. "Evzha, would you . . . ?"

"Yes, yes," she said and translated his message like a dutiful servant.

Rabbi Adler congratulated us on building a bridge to the twenty-first century with our presence. Tonight he wanted to deal with a difficult subject: the Holocaust. He got along fine until he tried to explain how the Germans determined who was a Jew.

"Rabbi, I must interrupt," Evzha called out.

Finally! Prepare to be demolished, I thought, wanting to laugh out loud.

"The Nazis, they are dead fifty years. But only a few minutes from here, there are men in black uniforms who collect records of all the Jews in Prague and how much blood they have in them. Only instead of Nazis, they call themselves Orthodox Jews."

It was wonderful stuff. I was creaming in my pants. Take that, you petit bourgeois philosopher, you propagator of "acceptable morality," you homophobe!

As Evzha repeated herself in Czech, Adler grinned and leaned over to assure his wife, "It's all part of the act." I guess the guy enjoyed being made a fool of.

"She's rude," his wife buzzed through clenched teeth. "We're all Jews."

She led him off in a huff shortly after kiddush, which was served in antique shot glasses with gold trim. In the rabbi's honor, Maria had baked one of her leaden cakes: chocolate-ginger-spice-pound or something like that. Thank God some things never changed. Lenka snapped a plastic knife trying to cut through it.

I was waiting for Lubos to finish talking to Tomas, who was coughing and spluttering so violently he could barely speak. His entire frame shook as he covered his mouth with his tiny frail fingers, more like fringes than fingers.

Evzha punched my arm. "You're becoming a regular," she said and smiled. "You with your friend."

I actually blushed.

Finally Lubos said good night to Tomas and we left.

"Tomas said me he has made second application for Jewish conversion," Lubos told me, "but Rabbi Kahn refuses again. This time because of medicine the boy takes for growth deficiency that may color his personal responsibility in converting. Still, Tomas says, no problem, he will keep working on it, even if other boys in his school laugh on him. He says they cannot help being anti-Semites. It is in their ancestry."

"What about his ancestry? Has he forgotten that he's a blond?"

"He is angry about his hair. He told me he wishes he has brown hairs like you."

I'd forgotten I had brown hair these days.

"Little Tomas tells me he has found girlfriend. Though she is not actually Jewish, he dates her. Her name is Sarka, classic Czech name, but he calls her Sarah. And he says assuredly she must have Jewish ancestry because she has black hairs." We waited at the corner for the traffic to clear. "Oh, Lubos has terrible luck in romance," he sighed, twisting one of his curls. "Maminka says it is because I am lazy."

"With men?" I asked.

He jerked his head back. "Er, no. I am not homosexual."

"I was kidding," I said quickly. Why did I feel embarrassed again? Sure, I'd thought about sex with Lubos, but I preferred him as a friend. Anyway, his breath smelled.

When the light changed, Lubos asked me how to recognize a homosexual.

"Lots of ways," I said, glad to babble about anything besides what we'd just talked about. "After a while, you learn the signs, like how you can tell if someone looks Jewish."

"It's true. I did not recognize you as a gay. But yes, I think you look Jewish."

I blushed. "I never tried to hide that I was gay. It just didn't come up."

"Surely," he said. "Of course Evzha and her girlfriend, they are homosexuals."

"Evzha's a lesbian?" I couldn't have been more surprised if he'd said she was an American. Evzha? She was almost a rabbi. How could she be a lesbian? Who was her girlfriend? Then an image flashed in my head of Evzha clutching Lenka, her "assistant."

"Everyone knows," he said. "But she never talks about it openly."

So even the fearless Evzha had her limits. This supposed maverick, so eager to spring to the defense of Reform Jews and Nazis, was a closet case. She and her Lenka.

She was a hypocrite, a faker like all the rest of them, like that Rabbi Kahn even.

"You know, I think I'll skip Meduza tonight," I said. There didn't seem to be much point.

■

I STOPPED GOING to Evzha's. One night I met Lubos at Meduza after services to help him translate a Jewish book written in English. He needed it for his thesis.

"Has Evzha asked about me?" I said, hoping she had.

"Evzha would not ask about an American," he explained.

On Friday nights I drank overpriced beers at Aqua Club and watched drag queens. One night, I was standing there thinking what good company I was for myself when Jason, that half-Gypsy, tapped my shoulder. At first I thought he'd found the place by mistake.

"*Opravdu?* I mean, really?" he said, delighted. "Fuckin' awesome!"

I liked the way he danced, nothing like a Gypsy. More flat-footed, a grudging acknowledgment of rhythm. Also, he lived nearby.

Jason led me by the hand through his two rooms, his "crib." "This is my bed," he said, bouncing on it and taking off his shoes. He was a bit heavy, but not in an unattractive way. I pressed my nose to his skin and inhaled his sweet and muddy scent.

As we wrestled naked, he panted, "Someone's getting fucked." I went first, then it was his turn, the half-Gypsy who wore Levi's and college sweatshirts instead of vests and pantaloons with gold stitching and mirrors. I found him sexy that way, a Gypsy in jeans.

Maybe that's what I needed, a Jewish boyfriend.

The next week I tried calling Jason, but he wasn't home. Friday night rolled around and I didn't feel like going out, but I had nothing else to do. So I thought, fuck it, I'll try out Rabbi Kahn's Alt-Neu Synagogue.

The Alt-Neu Synagogue, a redbrick fortress with a steep crenellated roof, stood out against its lacy white Baroque neighbors carved with nymphs and flowers. On weekdays it was a museum and charged admission. A red gutter-pipe ran like an artery alongside the door, which faced an alley paved with broken cobblestones. Theirs was the oldest continually running service in Europe. Even the Nazis hadn't stopped them.

An Israeli bodyguard with a white plastic earpiece blocked me from going in until I told him in English I was Jewish.

I hopped down a short flight of steps into the main sanctuary, with rough walls like a desert cavern. The air smelled of baked clay, and the only light came from a few narrow slits near the ceiling and candles stuck onto iron candelabras with sharp hooks at the ends. I couldn't tell the front of the room from the back until I heard the women's voices drifting through a narrow mail slot cut into a wall; that was the back. One of the old men crowded around the central wooden altar must have been the infamous Rabbi Kahn. Worshippers came in, froze wherever they felt like it, then started rocking on their heels and moaning.

I didn't recognize the melodies they used and no one offered a book for me to follow along. I just stood there and watched the fanatics until suddenly the men folded up their prayer shawls and closed their books. I didn't move. The longer I stood quietly, the more afraid I felt next to those old men in that room, which seemed to vibrate with a strange, forbidding power, dark and full of awe.

I could never have been a prophet. I'd defiled myself and there was no hope for me unless, like Isaiah, I cleansed my profane lips with a blazing coal.

∎

A FEW WEEKS before Christmas, I made arrangements to leave Prague. My plane ticket home was open-ended, but what about the rest of my life?

All over the city wooden tables appeared on the snowy street corners beside blue tubs of dark gray carp. Women stood in long lines to select a fish, which a young man in a blood-splattered apron would catch in his net and set flapping on the table. The fishmonger would then press the gasping carp by the neck, conk its brains out with a mallet, and slice off its head while the lips still opened and closed. Afterward he handed the women their bloody fish sections in plastic bags to freeze for the traditional Christmas meal. Lubos said he and his mother once bought a live carp and kept it in their bathtub. When Christmas Day came, he didn't have the heart to go through with the execution so he set the fish free in the Vltava River, down with all the garbage and, according to urban legend, Stalin's head.

On my last day in town, I met Lubos in Old Town Square and visited my favorite cathedrals, then gobbled up a sausage from a stand. I never ate sausage at home, but here they had a special sweet flavor. Lubos wouldn't touch them because they weren't kosher. Instead he bought an ice cream in a café on the Square. "They sold this same kind in time of Communism," he marveled as he licked his wooden spoon. "Each week they sold only one flavor, and it had a special color, very brightly artificial. Everywhere in Prague you saw these same pink ice creams on ground. Even in summer, it took them hours to melt."

I hardly saw Lubos anymore. He was always doing re-

search in the library, or attending synagogue. He kept talking about making the big trip to England. "I have long felt I
am different from my friends. I may as well join this nation
of outsiders," he said. "Also, Maminka gives her blessing.
And once I have converted, perhaps I shall travel to Holy
Land to study in some yeshiva in Jerusalem. Oh, that would
be fine."

We joined the mob of tourists who gathered under a
gray-green sky to watch the astronomical clock strike on the
hour. At the edge of the crowd, a pair of cute Mormon young
men with identical haircuts, white shirts, ties, and backpacks handed out literature.

"So now what do we do?" I asked as the sun sank behind
the clock tower.

He seemed embarrassed. "Er, tonight is Friday. Many
synagogues are not far . . ."

I cut him off. "I'll go with you, but only if we go to
Evzha's."

"Really?" Lubos clapped his hands.

Evzha had moved to an apartment in Old Town, just
down the street from the Spanish Synagogue, still under
restoration, as it probably would be forever. Lenka let us in.
She'd just returned from England and her face glowed like
she was pregnant.

The room was painted white and carpeted gray. The
empty Torah cover was enshrined in a wooden china cabinet. I heard, "You are returned from the dead," and turned to
face Evzha standing behind me and chewing her lip. She
was shorter than I'd remembered, and just then she struck

me as being so resolutely herself that she could never have been mistaken for anything else. Like the craggy Alt-Neu shul, so very deeply *Jewish*.

"I've been out of town," I said, not afraid to meet her eyes for once.

She rolled her eyes. "Enough excuses. Find a chair." The floorboards swayed under her footsteps as she padded away.

I made a point of being friendly to everyone besides Evzha, wishing Lenka a Good Shabbes, complimenting Maria on her carrot cake. I shook hands with newcomers and Zara the Amazon, who told me she'd gotten a grant. "Oh, *good*," I said with special emphasis. I didn't see Tomas and was afraid he might be gravely ill until Lubos explained that he now attended the Jerusalem Synagogue, where there were so few congregants no one cared if he was mocking them. "Perhaps I will try there also," said Lubos, putting on his yarmulke. He'd bought a black one with silver threads, which he wore in his room with the door closed. "They are more traditional than Evzha."

I sat next to an old man from New York who'd moved back here to die after a fifty-year exile, because "this is my home," as he said in his Brooklyn accent. "They think I'm an American. I speak Czech like an American now and I didn't even know it. They all try to cheat me, in all the stores. But this is where I belong."

Strangely, there were times when the city felt like my home too. I ate at expat restaurants, drank at gay bars, read American magazines at the Globe and the Bookworm. I got mail at the American Express office. The "girls" behind the counter all knew who I was and shared secret smiles with me as they pretended to ask for my name. I tried to come less or at odd hours to confuse them, but they always knew who I was.

A rabbi from Australia was supposed to have led services, but he'd been detained at the border because he hadn't realized he'd needed a visa. I watched Evzha and her girlfriend closely, but I didn't see any signs of endearments until Evzha chose Lenka to slice the challah. Zara donned her matching yarmulke and tallis and gave a short sermon about the Jews' favorite Habsburg, Franz Josef. He'd earned a place in their hearts by allowing them to have last names for the first time so they could blend in with everyone else. Their choices were limited to Big, Small, White, and Black (*Gross, Klein, Weiss,* and *Schwartz*). Evzha applauded and said, "Very nice, Zara."

Tomas dropped by during kiddush. When he found out I was going home to New York he begged me to buy him a menorah. He promised to send me money.

"I don't need your money," I said. "What kind do you want? Gold? Silver?"

"Traditional," he said and downed a shot of kosher red wine.

I felt sorry for him. "Why do you want to be Jewish when they don't want you?"

"I have no choice," he said with a weak smile. "I feel it in my skin."

The man from Brooklyn apologized to Evzha for sleeping through Zara's sermon.

"Who cares?" she said. "As long as you come. The whole point is community."

"What about the members who aren't accepted by the community?" I said. "Like gays. If you follow the Torah strictly, you're supposed to cast those members out of your community. You're supposed to stone them."

"I'm glad you asked this question," Evzha said and repeated my challenge aloud in Czech so everyone could hear. "Let me tell you a story about Hillel and Shammai."

Here we go, I thought. Hillel and Shammai, good cop/bad cop, Laurel and Hardy, Siskel and Ebert. You couldn't have one without the other.

"In Old Jerusalem there were two great rabbis who disagreed, Hillel and Shammai. Shammai believed you should obey all rules of Torah exactly. If there was an easier way to keep a rule, he chose the harder way, just to be sure he didn't break the law by accident. But Hillel said, 'Look, God doesn't care which way is easier or harder. He gave us the Torah as his gift. He wants us to choose the way that will make our lives better.' "

"You're saying we're free to choose which laws we want to follow?" I asked. "How can you call that Judaism? It's not the real thing."

"Real? Hundreds of years ago our ancestors sacrificed animals three times a year and a few of them were crazy enough to believe that because they heard voices in their head God was talking to them. That's real? They say that before he died, Moses asked God to see the future of Judaism. So God shows him Hillel with all his students arguing about a text. 'What the hell is this?' Moses asks. 'That's your Judaism,' God says. 'They've evolved, but it's the same thing as what I gave you on Sinai.' Now when Hillel heard this story, he asked for the same favor. So God took him to a modern yeshiva in Jerusalem, which Hillel recognized down to the last detail, and he wept."

"You still didn't answer my question," I said after she translated her sermon.

"Didn't I?"

"I mean, you didn't come out and say if you believed in excluding gays."

"Didn't I?" she repeated with a wink and folded up a chair.

At the end of kiddush, I tried to bid Evzha a casual good-bye, but she pinched my arm and said, "Will we see you next week?" I didn't answer quickly enough and she added, "Why do I bother? I'll never see you again, just like that Gypsy who used to come here. You Americans are all Gypsies. The first group who came in '91, they were great, very enthusiastic, involved. Now they couldn't be more selfish."

I took a last look over my shoulder just before I left. Evzha had her back turned to me and was yelling at her girlfriend in Czech.

On our way to the metro, we passed one of the boys in bloody aprons hosing down his wooden table. In a tub by his feet, dark gray carp swam in quiet circles. "I would like to go to America," Lubos said, "to go to a land where it is not strange to be Jewish."

"Eastern Europe has been home to Jews for centuries," I pointed out.

"But we are in Central Europe," he said.

"You're more Jewish than they are. More than I am. You chose it."

"There is no choice," he said. "In Holocaust, you would have died, not me."

When we said good-bye outside my apartment, he handed me a folded slip of brown paper. Inside were several bills, one, five, ten, twenty, and fifty marks. Terezin marks, play money for a concentration camp. "I collected them when I was young," he said shyly.

I handled the weirdly beautiful money by the corners. Each bill featured an oval portrait of Moses holding the Ten Commandments. There were different colors for the different denominations, pale green, orange, pink, and blue. They'd all been printed in 1944. I tried to imagine where the bills had come from, who'd owned them, what they'd been used to pay for, and how they'd come to flutter into my hands.

"Lubos, you can't give me this," I said, feeling dizzy. "It's too precious."

"I can find more. I have a collection. I know a special source," he said. Where was that? Why did he have this money? "You keep it."

I was going to argue, but I looked at him and choked up. I didn't know if he was Jewish, but he was strange and so was I and he was my friend. "Thank you," I said.

■

NINETEEN NINETY-FOUR WAS a long time ago. I'm holding two silver tubes of flesh-colored pigment I found at the back of a drawer. With a little water the paint would start right up again. Instead I cradle the tubes in my palm for a moment before throwing them in the trash.

When I first came home, it took me a while to adjust to the big portions. Also, what was polenta? And who was Forrest Gump?

Here in New York, I draw on a computer for a chic graphic design firm that frowns on green hair. I've become used to doorman buildings with elevators and paying five bucks for beer. If I turn on the toaster oven and the TV at the same time, nothing explodes.

I've joined a gay synagogue that meets in a church. I go to services on Friday nights and once I saw an American there I recognized from my expatriate days. We nodded but didn't speak, as if the alchemy of conversation might whisk us back to the never-never land we'd escaped. I'm looking for a boyfriend, and though I haven't had much luck yet, my therapist is teaching me to visualize.

Lubos used to send letters, but now he e-mails me from a Hotmail account. He never went to England, but he still attends services and says that my Gypsy has moved to Budapest, where he works for George Soros. Zara the Amazon has broken off from Evzha to form her own club, "for philosophical reasons." She has about ten members.

In other news, Evzha still has her girlfriend. Once Lubos sent me an article about Evzha that made no mention of her lesbianism. In the accompanying photo, she didn't smile, just looked up eerily from the shadows like a prophet, and I guess she is one. (Maybe that's why she's so difficult to have a conversation with.) There was an account of a former fiancé, a Mongolian dissident who'd agreed twenty years ago to convert to Judaism so they could get married. Before that could happen, the government expelled him from Czechoslovakia. Today he lives in Mongolia and is married with a family.

ACKNOWLEDGMENTS

I would like to express my thanks to my talented fellow students and teachers at Columbia, especially Jonathan Franzen, Mary Gordon, Binnie Kirshenbaum, and Ben Marcus. I'd also like to thank Hardy Griffin, Mark Derenzo, and Rob Williams for their tireless reading of drafts. Thank you to everyone at Random House, and a special thanks to Veronica Windholz, Adam Korn, and to Bruce Tracy for being a terrific editor. To Melanie Jackson and Andrea Schaefer for their hard work on my behalf. To Frish Brandt, Eileen Pollack, and Gordon Powell for life lessons learned. To Kimberly Ewald Callas, Rachel Erdstein, Paul Fisher, Wendy Frey, Leah Markowitz, Marc Olender, Brian Rubin, Pavel Sedlacek, Ivo Vesely, Milan Walter for friendship. To Jeff Jackson for the fantastic website. To my family and to Anthony Palatta for their love and support. And for inspiration, thank you to Christopher Isherwood.

ABOUT THE AUTHOR

AARON HAMBURGER was recently awarded a
fellowship from the Edward F. Albee Founda-
tion and won first prize in the David Dornstein
Memorial Creative Writing Contest for Young
Adult Writers. His writing has appeared in the
Village Voice, Out, Nerve, and *Time Out New
York.* He holds degrees from Columbia University and the University of Michigan and teaches
in Brooklyn. Currently he is at work on his first
novel, which is set in Jerusalem. He lives in
New York City.